P9-DCX-434

DIFFERENT WATERFRONTS

DIFFERENT WATERFRONTS

A Wooden Boat Reader

Peter H. Spectre

Illustrated by
William Gilkerson

Tilbury House, Publishers — Gardiner, Maine

Tilbury House, Publishers
The Boston Building
132 Water Street
Gardiner, Maine 04345

Copyright © 1989 by Peter H. Spectre
Illustrations © 1989 by William Gilkerson

All rights reserved. No part of this book may be reproduced in
any form or by an electronic or mechanical means including
information storage and retrieval systems without permission in
writing from the publisher, except by a reviewer who may quote
brief passages in a review.

Most of the contents of *Different Waterfronts* appeared in a
slightly different form in *WoodenBoat*. The author and publisher
gratefully acknowledge the cooperation of Jon Wilson and the
entire staff of *WoodenBoat*.

"Bookends Theme," © 1967, 1968, Paul Simon, Charing Cross
Music (BMI)

Library of Congress Catalog Card Number 89-85317

ISBN 0-88448-077-1 (cloth)
ISBN 0-88448-079-8 (paperback)

Designed by William Gilkerson
Composition by High Resolution, Inc., Camden, Maine
Printing and Binding by Halliday Lithography, West Hanover,
Massachusetts
Paperback binding by Dunn & Co., Inc., Clinton, Massachusetts

Contents

Dedicated to the memory of Myer Brooks,
my grandfather

Acknowledgments

Because much of the material for many of the stories in this book was gathered on the fly, my heartfelt thanks go out to all of the boatbuilders, designers, and wooden boat enthusiasts who put aside, without a moment's notice, whatever they were working on to answer my questions. To a person they were patient, informative, and hospitable.

Special thanks are due my colleagues at *WoodenBoat*: to Jonathan Wilson, for his confidence and trust; Terence Driscoll, for his challenge in the post office to get off the dime; Maynard Bray, for his suggestions and insistance on accuracy; Jennifer Elliott, for her encouragement; and Sherry Streeter, for her ability to make the written word look good. Especially to Meg Maiden and Mary Lou Dietrich for helping me keep track of the details.

I owe an immense debt of gratitude to my friend and colleague George Putz, who in the course of thousands of hours of intense conversation and hilarious commentary provided insights and ideas that crop up everywhere in my work.

Others who have gone out of their way to help me over

the years are Joseph Gribbins, editor of *Nautical Quarterly*, who published some of the stories between these covers; John W. Lampl of British Airways, who smoothed my travels to England; Kathleen Brandes, who never failed to have a good thing to say; JoAnn King, who shared her valuable research on Howard I. Chapelle; and Fred Brooks, who kept things from getting too serious.

Hats off to Llewellyn Howland III, my agent; Logan Johnston, Sarah Clark, and Liz Pierson of Harpswell Press; and William Gilkerson, an artist of great skill.

And, of course, thanks to my family — Eileen, Maureen, Nathan, and Emily.

Peter H. Spectre
Compass Rose
Camden, Maine

Introduction

Here is a collection of stories about a phenomenon of the 1970s and 1980s known as the Wooden Boat Revival. I became involved in this event — or perhaps, I should say in the chronicling of these events — starting in 1972, when I was the editor of a small nautical book publishing company on the coast of Maine. One day, Dave Getchell, the editor of the *National Fisherman*, a commercial fisherman's newspaper, walked into my office with a proposal: Let's join forces and publish a marine version of the then-very-hip *Whole Earth Catalog*. I gave the matter perhaps thirty seconds' thought and signed on. After all, I was an avid reader of the *WEC* and enthusiastically subscribed to its philosophy, which held that those who had access to the proper tools for the hand and the mind would have control over their personal lives.

Our book would be a seagoing *Whole Earth Catalog*, a Whole Sea Catalog (or something like that), an annotated guide to the publications, products, and services that were indispensable to being on or around the water in a traditional, or at least commonsense, manner. Not a consumer's guide to buying stuff off the shelf; rather a sourcebook for people of independent mind who wanted to become involved with the sea.

So we set to work, making outlines, setting schedules, gathering material, contacting writers, doing everything a pair of responsible editors would do in the preparation of a new publication. It was all rather sane and predictable, but boring, which would have been fine except this was the early 1970s when everything was supposed to be insane and unpredictable, and exciting. If you were a sentient person in that era, then you know what I mean. Dave, therefore, went out to find a third person who could set things right.

Our man was found on an island in Penobscot Bay. Many months were to pass before I met him, but in the meantime I heard through third parties that, among other eccentricities, he talked to trees. ("Hi, tree, how would you like to become a boat?") I knew we were going to have a publication to be reckoned with when this fellow, an ex-Oregonian named George Putz, finally came off his island ("Taking the ferryboat to America," he called it) and stopped by my office. Our first conversation went something like this.

Spectre: Well, what have you been writing about for the Whole Sea Catalog (or something like that)?

Putz: Oh, a little of this, a little of that.

Spectre: What about tools? Doing anything on boat-building tools?

Putz: Yes. A bunch.

Spectre: What are you going to say?

Putz: Well, you can't get decent tools, you know. You can go into a hardware store and they throw blister-packed trash at you. If there's any steel at all in them it isn't tempered steel. And most of the time there's only one size of each tool — medium and useless. Who ever heard of medium for crying out loud? Everything is either small or large. Look at a proper tool kit and the medium-size tools are the least worn. And of course the bloody good tools that used to be available are all hanging on restaurant and barroom walls. Oh sure, you can send off to these fine tool catalog outfits and get English and German planes at thirty dollars apiece, five-hundred-dollar workbenches, mono-grammed screw extractors, and full-size drawings for a seventeenth-century mandolin, but try to get a boatslick or a lipped adze, show me a ship auger and I'll quit smoking, lead me to a boatbuilder's bevel, backing iron, or spud and I'll take esoteric vows, and materials to work with, Great Hornitoads you can't get the wood, and no copper rivets and roves, it's a conspiracy, some heinous troll is sitting atop a mountain of *our tools, our wood,* and we gotta find the bastards to liberate what is ours, to find peace and freedom and the knowledge that we can do it ourselves once again, to know joy again in the beatitude of one's very own shop where personal expression once again blossoms across the land, oh lordy . . .

Spectre: Right. Do you take cream or sugar in your coffee?

What George meant to say was that we were living in an era bereft of quality goods for the construction of boats of integrity; real boats built by old-style craftsmen, not plastic craft manufactured by unskilled workers and trimmed out with vinyl and chrome. We were also living in an era that was becoming increasingly bereft of an appreciation for the traditions of fine craftsmanship.

Our approach to craftsmanship in boats, both commercial and pleasure, mirrored our society's attention to craftsmanship in all respects. Generally speaking, a society that would accept a half-baked boat would accept, say, a half-baked house. It followed, then, that if there should be a renaissance in our boats, there would probably be a renaissance in, say, our houses. (In retrospect I see nothing wrong with that assessment. We have had our revival of wooden boats. We also have had our revival of quality built houses, natural-fiber clothes, genuine fountain pens, classically inspired public buildings, even regionally brewed beer with character.)

The *Mariner's Catalog*, which is what we decided to call our weird little publication, was my introduction to the idea that it was time to pay attention to the decline of traditional boats and boatbuilding and the attempts of a minority to effect a revival of these beautiful and always worthwhile craft.

Not to say that we were always serious in our approach to the subject. *Anarchistically eclectic* is probably a better term. If a topic were even remotely concerned with boats and the sea, George and I would discuss it. (Dave Getchell bowed out of the *Mariner's Catalog* after a couple of years, went back to the *National Fisherman* full-time, and eventually helped found the *Small Boat Journal*.) We even got into the subject of higher-quality beer, under the assumption that anyone who was serious about boats had to be serious about beer. ("The ideal mariner's beer could very well be chung," wrote George. "Chung is an ale from Nepal that you can make as you want or, horrors, need, that does not require bottling or aging, that is laughably cheap, that is good both hot or cold, and that can keep you dangerously incompetent throughout your entire cruise.")

But after seven years and seven completely different editions, we quit. For one thing we never quite saw eye to eye with our publisher; for another we were burned out by the reams of correspondence such an endeavor required; for yet another, toward the end we felt as if we were being typecast as a couple of anarchistically eclectic lunatics whose irreverance was a menace to modern nautical society.

Meanwhile, in 1974 an interesting character named Jonathan Wilson had started a bimonthly magazine called *WoodenBoat*. While we thought the magazine took a rather parochial view — we took our boats in whatever material was closest to hand — it seemed to be quite effective in getting to the heart of the matter. One early January evening in 1980, I got a call from Wilson. Would I be interested in looking into the circumstances of the recent abandonment of the schooner *John F. Leavitt* and writing a five-thousand-word article? The deadline was two weeks away.

My first reaction was to say no. After all, I did not think of myself as a journalist. I was an editor. Though it was true that I wrote extensively in the *Mariner's Catalog* and had had articles published from time to time in the nautical press, I had always written from my own knowledge. I had never gone out with a blank notebook, cold turkey, to interview strangers. I had never worked to such a tight deadline.

My second reaction was to say yes. Like most others who supported the preservation of traditional concepts and occupations, I had been thrilled by Ned Ackerman's decision to commit himself to the construction of a new wooden schooner in Thomaston, Maine, designed specifically to revive coastal cargo-carrying under sail. I had been shocked to hear that Ackerman had abandoned his schooner, the *John F. Leavitt*, at sea under strange circumstances just a few months after the vessel had been launched. I wanted to know the true story as much as anyone else. What the hell. If Jonathan Wilson wanted to pay me real money to satisfy my curiosity, then I would do it. (If you would like to satisfy yours, the story of the senseless loss of the *Leavitt* can be found in the March/April 1980 issue of *WoodenBoat*.)

Few people can point to a moment in their lives and identify it as a turning point, but I can. The moment I walked into the lobby of the Camden Harbour Inn in Camden, Maine, and asked Ned Ackerman what had happened to his schooner, I stopped being a book editor and started being a journalist. No longer one who sat at a desk and read reports written by others about what was going on in the world, I became one who went out to discover these things for himself. It was like going from eating steak to roping steer, or in my field, from sailing boats to building them.

A few months later I joined *WoodenBoat* magazine on a full-time basis. Jonathan Wilson paid me to travel around the United States and Canada, even Great Britain, to look into the state of wooden boat building today and to follow the ins and outs of the revival of traditional maritime craftsmanship. I got to hang around boatshops, crawl along the waterfront, talk to people who may not have been, and probably never will be, household words but were fascinating characters nevertheless. I had a grand old time.

The stories that follow are among some of my assignments during the last ten years. They are about people who have worked hard, sometimes struggled mightily, to keep alive a traditional way of life and traditional objects that probably do not mean much in economic terms for a society such as ours. But they do mean a great deal about who we are and where we should go in the future. Wooden boats, after all, are metaphors. . . .

The Wooden Boat Revival

Obituaries are seldom written for inanimate objects, but some time in the late 1960s — what amounted to an obituary for wooden boats was prepared by an anonymous member of the New York Boat Show public-relations staff. The gist of the notice, which was picked up by most of the nautical press of the time, was that at that year's show all of the boats on display were built of fiberglass. After centuries of development, the wooden boat as a mainstream commercial product was for all intents and purposes dead.

Fiberglass-reinforced plastic was hailed by most as the miracle material, even though L. Francis Herreshoff, the wit of Marblehead, observed that the inside of fiberglass boats looked like frozen snot.

I would be the last to suggest that the New York Boat Show is a representative institution, but in this case it was the bellweather of a failing industry. The death of wood as a boatbuilding material was inevitable, or so it seemed. We were living then in a period when everything was possible — if we could declare war on poverty and expect to win, if we could shoot a man to the moon and bring him back,

1

if we could have guns and butter and an expanding economy without inflation, then we could have universally available boats guaranteed to last forever. It was the culmination of the American nautical dream: fiberglass boats for the masses.

There really was a fiberglass revolution, but as in every other revolution there remained a cadre of people who would not accept the inevitable. Their numbers have increased and decreased over the years, and the waterfront's perception of them has changed from time to time (the doubters of the 1950s and 1960s became the elitists of the 1970s and 1980s), yet they have been around for a generation now, patiently waiting for the Second Coming of Wood. At first they were characterized by their hatred for fiberglass boats — they called them plastic bathtubs and Clorox bottles and worse — but the passage of time seemed to mellow most of them. They had their wooden boats and the masses didn't and that was just fine. They were like the people who wear wool. In fact, many of them *were* the people who wear wool.

Some of these people liked wood simply because it was wood. They liked wood's smell, feel, random grain, elegance. Others were putterers who liked to fiddle with boats more than sail them, and they therefore had little interest in fiberglass boats because there was so little that had to be done to them. Others were amateurs who wanted to use their workshops for building boats instead of knickknack shelves and bird feeders. Still others were hard-core professionals who would never give up as long as there was cedar in the woods and copper in the mines.

There were also the historic preservationists, whose mission was to ensure that the old designs and traditions would not die out but would remain not only in museums and libraries, but also on the waterways. There were the fishermen, particularly the lobster fishermen, who kept their wooden boats long after others had given them up, though in recent years their numbers have been declining rather precipitously. And then there were the mystics, the people who found magical properties in wood — who touted wood as Nature's Own, a biodegradable material that is renewable, self-sustaining, a fit accompaniment to the innermost yearning's of man's soul . . . well, you know what I mean.

Back in my lost youth in the 1950s and 1960s, I was busy with my own preoccupations, as were many others. We were fooling around with boats — wooden boats, in fact — and because we were generally broke at the time, we didn't care what new boats were built with. We were involved with cheap old boats, and as time passed our cheap old boats became cheaper, depreciated by everyone else's lust for fiberglass.

But as the salesmen of new fiberglass boats were quick to point out, old boats require considerable maintenance and occasional rebuilding with the passage of time. This wasn't much of a problem at first, because a large part of our experience with wooden boats was their maintenance and repair. We were as much in love with spring fitting out as with summer sailing. Refastening, recaulking, painting, and varnishing were satisfactions of their own.

To install a knee, however, or caulk a seam, bend in new timbers, or replace a keelbolt required things that were fast disappearing — tools, materials, skills. In less than a decade, the fiberglass revolution destroyed economy of scale as it applied to wooden boats. What was the point of manufacturing cut copper boat nails if the demand for them became so small as to make the price high and the profit minuscule? Why stock esoteric boatbuilding tools like adzes and caulking mallets if a chandler had to buy them in lots of a dozen or more and might sell only two in a year? Why take on apprentices in a boatyard if even the old-timers couldn't find enough

3

work to keep them busy?

Our wooden boats may have been cheap, but the tools and materials required to keep them in good condition were becoming either too expensive to buy or impossible to find at any price. The local chandler in the space of a few years had become the purveyor of fiberglass patching kits, polypropylene rope, blister-packed electroplated screws, and synthetic polishing wax. Most of the master boatbuilders had retired before passing on their skills to the next generation. By the end of the 1960s those who wished to stay with wooden boats were finding themselves increasingly alone. What's more, they were increasingly seen as absurd romantics, negativists, waterfront Luddites.

It was about this time, "a period of nautical despair," according to Fred Brooks, that the remaining lovers of wooden boats started to dig in. I first noticed the phenomenon in the pages of the *National Fisherman*. *NF* was a strange, ragged sheet trying to cover two things at once to keep from going under — commercial fishing, and boats and boatbuilding. Commercial fishing in the United States was in a decline because of foreign competition and other complex matters, and anything associated with the industry, including newspapers, was in dire straits. To hedge their bets, the owners and editors of *NF* were publishing material about pleasure boats.

NF's coverage of boats and boatbuilding was atavistic, just like the fishing industry of that period. The old ways and days dominated the newspaper, so much so that you could find articles on boats being built in 1968 illustrated with photographs or drawings from 1936. For romantics, it was great stuff. The real thing, we thought. We loved to read about old Zeke down to Lubec who couldn't care less about plastics and other contemporary concoctions, who built crooked peapods out back behind the fishhouse with an adze and an old Barlow knife, while his old wife Mellie sat in a rocker on the porch, knitting lobster-pot heads with broken whalebone needles. Meanwhile, his son Luke ran around Passamaquoddy Bay in a leaking old haulup-propeller dory chasing sardines for the local cannery.

The star writer for the *National Fisherman* was John Gardner, who had been a regular since the early 1950s. He was a wooden boat builder of the old school, a Maine native, a skilled and eloquent man. Gardner's title was technical editor, which did not mean that he wrote about net-mesh gauges or specifications for diesel-engine power takeoffs. He wrote instead about boats and boatbuilding of the past, with an emphasis on how to adapt them to the present. Yet, despite his reputation now as the dean of wooden boat building, then he wrote often about fiberglass, ferrocement, and metals. His message was less about saving wooden boats and more about reproducing superior designs of the past in any material you could lay your hands on. But his wooden boat material was the most memorable.

Gardner turned on a lot of people. His writing in *NF*, along with that of Weston Farmer, Pete Culler, and others, involved the readers, especially when the articles were of the how-to-build variety. He was following in the tradition of Howard I. Chapelle, a maritime historian who did the bulk of his work in the 1930s through the 1960s and whose writings provided guidance and inspiration to a vast number of people.

Through John Gardner and the *National Fisherman*, wooden boat lovers discovered they were not alone. They traded information on sources of supply, learned about new stuff (epoxy glue) and new applications for old stuff (plywood covered with synthetic cloth). And in almost every issue of the newspaper they were treated to the plans and building instructions for a least one boat.

Gardner reminded his readers again and again that some watercraft were of such a design that they demanded wooden construction and were of such inherently good design that they should be preserved and their use encouraged. He wrote primarily of dories, wherries, flatiron skiffs, sharpies, Whitehalls, Adirondack guideboats, peapods — small boats that are easily built and maintained by one person. He called them *traditional small craft*, and he promoted their use because he saw them as the perfect recreational boats for amateurs to build. If the professional builders were to concentrate on fiberglass boats, then amateurs were the only ones to keep wooden construction alive.

People began to send Gardner photographs and letters about the boats they built in response to his urgings, and the *National Fisherman* began to publish them, sometimes as separate articles and sometimes with comment and praise by Gardner himself. By the early 1970s this traditional small-craft revival, primarily wood, was in full swing.

In the meantime, Mystic Seaport Museum in Connecticut called on John Gardner in 1969 to help oversee their small-craft collection and set up a working boatshop. Gardner made many innovations at Mystic, including classes for amateur builders and an annual small-craft meet where enthusiasts could gather to show off their boats and learn about others. Founded in 1970, the Mystic Seaport Small Craft Workshop brought together for the first time a large group of people who had felt for years that they were alone in a sea of ugly plastic boats. What was this? They found they were not alone; in fact, they were card-carrying members of a Movement.

While John Gardner and others were exhorting the faithful in print, people like Dick Wagner of Seattle, Washington, were influencing them by deed. Wagner was living on a houseboat in Lake Union, right in the heart of the city, where he had a small fleet of wooden sailing and rowing boats for rent. After awhile, as interest built, he began selling boats as well, all the while acting as a clearinghouse of information and advice. He turned on an entire community almost singlehandedly. In the ten-year period between 1968 and 1978, he estimated that he had ten thousand customers, plus an equal number of tire kickers and thousands of phone calls. His Old Boathouse was soon known around the country, even supplying wooden boats to people in the East and the Midwest, and became the genesis of the West Coast's Traditional Wooden Boat Society and Seattle's Center for Wooden Boats.

If this discussion seems to focus too much on small wooden boats, it is because small craft have always been at the heart of the renaissance of wood. Yes, larger wooden boats were being built in the 1960s and 1970s by both amateurs and professionals, but the enthusiasm came from the fans of small boats, perhaps because they were affordable and buildable, but also because they represented new territory for exploration. The wooden boat movement has always looked to the past for inspiration, yet the large-vessel past had been well worked by establishment historians like Howard I. Chapelle and William A. Baker. Small craft had been largely ignored. Here was a new field, a subject with as much romance as the Friendship sloops and the Gloucester schooners of Chapelle's scholarship, and an opportunity for some to become experts in an area that was an informational vacuum.

But the larger boats cannot be ignored. Quite a few large boatbuilding yards remained from the good old days of wood, especially in Maine, where craftsmen with names like Hodgdon, Gamage, Wallace, and Morse still built commercial hulls and yachts for those who thought they deserved the very best. In building pleasure boats they served the carriage trade, the type of owner who didn't think much about cost. It's stretching the argument, however, to suggest that this custom-boatbuilding business was a significant part of the Wooden Boat Revival, since it never really died — only declined — and few newcomers under the influence of the wood renaissance have ever tried to enter it. And for good reason: the building of large, expensive yachts in wood calls for years of experience and lots of capital.

This didn't stop people from trying to revive and restore large old wooden vessels. As interest in wooden boats increased, along with the prices of new fiberglass boats, many big wooden yachts and workboats that could be converted to pleasure use were given new life both by those who lived hand-to-mouth and those who could afford to spare no expense.

In the early 1970s, the interest in traditional wooden boats, large or small, began to come together on a lot of fronts, enough so that increasingly frequent use of the words *revival* and *renaissance* and *movement* (sometimes even *fad* if a cynic were talking) could be found in print. The vortex was in Maine, where a new magazine and a new boatshop were to have immense influence.

They laughed in 1970 when the newly launched *Sail* magazine challenged the conventional nautical publications by intentionally ignoring powerboats. (It was thought that there wouldn't be enough circulation or advertising to support such a narrow view.) They called for a psychiatrist to examine Jonathan Wilson's head when he started *WoodenBoat*. By any standard, his bimonthly magazine should have failed with its first issue. Instead it became one of those inexplicable miracles.

Like the chicken-and-egg debate, it is impossible to sort out whether the surge in popularity of wooden boats was caused by the existence of *WoodenBoat*, or whether the continued existence of the magazine was the result of the Wooden Boat Revival. Born in the back of a truck, feebly capitalized, put together by a staff that initially knew nothing about publishing and distribution and lived hand-to-mouth for years to make it work, located way Down East at the end of a road to nowhere, driven out of its offices by fire and published in a succession of buildings and barns until a permanent place could be found, *WoodenBoat* went from a circulation of two in the fall of 1974 to more than one hundred thousand a decade and a half later.

Part of *WoodenBoat*'s success is directly attributable to the content of the magazine. But another part can be attributed to the other boating magazines, which since the emergence of fiberglass have become fixated on that substance and many of its corollaries in interests and commercial opportunities. In the past the boating magazines were filled with practical advice on boatbuilding, repair, maintenance, marlinspike seamanship, and the rest of the arts of the sailor. Today they are essentially consumer magazines, giving readers raw (but suspect) data on how to evaluate what they might like to buy next. Even if you have a fiberglass boat, you will find more information on sailorizing in *WoodenBoat* than you will in most other boating magazines.

At the time *WoodenBoat* was being established, Lance Lee, a former instructor at the Outward Bound School in Maine, decided to do something about wooden boatbuilding education. (It's worth noting that Jonathan Wilson also worked for Outward Bound, repairing their boats, before he went into the magazine business.) In the past, boatbuilding skills were passed from one generation to the next by apprenticeship. Young men went to work in boatshops as apprentices; after developing basic skills they became journeymen. Following years of hard work and subtle experience they were judged good enough to be called masters, to whom the next generation of young men would become apprentices. This logical, rigorous system of training broke down when wooden boatshops, one after another, folded after demand for their product dropped off. Those that remained were so small they couldn't even afford one unproductive apprentice. (It should be noted that certain government regulations — minimum wages and some OSHA rules, as well as various insurance provisions — also worked against the ancient apprentice-ship system.)

A period of ten to fifteen years passed during which very few skilled boatbuilders were turned out while numbers of old-timers retired or died. On the one hand this wasn't a great problem, because there was no real demand for wooden boats that might have been built by newly trained journeymen. On the other hand, as the interest in wooden boat building developed, especially among young people in the early 1970s, it became more and more difficult for the unskilled to gain training. At the same time, a large number of people began wanting to learn how to build boats for the sake of the act itself, not just to sell them to others.

Motivated by the desire to teach practical, usable skills to young people and also by the need to perpetuate methods and techniques that were fast dying out, Lance Lee founded the Apprenticeshop at the Maine Maritime Museum in Bath, Maine. He later went on to found the Rockport Apprenticeshop of Rockport, Maine.

The Apprenticeshop became a very successful melding of instruction and hands-on experience, where students built boats from the beginning to the end and saw the products of their labor sold to help defray the costs of running the school. When they finished at the shop, the apprentices would have mastered basic boatbuilding skills; some went on to professional boatbuilding, others took up different lines of work.

The Apprenticeshop was a success in the new world of post-fiberglass wooden boat building, and it caused many other organizations, both public and private, to set up training programs of their own. Some succeeded, some failed, but all contributed to establishing a pool of skilled young boatbuilders who fanned out into the countryside, going to work in professional shops, setting up their own shops, and spreading the gospel.

WoodenBoat magazine and the Apprenticeshop have become certifiable institutions of the Wooden Boat Revival, but they're not the only ones. Several other influential organizations have sprung up in the last couple of decades, among them the Traditional Small Craft Association, the Traditional Wooden Boat Society, the Center for Wooden Boats, the Antique and Classic Boat Society, the society for the preservation of this, the school for the promotion of that, the foundation for the encouragement of whatever. Their members are more than wooden boat enthusiasts. They are believers in the power of wood.

Who are these people who have turned their backs on the much-touted superiority of fiberglass in favor of more-demanding wood? Where did they come from?

For certain, many of them are people who never gave up. They like wood, dislike fiberglass, and that's that. They grew up with wooden boats, and the look, feel, and smell of wood are a large part of their definition of what a boat is all about. (Smell plays a significant role in people's love of wood — the sweet aroma of cedar, the sharp perfume of linseed oil, the raw power of pine tar — yet there are ironies here. I wonder how many are aware that the smell that almost always brings tears of nostalgia to their eyes is in reality the odor of incipient rot.)

I am convinced, though, that the real roots of the Wooden Boat Revival are embedded in the romantic back-to-the-land movement of the late 1960s and early 1970s. It is no coincidence that the *Mariner's Catalog* — an early revivalist publication — was an offshoot of the *Whole Earth Catalog*, that Jonathan Wilson, founder of *Wooden-*

Boat, dropped out and lived on a subsistence farm while he built small craft, that the students at the Apprentice-shop live communally, that the annual festival at Port Townsend, Washington, resembles as much a countercultural street fair as it does a showplace for restored and newly constructed wooden boats.

The back-to-the-landers dropped out because they were unhappy with the direction of modern society. Sterility, regimentation, bureaucratization, depersonalization, artificiality — the whole works made them nostalgic for what they perceived as a gentler time when folks were self-sufficient and in tune with their surroundings, and had permanent traditions and values. Small is beautiful. You are what you eat.

On one level, at least, the entire movement was a flash in the pan; the hippie of yesterday is the arbitrageur of today. But that yearning for things plainer, fresher, and more natural continues to influence most of us today. We want *real* things and *real* experiences.

Many of today's wooden boat revivalists began as philosophical refugees from the twentieth century. Like the back-to-the-landers, they sought to get in touch with what they thought was real, and gained inspiration from the old-timers who hadn't quit and probably never will. The revival was started by a bunch of backwater romantics who allied themselves with those old-style boatbuilders who were willing to go along. If you don't believe this, find an established wooden boat builder of the old school and ask him how many of the visitors to his shop in, say, 1971, were so-called hippies speaking of craftsmanship and how many were white-collar workers talking about a boat for weekend sailing with the wife and the kids.

"We've lost our past and must find it," was almost a slogan for these people. They combed the waterfront for those boatbuilders and designers who represented the best of the old craftsmanship, and then set out to emulate them. As a result, builders and designers, especially those who did their best work before World War II — the Herreshoffs, John Alden, Fenwick Williams, John Atkin, William Crosby, etc., — gained revived reputations and became almost cult heroes to the Movement. Before 1970 not many boat lovers had ever heard of such boatbuilders as Pete Culler, Sonny Hodgdon, Bent Jespersen, Aubrey Marshall, Clark Mills, Roy Wallace, Ralph Stanley, and Frank Prothero, but among revivalists they have become legends.

But when you get right down to it, the wooden boat movement doesn't amount to much when compared to everything going on in the rest of the boat world. For every new wooden boat built today, there are thousands of fiberglass and aluminum craft emerging from the factories. We are witnessing a low-tech phenomenon in a high-tech society. Most wooden boat activity is tucked away out of public view, carried on by individuals and small groups going quietly about their business. Within a fifteen-mile radius of my home on West Penobscot Bay, Maine, there are many small professional shops turning out plywood dories, lapstrake-planked peapods and wherries, guideboats, yacht dinghies, oars and paddles, lobsterboats, and good-sized yachts. There is a small shipyard in nearby Rockland that built a brand-new ninety-three-foot passenger schooner a few years ago, plus countless private projects underway in cellar workshops and backyard barns.

Very few of these projects are ever acknowledged publicly, but all of them taken together put the lie to the assertation that wooden boats are dead.

The Legacy of Howard I. Chapelle

Back in 1969 or 1970 — the exact date escapes me — I attended a conference on maritime history at the U.S. Naval Academy in Annapolis, Maryland. For the most part it was a typically dull, jargon-ridden exercise in academic dreariness. I remember wondering which could be worse: having to read learned papers on the composition of lag bolts in late-nineteenth-century torpedo-boat destroyers or having to listen to the authors of the learned papers read them out loud while three-quarters of the audience twitched in somnolence.

But I hadn't come for the formal sessions. As an editor working for a publisher specializing in nautical books, I had come for the coffee breaks and the cocktail hours, those intimate moments when one might meet firsthand the people who could provide grist for my particular mill. Famous historians such as Morison and Baker, Tate and Albion, Labaree, Leavitt, Brewington, and Chapelle.

Samuel Eliot Morison. Was he there? I can't remember; but if he wasn't, he should have been. William Avery Baker. Was he there? What does it matter? Chapelle was, and everyone knew it.

When Howard I. Chapelle, at the time senior historian of the Smithsonian Institution, walked into the room, all conversation stopped, all heads turned, all due respect was paid to a legend in his own time. On the verge of turning seventy years old, Howard Chapelle — "Chap" to his friends and colleagues — was literally and figuratively a giant in the field of maritime history. Tall, white-haired, with a heavy featured face relieved by a thin, white mustache, he was a man with the very rare quality of *presence* — a presence so strong that, of all the luminaries who were in the room at the time, his is the only image that still remains fixed in my mind.

I had no competition. When I started exploring the field I discovered that I was all alone. . . . No one else was interested in the old sailing vessels, especially the smaller ones. — Howard I. Chapelle

In the 1920s, when Howard Chapelle was a young man, few people were paying much attention to traditional American maritime culture. The Great Age of Sail had ended years before, and the Lesser Age of Sail was being slowly ground down to a rather pathetic collection of aging and economically marginal vessels employed in commercial fishing, coasting, and in a few instances, deepwater tramping. The immediate cause of this decline was the shipping slump that followed World War I, but the principal, underlying causes were the efficiencies and conveniences of the engine-powered vessel and the parallel development of shoreside transportation, especially the trucking industry. Sail, whether in small craft or large vessels, couldn't compete with steam, diesel, and gasoline.

Smart money and smart people were going modern. The old vessels were being laid up, junked, scrapped, sold foreign, converted to restaurants and ballrooms, and in many cases, simply run up on mudflats and abandoned. The smaller working craft — the Friendship sloops, the Banks dories, the whaleboats, the oyster sharpies, the peapods, the wherries — made obsolete by power launches and draggers and who knows what all, were being propped up on shore or in barns and being forgotten. Not-so-smart money and not-so-smart people were hanging on to the old ways and the old vessels as best they could, but the handwriting was on the wall: A new age was dawning; an old age was just about dead.

It is impossible to get into the mind of Howard Chapelle. Nobody can put a finger on why he decided at an early age to document the traditional maritime culture that was dying before his eyes. Curiosity? Nostalgia? Monomania? The lack of something better to do? Who knows? All that can be said is that while virtually all of his contemporaries went modern, so to speak, Chapelle took a long, thorough, hard look at what was left — the still-working craft, the hulks, the half models, the not-quite-abandoned skills, the plans, the memories of the old-timers — and documented them. Chapelle and a very few others seemed to understand intuitively that the study of the maritime past must begin with the preservation of the maritime present. If records and artifacts and memories were not preserved, there could be no evidence for historians to sift, no concrete material on which to anchor a theory, no demonstrable proof to clinch an argument.

Almost anyone who has been interested in wooden boats in my era grew up with American Small Sailing Craft *within close reach. Look at my copy as I sit here. It's about 18 inches away from me! That book and* Boatbuilding *were easily the two most influential books for anyone interested in traditional small craft.* — Benjamin A. G. Fuller, Curator, Mystic Seaport Museum

Howard Chapelle had no way of knowing it, but his work, more than anyone else's, would have a great influence on the revival of interest in traditional small craft and wooden boats that began in the late 1960s and continues today. Two books, both by Howard Chapelle, lay at the heart of the movement: *Boatbuilding* and *American Small Sailing Craft*. The first published in 1941, the second in 1951, they may have been a few decades or more before their time, but their time came nevertheless.

Boatbuilding was ostensibly a practical book. It took the reader step by step through the building of wooden boats of three types: flat-bottomed, V-bottomed, and round-bottomed. Immediately upon publication it was hailed as *the* book to have, and it has held that reputation ever since, even though critics pointed out that it was poorly organized, expert boatbuilders pointed out that some of the procedures described were a little dicey, and readers pointed out that more information was left out than was put in. The strengths of the book, however, were that it was about old-style plank-on-frame boatbuilding and, for the most part, described how professional shops built boats in the 1920s and 1930s. Since Chapelle was not a boatbuilder himself and relied on professionals for his information, he had — perhaps unwittingly, perhaps not — created an anthropological document, a road map to the past for those who might wish to go in that direction.

American Small Sailing Craft was, in effect, a companion volume to *Boatbuilding*. A study of vanished or vanishing indigenous boat types, it illustrated and described, through plans, the development of the design of small working craft from Colonial times to the 1930s. Chapelle laid them all out, the obscure and the unobscure — the catboats, the sloop-boats, the skipjacks, the garvies, the sharpies, the beach boats, and all their permutations. Each boat was presented through excrutiatingly detailed plans, with builder's offsets, which suggested to the reader that these craft need not be obsolete or extinct. Anyone, amateur or professional, with a copy of *American Small Sailing Craft* in one hand and *Boatbuilding* in the other could resurrect any boat he pleased.

In fact, that was one of the premises behind Chapelle's books in the first place. His introduction to *American Small Sailing Craft* was a reasoned argument in favor of a reexamination of the old workboat types for pleaure sailing. "As opposed to the mass-production boat," he wrote, "the idea of employing the cheap work-boat appears both practical and attractive: by use of work-boat types the owner can obtain a boat suited to his home waters and weather; he can have a distinctive boat, built in many cases by himself or with local aid and with available materials; and he can avoid the appearance of sameness that now afflicts our yachting fleets."

There was always and will always be a class of people who are dissatisfied with the *appearance of sameness*, and for them, the works of Howard Chapelle were a godsend. His books documented salty boats, classic boats, traditional boats, good boats, sensible boats — they've been called all that and more — and hailed them not as the end of things but as the beginning of things.

Chapelle was an amazing man. He was able to go into the field and come back with hard data and come pretty close to closing a circle. — Lance Lee, Director, the Rockport Apprenticeshop

To understand Howard Chapelle's contributions one must understand first and foremost that he was both a naval architect and a maritime historian. Born in Tolland, Massachusetts, in 1901, he grew up in New Haven, Connecticut, where his father owned an oyster business. He was given his first sailboat — a New Haven sharpie, an oyster workboat, of course — when he was twelve years old and became hooked on what can best be described as the alongshore life, the maritime culture where the land meets the sea. (In later years, Chapelle was notable for his dislike of offshore sailing, even though his public reputation seemed to indicate otherwise.) More specifically, he became fascinated by boats and ships and at an early age resolved to become a naval architect, or rather a small-craft designer.

After high school, Chapelle enrolled in the Webb Institute of Naval Architecture, but dropped out before classes began because of poor health. It was just as well, given his interests, since small-craft design, unlike naval architecture, is more of an art and less of a science. Webb was a scientific institution that trained its students in big-ship design and engineering and left art to the artists.

There would be no more formal education for Howard Chapelle. In 1919 he began effectively a ten-year apprenticeship without indenture, knocking about from boatyard to design office, shipyard to library. He learned boatbuilding in the shop of George Buckout of Poughkeepsie, New York, and shipbuilding in a yard in Jacksonville, Florida. He learned seamanship on a lumber schooner on the Cuba-Bahamas run, and marine engineering with the Gibbs Gas Engine Company of Jacksonville, Florida. Most especially, he learned naval architecture in the offices of some of the greatest designers of the time: Charles Mower, William Gardner, William H. Hand, Walter McInnis, and John Alden.

On the one hand, this sounds like the résumé of a young man who either didn't know what to do with himself or wasn't good enough to keep a job for more than a few months at a time. On the other hand, it sounds like the résumé of a young man who wanted to gain as much experience as possible in a very short period of time.

In retrospect, the latter must have been the goal, since during those years Chapelle was also seeking out in his spare time the company of such influential naval architects as Commodore Ralph Munroe and Nathanael G. Herreshoff and other nautical sages, known and unknown. He even traveled on his own account to England in 1924 to study Admiralty draughts preserved in Whitehall that pertained to American ships and boats.

Before he was thirty years old, through a process of self-education, Chapelle had established himself as a practicing small-craft designer and as a serious scholar of the history of naval architecture. The proof? In 1930 he set up his own design shop and published his first book, *The Baltimore Clipper*. Uncredentialed, yet with a richer education than most other people his age, he was on the verge of a roll that would make him, in another decade, preeminent in his field of interest.

It began, about 1924, as a self-educational project to explore the "art" of small boat design, on which there had been little published. As time passed and more and more material was found, the beauty, distinction, and practical good qualities of many types became apparant, and the matter became one of greater personal interest. — Howard I. Chapelle

The thing to remember about Chapelle is that he wasn't a designer and he wasn't a sailor. He was a historian. — Melbourne Smith, artist, shipbuilder, ship designer

Well, yes and no. Howard Chapelle was indeed a designer. He had worked for several well-known naval architects and even hung out his own shingle for a while, but his work was not of an original sort. Rather, he adapted historical types for modern use and sometimes encountered problems when he did so. The most famous of his designs, for example, the topsail schooner *Swift*, which he produced for William A. Robinson, turned out to be an initial failure. Based on an eighteenth-century brig, she had stability problems when launched and required modification before she could be used. (There are those who claim the problems arose because Chapelle didn't like to do stability calculations, having been of the school of thought that holds, "If she looks good, she must be good.")

It is also true that Chapelle didn't like sailing all that much. He liked the idea of it — even designed and built his pinky *Glad Tidings* for a projected voyage to the West Indies (which he never undertook) — but the reality was something else. Daysailing in small craft was mostly his cup of tea.

A historian? Of course he was a historian, though not necessarily in the formal, academic sense of the word.

It would be an exaggeration of the grossest sort to suggest that maritime history in Chapelle's time (or even our time, for that matter) amounted to much more than a low rise on the academic landscape. Few people studied it, still fewer taught it, even though the history of America until recent years was maritime or maritime derived.

In Howard Chapelle's era, the 1920s through the 1960s, maritime scholarship belonged to the nonprofessionals — not that the work being done was necessarily unprofessional, but that the people who were doing it were not professionally trained historians. Genuine professional maritime historians were few and far between. In their absence, the field, such as it was, was dominated by a few extremely proficient and knowledgeable amateurs.

Chapelle was a perfect example of the type. He didn't have a bachelor's degree in history, never mind a master's or a doctorate, yet he wrote books and learned papers, served on committees, and did original research. He was at various times a regional director of the Historic American Merchant Marine Survey (a Depression-era

Works Project Administration program), a consultant on the preservation of such historic vessels as the *Philadelphia* and the *Constellation*, one of the founding editors of the *American Neptune*, a Guggenheim Fellow, consultant to the Food and Agriculture Organization, and curator of transportation at the Smithsonian Institution. *But he didn't have any academic training.* He simply was imbued with the idea that this culture, these artifacts, were disappearing on his watch and that it was his duty to conserve as much as possible.

Chapelle's methodology was quite straightforward: document as much as possible, as quickly as possible, before he dropped. As a naval architect his specialty was taking the lines off existing vessels or their half models, recording details about rigging and hardware, analyzing the hull shapes of various boat types, and comparing, contrasting, and developing an appreciation for the evolutionary development of American ships and boats. He traveled extensively — in the early years for the most part on his own dime — and developed a wide range of contacts and informants, people in the heart of the maritime community who knew what was what.

He was involved in research of the most basic sort. Indeed, he studied in libraries and archives, but his prime sources were the shipyards, boatshops, wharves, and warehouses. Howard Chapelle was doing what almost no other maritime historian was doing. He was singlehandedly defining the scope of the history of naval architecture.

Not without a certain amount of controversy, both during the years when he was engaged in research and later when others had time to examine the product of his labors. Chapelle's reputation notwithstanding, there were flaws in his research and inaccuracies in his published findings and plans. Perhaps because he lacked a scholar's education or because he was in a hurry — or perhaps both — he sometimes didn't get the facts right, and sometimes, in the absence of the facts themselves, he did a little interpretation, guesswork, intuitive supposition. Sometimes, probably because he was a naval architect himself, he would slightly alter the design of a historical vessel when he drew her plans for publication. He might have been drawing the lines to make them conform to what he thought they should be rather than what they actually were.

Anyone who has spent a reasonable amount of time with Howard Chapelle's work — built a boat from his plans, for example — will have discovered problems of one sort or another. The table of offsets might have transposed numbers, one view of a vessel might not completely match another, the source for Chapelle's data might not have been provided, a plan that may have been traced from an Admiralty draught might have been refaired in such a way as to alter slightly the appearance of the hull.

"If you look at the original lines of the clipper *Sea Witch* that were drawn by John W. Griffiths and compare them to Chapelle's redrawing in *The Search for Speed Under Sail*," says designer Melbourne Smith, "you'll see that Chapelle increased the depth by 18 inches. He made many, many changes in the vessel. I don't know why he did it." Other researchers have found similar difficulties.

On the other hand, all this must be balanced by the prodigious amount of work done by Chapelle. If he hadn't done it, inaccurate or not, we would now have nothing.

Howard Chapelle was a great pioneer whose influence has been profound on both sides of the Atlantic. A good deal of the current interest in small craft and almost all the interest in the development of hull form in sailing craft is due to him. — Basil Greenhill, former director, National Maritime Museum, Greenwich, England

I have all his books right in front of me while I work.

I use them so much the spines are worn off. I have to use a marking pencil on them now to tell which one is which.
— Melbourne Smith, artist, shipbuilder, ship designer

The influence of Howard Chapelle is incalculable. Most historians, if they are lucky, publish the results of their research and hope that a few of their colleagues will read it and perhaps adopt it as required reading in a graduate seminar. None of them would realistically expect any practical results to flow from their work. Would a scholar of, say, Early American stagecoach design and construction live to see the day when vast numbers of people would start building replicas and adaptations of Early American stagecoaches? Hardly likely. But consider just a few of the things that have happened as a consequence of Howard Chapelle's work.

Almost every maritime museum and historical society worthy of the name has a wooden boat building program of some sort, and most of the boats they are building are based on designs recorded by Chapelle.

The first boat professionally built by Jonathan Wilson, founder of *WoodenBoat* magazine, was a peapod illustrated in *American Small Sailing Craft*. In fact, the very founding of *WoodenBoat* came about following Wilson's immersion in Chapelle's works.

Many of the crop of currently fashionable replica ships are based on designs brought to light and analyzed by Chapelle: *Pride of Baltimore* (Baltimore clipper), *Spirit of Massachusetts* (fishing schooner), *Californian* (revenue cutter), *Vernon Languille* (Tancook whaler).

At any of the scores of gatherings each year of traditional small craft everywhere in the country — East, South, North, West, Great Lakes, Chesapeake — a huge percentage of the boats are either straight from the pages of *American Small Sailing Craft* or are modern derivations of designs found therein.

Where once there was Howard Chapelle, primarily, and a handful of others, secondarily, documenting American boat and ship types and writing about their findings, there is now an entire army combing the waterfront with notebook and measuring tape in hand.

In Great Britain, Europe, Canada, Australia, New Zealand — anywhere in the world where books are sold and people can read — there are traditional American boats being built and used, primarily because their plans are readily available in Howard Chapelle's books. You can find Banks dories in England, peapods in New Zealand, and sandbaggers in France without even looking very hard.

Howard Chapelle's work lured me into what I do, primarily because of the shapes of the boats that he recorded. — Jonathan Wilson, editor and publisher, *WoodenBoat*

Who wouldn't succumb to the lure of the boats recorded by Howard Chapelle? (The temptation here is to call them Howard Chapelle's boats. It is true that he did not *design* them in a technical sense; nevertheless, many of these designs would not exist if he had not included them in his books, and therefore they must be his.) These are the boats of our maritime past. They carry the stamp of the sea, the power of unbroken practical evolution, the sense of being what they are for no other reason than to serve a particular purpose in a particular place at a particular time. They are boats of *context*.

You can look at Chapelle's plans for any number of types of craft and almost determine intuitively what they were for. The New Haven sharpie — narrow and flat-bottomed for fast sailing in shallow water. The Block Island boat — fat and deep for seaworthiness and capaciousness. The Whitehall — fine-lined and finely formed for elegant quickness. These are boats with distinction, modeled to do a job and make their owners proud while they're doing it.

Of course, there is no longer a practical need for Howard Chapelle's boats. Fishing is no longer done under sail; pilots are not dropped off or picked up under oar. Peapods, wherries, Hampton boats, Newfoundland trap skiffs, Bermuda sloops, Chesapeake log canoes — none of these craft are required to do what they were developed to do. But they fascinate us still because of their integrity and honest aesthetics.

The aesthetics — they are the heart of the matter. Howard Chapelle's boats have a look, make a statement, convey an emotion. His plans and drawings are so sharp, so full of detail, so visually appealing that you would have to have a heart of stone not to be attracted to them.

At that meeting of maritime historians at the Naval Academy so long ago, I remember someone asking Howard Chapelle why he devoted so much time to such an obscure discipline as the history of American naval architecture. His response reminded me of the mountaineer's reply, "Because it is there," to the question, "Why did you climb that mountain?" Chapelle said he was fascinated by the subject and couldn't imagine doing anything but studying it. His legacy and our good fortune are that he was and he did.

Without access to the research of JoAnn King, this look at the work of Howard Chapelle would be thin soup indeed. Ms. King is an information consultant and free-lance researcher with a PhD in American Studies from George Washington University. Her dissertation was on Chapelle.

John Gardner
in His Own Words

John Gardner is the heart and soul of the traditional small-craft movement. He is a boatbuilder, boat designer, small-craft historian, museum curator, technical editor, teacher, author, public speaker. Few in our field can claim such a breadth and depth of experience and expertise, and few can claim to have influenced so many people so thoroughly.

But every person holds surprises, and John Gardner is no exception. Publicly he comes across as a man who gets up in the morning, thinks about boats, talks about boats, builds boats, then goes back to bed at night and dreams about boats. There may be some truth to that, but there is also the private John Gardner who is at ease with larger issues, who has spent a good part of his life trying to gain a larger perspective and who, for the most part, has been successful at it. The achievement of balance as an individual — with equal application of manual and intellectual skills — seems to have been his lifelong goal, which means that he is as comfortable discussing social theory as he is talking about the origins of the Swampscott dory. His implied message is that it is perfectly all

29

right to become a specialist, but not to the extent that you ignore the rest of the world.

This interview took place in the fall of 1980 at John Gardner's home in Mystic, Connecticut. The results of our conversation are published here without the questions so they will not get in the way of the story. What is worth reading is what he said, not what I asked him.

Unfortunately, the one thing this interview failed to reveal is Gardner's humor. On one level at least he is one of the wittiest people I have met, though the nature of his humor can only be understood on a person-to-person basis. He possesses the classical Yankee dry wit, which relies on understatement coupled with twinkling eyes or a wry grin, a style that cannot be conveyed by the written word. Take my word for it: he has the gift as few others do.

"My recollections go back to very early in the century. I was born in 1905 in Calais, Maine, which is on the St. Croix River at the head of Passamaquoddy Bay, where it forms the border between Maine and New Brunswick. I come from a long line of land surveyors. My great-grandfather was one, as was my grandfather and my father.

"We lived on a farm on the river about three miles below Calais. The farm ran down to the water and a mile back. As a boy I had boats on the river. There were great tides, twenty-six to twenty-eight feet, and the river at that point was about a mile wide, so when the tide was out there would be a half-mile of mud flats. Keeping a boat with tides like that took ingenuity. I had a pole about thirty feet long stuck in the mud flats and a square float — four boards nailed together — around the pole that would go up and down with the tide. I tied my boat to that. I also had a boat similar to the one Chapelle called the *Farmer's Daughter* with a wooden wheelbarrow wheel at the bow, which allowed it to be pushed over the mud flats.

"We built boats and used boats. My grandfather, before my time, had a pinky, which he used a great deal, and even while I was small he still went down river in the fall to catch fish for the winter. In fact, there were many boats on the river at that time. There were lumber schooners, excursion boats, and steamboats. Calais was a thriving, enterprising, prosperous place, a center for the lumber industry.

"We cut our own boat lumber from our woodlot, usually at the same time we cut our firewood for the winter. We saved the good sawlogs and hauled them to a mill and brought the lumber home. My grandfather made everything. He made boats, he made hay racks and cart wheels, he built buildings and shingled roofs. He had been a carver's apprentice in Charlestown, Massachusetts, and was an accomplished woodcarver. I learned woodworking from him and my father as part of growing up.

"When I was young I used to spend quite a good deal of time at a nearby boatshop owned by the Whelan boys, so called although they were still called the Whelan boys when they were long past seventy. Jim and George were their names, though they were locally known as Pete and Repeat because they always repeated each other when they talked. They were Irish, Catholic, and Democrats, which put them apart to some extent in that area. They built all types of boats up to fifty or sixty feet for commercial or pleasure use, and all by hand. The shop had no power at all. Pieces were ripped out of rough-sawn lumber with handsaws and then planed. They used adzes and broad axes. I was influenced by these men. I was also influenced by a very skilled carpenter by the name of Tommy Webster, who lived up the road. He built my father's house with my father's assistance, without plans. The shelves and pantries were finished just like the interior of a vessel.

"I never apprenticed as a carpenter or boatbuilder, but

I picked up the skills as I went along. My first attempt to rig my own boat came early on, when I took one of my great-grandfather's sea chests from the barn down to the brook and tried to sail it like a boat. From there I became a pretty good boatbuilder and built several craft before I got out of high school — rowboats, sailboats, nothing too difficult. Once I decided to build a dory and sent to the Maine State Library for a book with the lines of a pretty big dory. I scaled it down proportionally with the result that it was too tender. So to remedy the defect I built two airtight sponsons shaped something like crescent moons and attached them to the sides. The boat became very stable and rowed nicely but looked odd. I took it down to the Whelans, who scratched their heads but admitted the arrangement worked pretty good.

"I went to school in Calais, and after graduation I went to normal school in Machias. I took the standard two-year teacher-training course and then taught school for two years. I decided to become a teacher because I was encouraged to do so at home — both of my aunts were teachers — and it was the most convenient thing to do, I guess. Believe it or not, I was also motivated by football. Perhaps one of the most exciting moments of my life was when I made the varsity football team in my high school sophomore year at Calais Academy. In those days you had to supply your own uniform. I sawed and split and piled four cords of hackmatack wood to buy a pair of football pants. In my freshman year at Machias Normal School I was one of the group that organized the school's first football team. But football wasn't the only thing. I had a lot of drive back then. I initiated and was editor of the *Washingtonia*, the school magazine, was president of the student body, and did just about everything else.

"During one of my teaching years, I went to summer school at Columbia University in New York, which at the time was the leading teacher-training institution in the country. Only graduate courses were offered, but working teachers were permitted to take two years of graduate work that qualified them for a BS in education. So I stayed on at Columbia and took the two-year course, and then went on to get my master's degree in 1932.

"I got out of Columbia in the depths of the Depression. I was there in New York when they were selling apples on street corners and the financiers were jumping out of windows on Wall Street. It was a tough time to go to college and a tough time to get a job afterwards, even though I achieved honor rank.

"But in the meantime, in 1930, I had got a summer job as a counselor at Pine Island Camp in Belgrade Lakes, Maine. I worked there summers during the 1930s while I was at Columbia and afterwards when I was kicking around like most others during the Depression. I was in charge of the workshop, which was one of the features of the camp. We built model boats and yachts and sailed them. I also built several full-size boats there, such as a C. D. Mower sailing dinghy whose lines had been published in *Rudder* magazine. I was put in charge of the shop because of my background; I had the skills and the interest. I was also qualified because I understood both inland craft, like canoes, and saltwater craft. Calais, where I grew up, was intermediate between upriver — the woods — and downriver — the ocean. I understood both worlds. I found the camp to be a delightful experience and gained much inspiration from the work I did there.

"But full-time work eluded me. When I graduated from Columbia I had a first-class education. My expectations were that I would get a rather fancy job, but there weren't any. So I knocked about quite a bit and spent some time at home. I worked in the woods as a lumberman. I contracted and peeled pulpwood. I peeled a hundred cords of pulpwood one summer. I didn't teach at all — just knocked around at a lot of different things.

"My life as a boatyard worker began when World War II broke out. I happened to be in Lynn, Massachusetts, at the time and signed on at the Graves yard in nearby Marblehead because they were building Coast Guard picketboats as fast as they could and needed experienced workers. They never questioned my ability; I guess it was because I was from Maine and seemed to know what I was talking about.

"The picketboats were thirty-eight feet long and had been designed by Walter McInnis. We built seventy-two or seventy-three of them. I was on the night shift as a planker, since this was an assembly line operation. We were building two boats at a time, and I had two men who were hanging the planks and fastening them as fast as I got them out. Another crew was getting out the keel assemblies, lowering them on the forms and timbering them. Still another crew would finish them inside after they were turned over. We planked the boats upside down, and it was fast and furious work.

"When the picket boats were finished and things slacked off at Graves, I went over to Reed's Shipyard in Winthrop and went to work on a big, curious Navy barge, heavily built of Oregon fir. The yard was expanding like mad. I hung plank for a while and then was assigned to build a scale model of the craft for Washington. It was a typical government mess, with constant revisions to the full-size craft. I had to go out to the construction all the time and measure the changes and then rework the model. It was quite an elaborate job.

"Soon I got a call to go back to Graves, however. I returned to work on several different types of boats, and then started in on yachts because they were still trying to carry on with their yacht business even though there was a war on. I did yacht repair and other jobs; in fact, I built the tank-test model for the Hickman Sea Sled.

"It was wild over there in Marblehead at the beginning

of the war. We had blackouts because the submarines were right off the coast, and a civil defense force was organized locally. We were all given guns; I had an old elephant gun that belonged to Graves's father-in-law. The foreman turned out billy clubs for blackout wardens in the joiner shop. We stopped work on several afternoons to go to the gravel pit and practice with our guns. We were given posts behind various rocks on the beach in case the submarines should land. It was completely wild.

"By then I had given up on being a teacher. I was doing what I wanted to do, and the job was over at four o'clock on Friday. I had a great many intellectual interests that occupied me when I wasn't working. That was more or less the pattern until I went to work at Mystic Seaport in 1969. For example, I began to measure boats and take off lines. Some of those lines I put away until much later when I began to write. I then drew upon those resources that I gathered in Marblehead.

"I started taking off lines because I was interested in boats and their shapes, and I was interested in drawing them. I was also influenced by the people I worked with. I was working with a very fine boatbuilder, Charles Lawton, who was then considered to be the dean of his craft north of Boston. He was almost ninety at that time, still building boats at Graves. He had come down from St. John as a young man and had begun building boats in Boston as early as 1880. He worked at the Navy Yard before coming to Graves.

"World War II was the last hurrah of the old-time boatbuilders, many of whom came out of retirement for the duration. We had one boat joiner at Graves by the name of Dan Grant. He was a Nova Scotia Scotsman, an extraordinarily talented woodworker, sparmaker, carpenter. He could do anything. He made violins to pay the hospital expenses for one of his sons who had polio. He made very fine violins. He claimed he ruined his eyes working nights making them. He was a very ingenious man, and I count myself lucky for being able to work with people like that.

"I stayed at Graves until the end of the war; then I went to work for Simms Brothers in Dorchester, where they were building fine yachts for Sparkman & Stephens. Simms had formerly worked for Lawley, and his yard was sort of a home for old Lawley hands. We were double planking yachts fifty to sixty feet long. The outside layer was seven-eights-inch African mahogany and the inside was three-eights-inch white cedar with white lead between. The outside planking was so smooth and tight you couldn't see where the seams were. I finally left Simms in the late 1940s because it was too far from my home and the pay wasn't too good. I went to work at Dion's Boatyard in Salem. Relations there were very good. If you could do the work and you were reliable, Fred Dion didn't bother you. In fact, he gave me his youngest son so I could train him. I did all repair work — no new construction.

"From the late 1940s until 1969 I worked at Dion's, with the exception of two years during the Korean War when I worked at General Electric in the template room. I was essentially a patternmaker in the turbine division, though when business was slow I went out on the floor and tried my hand at welding and boilermaking. It was interesting work, but not too hard. I was generally done with my task in three or four hours, and for the rest of my shift I used to make things for myself or write.

"You have to understand that I was leading two lives. I was a manual worker to make a living but was engaged in intellectual pursuits the rest of the time. In the 1930s I had been doing a lot of reading in many fields, including boat design and building. I read the very fine articles in *Yachting* written by Howard Chapelle in the 1930s; they were quite definitely the foundation of all his work — those are the articles he contributed on the Friendship sloop and a series of other traditional American craft. I had Chapelle's book on boatbuilding, for example, which came out in 1941. I brought a copy in to work and showed it to Dan Grant. He said not to pay too much attention to it, because he had given most of the information to Chapelle, and it was old-fashioned.

"During this period I used to go to the Associates' meetings at the Peabody Museum of Salem, which group was very loosely constituted. We used to meet more or less regularly, and different people would talk and present papers — people like Samuel Eliot Morison and William Avery Baker. It was also during this time that I started to write about boats for publication. I wrote my first article for the *Maine Coast Fisherman* (which later became the *National Fisherman*) in 1951, and after my first piece on the Hammond dory appeared, I became acquainted with Howard Chapelle. We met and established a very close relationship, working together and exchanging information. For example, in the late 1950s I spent a week at his home in Maryland, where I learned much about Chesapeake Bay boat construction.

"Howard Chapelle was an extremely interesting man and had much influence on me and others. You hear occasional revisionist talk about him now, but I must say that he was an extraordinarily gifted man who made an enormous contribution. When I say gifted, I mean he could turn out prodigious amounts of work. He could draw boat lines, intricate boat lines, and carry on an animated conversation on an entirely different subject at the same time. He was the first man in our field, a completely virgin field. There was an abundance of material scattered around just to be had for the asking, and he attempted to gather in so much that quite naturally he sometimes missed things. Sometimes he arrived at conclusions intuitively rather than from laborious digging. Sometimes his intuitions were not accurate, although they could be enormously brilliant. He read extensively but kept few notes. Occasionally his references are not to be trusted completely. Yet you have to give the man credit; he did a tremendous amount of work when no one else was paying any attention to it. He got the thing started, but some of what he did has to be refined.

"Marion Brewington, another pioneer, was a meticulous researcher, extremely fussy about the most minute details. He and Chapelle in the beginning were quite close friends, and I knew them both. Some of the slips that Chapelle made, Brewington couldn't take. On the other hand, Chapelle said he just couldn't understand Brewington. Yet Chapelle was an extremely generous person, was always sharing his information. He was also argumentative, and his politics were quite conservative. You have to give Chapelle credit for what he did, and you need to be cautious about what you accept without checking. Incidentally, I believe that goes for all of us.

"But boats weren't my only interest. I was very much involved in Freudian psychology at that time and still have a whole Freudian library, which I don't read any more. I almost wrote a book on the Oneida Community. I still have the copious notes. I researched the obscure literature in the Widener Library at Harvard after getting special entrée through a friend. I spent hours in the Boston Athenaeum, the Hart Nautical Library, and the Boston Medical Library.

"At the same time I was a contributing editor of *Contemporary Issues* magazine, which was published in England and has since gone out of existence. I wrote under the pseudonym of Clarkson. I did a long study of the Rosenburg case, one of the first analyses of what was going on. I did a very long analysis of the early background of atomic energy, with the mistaken notion that it was going to solve all our energy problems. Some of the others connected with the magazine thought otherwise. But I was wrong, and I know it now. I contributed to other publications as well, including *Balanced Living*, published by The School for Living. This was on ecology — back to the land, organic gardening — long before the present interest in that sort of thing. All this took quite a bit of time and research. I received no money at all; I did it just for the interest. I was making enough at the boatyard to get by on, but you might say it wasn't a life of luxury.

"Very early on in my writing for the *Maine Coast Fisherman* I did a series of articles on the Whitehall boat, which marked the beginning of the Whitehall revival. Previous to that the boat was pretty much forgotten except for a short article Captain Charleton Smith had done for *Rudder* back in 1943. About 1958 or 1959 Kenneth Durant, after retiring from journalism, became interested in Adirondack guideboat history. He started out with the idea that the guideboat might have developed from the Whitehall, and got in touch with me. From then until his death in 1972 we had a very productive working relationship. We shared research and boatbuilding knowledge. He was researching in Hanover, New Hampshire, Cambridge, and New York, and he had contacts abroad. We were together accumulating a great deal of boatbuilding background, both history and development. Durant was working in conjunction with the Adirondack Museum, and it was through him that I began to work on and off with that museum as a consultant. And it was because of Ed Lynch, whom I worked with at the museum, that I came to Mystic Seaport in 1969.

"When Ed Lynch went to Mystic he decided he wanted to start a small-craft program. He arranged to have me hired. At the time I was still living in Lynn and working at Dion's in Salem, and it would be necessary for me to move to Connecticut. But it was a very promising job in many ways. I was getting older, and I could look ahead and see that the type of work that I was doing in the boatyard would be getting harder and harder for me. Although I liked the work at Dion's, it was fairly difficult, particularly in the wintertime, as we worked in unheated sheds. I was almost at retirement age. I came to Mystic for more money than I was getting in the boatyard, and it was a very interesting type of work, more or less a continuation, a culmination, of something that had been building up and growing for a long time.

"When I came to Mystic there was no small-craft program at all. I hunted around for a place and found an unoccupied corner of a storage shed where they had wagons and sleighs. I took that space and built a bench from materials I picked up around the seaport and started building a boat. I also started traveling around New England for the museum, buying up tools. There were many holes in the museum's collection. Tool collecting at that time had not quite reached the dramatic proportions that it has reached today, and I got a lot of good buys.

"That first year, 1969, I was invited to go to the Thousand Islands as a judge at the antique boat show, which was then in its fourth or fifth year. But there were no small craft. I saw St. Lawrence skiffs, which I had been interested in since I first went to work in Marblehead, and I suggested that they enlarge the program from one to two days and include small craft. The next year they did it. I got the idea from there that we should have some sort of small-craft meet at Mystic, with the result that in the summer of 1970, the following year, we had our first rowing workshop. That was the first meet of recreational small craft in this country, and it was the beginning of a continuing movement.

"That winter I decided to institute instruction in boatbuilding at Mystic Seaport, but not vocational boatbuilding. Ed Lynch had been toying with the idea of vocational instruction, but had discovered that there are all sorts of state regulations we would have to meet, which didn't seem feasible. It didn't seem to me that the regulations would prevent us from having instruction in recreational boatbuilding. We started our program in the winter of 1970-71. It was the first of its kind, to be followed later by Lance Lee's establishment of the Apprenticeshop in Bath, Maine, where he felt that boatbuilding could be used to mold character. He, too, succeeded, and the many other similar programs followed from those beginnings.

"As you can see, I have concentrated on small craft all of my life — unlike Howard Chapelle, for example, who studied the larger boats and ships as well — perhaps because that was what I was interested in as a boy, and in a certain way I am reliving my boyhood. I have always stressed practical experience in addition to theoretical study, perhaps because my father placed a high value on manual skills with woodworking tools. When I did a good job, I was praised for it. Maybe that's part of the reason I get satisfaction from using hand tools now. There is probably a psychological connection.

"Sure, I could have turned my efforts to recording the lines and details of larger vessels and luxury yachts, but my deeper interests lay with the smaller, simpler craft of my boyhood on the St. Croix River. And there were good examples of such craft still conveniently at hand in Salem and Marblehead thirty and forty years ago. I was drawn to them, as I was not to the larger craft, and it was easier, too. As it has turned out, there are many people now interested in building boats, and they do well to turn to the simpler, smaller craft of traditional design in making a start. My interests coincided with theirs.

"Traditional small craft are the field of my study and practical experience, but I have always been experimenting in new techniques within that framework. There are those who see this as something of a paradox — but innovation is traditional. If you will go back in the development of boatbuilding you will find that builders

41

were innovative and always ready to adopt anything that came along that was good. In fact, boatbuilders seem to be more innovative than sailors, who tend to stick with what is tried and proven. There's a good reason for that. Sailors don't want to go out to sea in an experiment and drown.

"Boatbuilders, on the other hand, want to do the job as quickly as they can. One of the bywords of the trade is, 'Hurry up. The man wants his boat.' You hear that a dozen times a day around a professional boatshop. Sometimes it is said in earnest and sometimes it is said satirically, but either way the emphasis among boatbuilders is to use techniques and materials that will get the job done quickly, yet produce a satisfactory boat.

"Innovation has always made the difference. Without the type of wood screw with a point on it that we have today, a great many traditional boats would not have been built. We all consider the Adirondack guideboat to be traditional. Yet it could not have been built until self-tapping wood screws and small copper tacks came along. Those fastenings were just as much an innovation a hundred years ago as epoxy resins are today.

"There is misunderstanding of the meaning I give to traditional boats. I have explained the concept a number of times, but it still doesn't seem to sink in for many people. To me, traditional boatbuilding means the type of boat construction that blossomed toward the end of the nineteenth century. That period was one of immense technical progress in every area, and it was the culmination of refined and perfected boatbuilding techniques extending back over a period of centuries. There was a proliferation of small-craft types for sail and oar perfected to the ultimate for speed and convenience. The boats were quite different in the Chesapeake than they were in the Gulf of Maine or the swamps of Louisiana or San Francisco Bay or Boston Harbor. Boatbuilding was to some extent an ethnic melting pot, and this all came to a head, blossomed, so to speak, toward the end of the nineteenth century before the advent of the gasoline engine.

"Yet the end came very quickly. In ten years, between 1900 and 1910, all the Hampton boats in Casco Bay were converted to gasoline engines because they would no longer have to depend on the wind. Americans are prone to adopt new things even when it's not advisable to do so. They might be sorry afterwards, but it doesn't stop them from doing it. Given this climate, then, all the refinements, all these diverse boat types, were no longer in demand because you could stick a gasoline engine in any old tub. Such craft didn't have to be hydrodynamically perfect any more.

"Everything changed, the old boatbuilders were no longer needed, they died off, and boatbuilding to the standards of the late nineteenth century died with them. Such boatbuilding had never been recorded, as it had been carried on by rule-of-thumb methods. It was almost an illiterate trade until fairly recently. So with the advent of the gasoline engine, plus many other changes in American life brought on by the automobile, the bicycle, and the canvas canoe, we came to the end of an era.

"When I talk about traditional boats, I mean that perfection of design and technique for boats of oar and sail that came into predominance in the last decade of the nineteenth century. Yet I also believe that if the boatbuilding of that time had been allowed to progress naturally as it had before then, it would have evolved gradually, picking up new methods and techniques as it went. Therefore, I see no contradiction when plywood and epoxy are applied to the perfected designs of the late nineteenth century. Not at all. It's a mistake to think that all progress came to an end at a certain juncture, and that there was no chance for improvement after that. We must not restrict ourselves only to what was done in the past. Definitely not.

"What do I think about the future of wooden boat

building? It seems to me at the present time in some areas it is taking on the characteristics of a fad, and I don't like it. A lot of people are jumping on a bandwagon. Some are doing it because they think it is a way to attract tourists or get some easy money from a foundation, and I wish it was not developing as fast, or along some of the lines that it is.

"I am also concerned about its vocational aspect. I have been making a certain amount of restrained comment concerning vocational programs, considering that there is little prospect that all who graduate will get jobs building wooden boats at wages they can live on. As you no doubt recall, I wrote a short piece for the fourth *Mariner's Catalog* advising young people interested in learning to build boats that perhaps the best way would be for them to teach themselves, while they held down a stopgap job of some sort to put bread on the table. Find a place to set up a bench, hang around boatshops and watch, read the books, start collecting hand tools, and begin with a simple boat with the idea of selling it. After a couple of years they will know if they want to build boats for a living, and should have enough equipment to start out in business in a small way if they do. They will have supported themselves in the meantime, won't be out any tuition, and will have learned much of value on their own.

"I don't want to sound negative about this. That is farthest from my intention. I think I see a better future for wooden boat building than what we have today, even though it will be primarily in the recreational field. I have felt that way all along. There will always be people who will want wooden boats for recreation, and many won't want to build them themselves. Consequently, there will always be a place for a few commercial shops building a limited number of wooden boats. I hope that in the process the best that was developed in the past will be preserved and passed on, but I should expect this heritage to be reworked and even improved to some extent to meet the needs and preferences of future times. Our obligation is to make sure that the richness of our small-craft heritage is passed on intact to the generations that will come after us."

The $15,000 Boston Whitehall

You see them every once in a while — handsome small craft; exquisite little things that sometimes are called traditional and other times are called classic and at all times are so beautifully proportioned and finished that you would have to be out of your mind not to want one. Their designs are either straight out of the late nineteenth or the early twentieth century or are derived from boats that were.

You know the types: graceful pulling boats with plumb stems, hollow entrances, long runs, and wineglass transoms. Fine-lined motor launches with oval coamings and counter sterns, the curved bench-seats upholstered with velvet-covered horsehair cushions and supported by turned cherrywood stanchions. Delicate-looking feather-light guideboats fitted with special-pattern bronze oarlocks, elegant spoonbladed oars, and carrying yokes carved to match the exact shape of the user's shoulders.

It should go without saying that these boats are built of wood. Cedar or white pine or mahogany for the planking. The best white oak for the stem, the keel, the deadwood, and the steam-bent frames. (Spruce roots for

47

the grown frames of the guideboats.) Apple or pear for the knees and the breasthooks. Cherrywood, ash, Honduran or African mahogany, sometimes even walnut for the trim. Oars and spars of straightgrained Sitka spruce. All finished bright, of course, with several hand-rubbed coats of oil or varnish — the more coats the better so the beholder can see that this boat is the real thing — a traditional craft built by a traditional craftsman who took years to learn his trade, not a plastic reproduction popped from a mold by an unskilled worker who doesn't know the difference between a quarter-sawn kingplank and a butt block.

Whenever you see one of these boats the first thought that pops into your mind is, "That's like a Heppelwhite highboy or a Stradivarius violin. I'd be afraid to put it in the water for fear it would be ruined." It's a thought, too often spoken, that makes Gary Weisenburger cringe. Weisenburger, for all his insistence on craftsmanship, feels that boats, however excellent their construction, should be used, not worshipped.

In the winter of 1987 Gary Weisenburger, builder of wooden Boston Whitehalls, seventeen-foot pulling boats with an auxiliary sailing rig, was in a boatyard in New London, Connecticut, doing exactly what he said he would never do again: building a fiberglass boat. Actually, he was finishing out a fiberglass hull, which was molded in another shop, but the effect was still the same. The stench of styrene, the howl of power grinders, the roar of shop heaters blowing hot air into a blue plastic tent that covered the boat and isolated it from the bone-chilling air of a cavernous steel yard building. Weisenburger's clothes were covered with polyester resin dust and his hair was streaked with it, making him look at least a decade older than his forty-one years. A man who could join together the pieces of a Whitehall's backbone so tightly that a razorblade couldn't fit in the joints, he had found making a living as a craftsman-boatbuilder virtually impossible. He had left behind a partially built boat in his own workshop and hired himself out for several months, perhaps even more, to earn real money to pay the bills and help his wife, a nurse, keep the finances of his small family in order.

"Let's get out of here," he said, ripping off his dust mask.

"Where?"

"Anywhere. But let's get out of here." He seemed genuinely uncomfortable to be found in such a shop by someone who had come to talk about art and craftsmanship and the pleasures of building fine wooden boats. We walked out into the cold, dry, sharp air and made our way to a coffee shop.

"This is a step backward for me," said Weisenburger. "I set out to become a builder of small wooden craft, and I did. Now . . . .

"Actually, I started my career in the housebuilding trade as a carpenter. I was self-employed. I've always had a penchant for being self-employed. I switched over to boatbuilding and repair in the mid-1970s because it was always something I wanted to do. I started in a boatyard in Groton, then three years at the Noank Shipyard, and another three years at the Essex Boat Works.

"Compared to house carpentry, boat work is a romantic sort of job, especially when joinerwork is involved. But my first job was to build a deck mold for a fiberglass boat. Masonite, fiberglass, body putty, that type of thing, and there was no romance in that. My next job involved repairing a wooden boat, and that was just fine.

"I've always loved doing challenging woodworking projects. The easy, quick-and-dirty projects never appealed to me. I like to make things that have fancy angles or curves on them. Simply hanging around a boatyard hollowing out the back of a rubrail and screwing it to a hull never appealed to me.

"Essex was my last full-time job, and I had it pretty good. I did a lot of planking and worked on some pretty fancy wooden boats, but there was glass work, too, because they used to rotate it among the carpenters. Anybody who gets his hands on wooden boats says to himself after awhile, 'I'm not going to do these fiberglass boats anymore,' and I wasn't any different. I couldn't stand glass work, so I finally cashed it in and went back out on my own."

Weisenburger had fallen victim to the lure of building small wooden boats. Having developed into a first-rate craftsman, he had visions of his own shop set up after his own fashion in which he would build only what he wanted to build, to the standards that he thought were appropriate — which is to say, of the highest order. In almost all ways, his story was similar to that of the rest of the people who were caught up in the small but intense revival of wooden boat construction during the 1970s and early 1980s. Like most of them, he was a romanticist. ("I was young and crazy.") Like most of them, he tended toward independence. Unlike most of them, he didn't have to speculate on his first job. He received a commission right off the bat.

"Actually, I got my first commission before I left the Essex Boat Works," said Weisenburger. "Bill Fisher, who owns Small Craft Incorporated, asked me if I would build a plug for a plastic reproduction of a Boston Whitehall. He hoped it would be a mainstay of his business, but as it turned out he only sold a few of them. The Boston Whitehall just wasn't meant to be built out of glass. It floated too high and required ballast to get it down to its marks.

"I built a boat instead of just a plug. Fisher gave me $1,000 for materials, and I put the labor into it and kept the boat when the mold was pulled. I worked on the boat when I had time off from the boatyard. I'd work nine-hour shifts at Essex, then come home and work until about 11

P.M., then get up the next morning at 5 A.M. and go down to the boatyard and work. I did this seven days a week. Building that boat was, in effect, holding down a second job."

Idealism knew no bounds. Weisenburger didn't work day and night because he wanted to make a pile of money. He did it because he was committed to wooden boat construction and wanted to work his way into such an endeavor full-time. He also did it because he had an intense fascination for Whitehalls.

"I build Whitehalls because they're boats I love to look at," said Weisenburger.

It's easy to see why. The epitome of the "gentleman's" pulling boat, the Whitehall is long, lean, strongly built, yet graced with a counterbalancing delicacy and elegance reminiscent of a thoroughbred racing horse. It is the boat of perfection in our mind's eye and always has been. John Gardner, small-craft historian, acknowledged this when writing about small boats of the past that were based on the Whitehall: ". . . seventy or 80 years ago, the reputation of the larger Whitehalls was so pre-eminent and good boatbuilders were so thoroughly steeped in the habits of Whitehall construction, that when they built yacht tenders, these naturally took shape as miniature Whitehalls." Even today this is true. Almost everyone's definition of a "yachty" pulling boat includes a long, straight keel, a gentle, sweeping sheer, a plumb or nearly plumb stem, a gently hollowed bow, a tucked after section, and, most importantly, a wineglass transom — all characteristics of the classic Whitehall.

Aesthetics alone aren't at the core of the exalted reputation of the Whitehall. Right alongside is the matter of performance. Wrote maritime historian Howard Chapelle, "Perhaps the most noted of the American rowing work-boats was the Whitehall. The type is mentioned in all literature relating to the lives of seamen in the days of the clipper ships and of the 'Down-Easters' that followed them . . . [It] was noted for its fine qualities; it rowed easily and moved fast in smooth or choppy water; it was safe, carried a heavy load easily, and was dry."

According to small-craft historians, the Whitehall was developed in New York City in the 1820s and quite likely took its name from Whitehall Street, where it is thought the first of the type were built. It was used variously as a harborfront workboat, a livery boat, a ship chandler's boat, a water taxi, and even for racing. The Whitehall's excellence was so obvious that it soon became a fixture in other American harbors as well, most notably Boston and San Francisco.

In the past, among practicing boatbuilders, those who built Whitehalls were held in the highest esteem. You had to be among the best to build a Whitehall. And today, among the wooden boat revivalists — both amateur and professional — almost the test, justified or not, of the extent of your craftsmanship is the ability to turn out a Whitehall that matches the standards of its heyday.

Gary Weisenburger had a pained expression on his face. "Building small wooden boats in a one-man shop, no matter how good you are," he said, "is a tough way to make a living. Given my own experience, it's an impossible way to make a living. But if wooden boat building dies out, it's not going to be because of me. I busted my ass for more than five years to do my part in keeping it going."

Indeed he did. In 1981 Weisenburger took his first Whitehall to the Wooden Boat Show in Newport, Rhode Island. He was testing the waters, so to speak, and the waters felt good. Besides getting considerable attention from the showgoers, he got a solid, money-down-on-the-table order for a second Whitehall.

"Without really analyzing the situation," he said, "I

figured I could build that boat and while I was doing it more orders would come in. As it turned out, it took me more than a year to build the second boat. It took that long because I wasn't getting enough money to build the boat, and I had to take on repair jobs to pay my bills. I repaired an old Chris-Craft, recanvased a canoe, and restored a steam launch. All that cut into the time I could spend on the Whitehall."

Even the repair jobs were marginally economical. "On the surface of it," said Weisenburger, "the steam launch job, which occupied a considerable amount of my time, looked as if it would be lucrative, but as all things work out, the job paid the bills and not much more."

But wait a minute. What's the going rate for a custom-built wooden Whitehall, all found — boat, oars, hardware, sailing rig, sails, trailer, ready to go? A boatbuilder must get $5,000 or $6,000 for something like that.

"Heavens no," said Weisenburger. "Right now the boat I have in the shop, which I can't afford to complete, is going for $11,000. And I'm not making any money on it. By rights, I should be getting $15,000, because that's what it's really worth and that's what I would need to get to make an honest living.

"As it stands now, I'm probably lucky to make six or seven dollars an hour building a Whitehall. Boatyards around here are charging their customers thirty-five dollars an hour for carpentry. Garages are billing the same amount for their mechanics. It's going to cost me $25,000 a year to send my boy to college. He's eight years old now, and that's what it will cost when the time comes, if not more. Why shouldn't I be able to earn enough money at my trade so I can send my son to school?"

Indeed, why not? But $15,000 for a *rowboat*? My word, you can get a sports car for that kind of money!

The value of things. That's the heart of the matter, of

course. You can call in a plumber to fix a pipe and get a bill for $100 or $200 and not like it at all but pay anyway, because the price is based on the current value of plumbing services. You can go to the lumberyard and buy an eight-foot spruce 2 x 4 for three dollars — a stick of wood, for goodness sakes, and a twisted, green one at that — and shrug your shoulders. That's the current value of 2 x 4s. You can go to an art gallery and see an oil painting — ten by twelve inches, perhaps, with ten to fifteen dollars worth of materials in it — and the price tag will be $5,000, $10,000, $15,000, whatever the artist thinks he can get away with. That painting might even be a representation of a boat. Given the superior aesthetics of a Whitehall, it might even be a representation of a Whitehall!

But a real Whitehall, one built to museum specifications (essentially the standards to which Weisenburger builds) — answer the question honestly: Wouldn't you choke on $15,000?

Gary Weisenburger's problem, his inability to make a living wage at his preferred trade, is central to the state of small wooden boat construction today. The cost of materials is extremely high (if a rough 2 x 4 can cost three dollars, you can well imagine what a single plank of select Honduran mahogany must be worth), and the number of labor hours that go into a single boat is sizable (five hundred or more for a Whitehall). Consider what goes into the typical seventeen-foot Boston Whitehall built by Gary Weisenburger.

The planking is yellow cedar or mahogany, the best that can be found. The backbone is white or yellowbark oak, built up in the old style, not laminated and therefore with no uncertain glue joints. All knees are cut from apple crooks harvested by Weisenburger in an orchard and cured for at least two years. ("There's a lot of time that goes into a grown knee. The price of each installed knee in real terms? Probably fifty to seventy-five dollars, and there are eighteen of them in a Whitehall.") Floorboards are teak. The centerboard is bronze, custom-cut and finished from a solid plate. Sails are Dacron and custom-made. Spars and oars, each made by hand, are yellow cedar or Sitka spruce. A custom-fitted canvas cover, a specially fitted trailer, the finest bronze fittings, the list goes on and on.

Each piece that goes into the boat is prefinished — several coats of varnish, eighteen coats of oil on the interior of the hull; each frame is steam-bent in place, then removed and beveled and oiled and red-leaded at the heel, then set back in place. All faying surfaces, including the backs of the butt blocks in the planking, are given at least two coats of red lead and then bedded in permanently flexible compound.

Figure it out for yourself. If Weisenburger's time is worth twenty dollars an hour — and it should be at the very least if you consider he is self-employed and has shop overhead to consider as well as his own wages — then labor alone would come to $10,000. Materials? At least $5,000 when all is said and done. So there you have it, a $15,000 Boston Whitehall.

"What makes this boat worth all that money?" asked Weisenburger. "It's how it is built. The beading along the seat riser, for example, is there purely for decoration, but John Gardner, who designed the boat after careful historical research, says it's supposed to be there, so it is. I cut the bead with a universal plane fitted with a blade I had to cut myself, then I had to drag a scraper along it to get a uniform shape along its length. All that took time.

"I've put a lot of time and effort into my Whitehalls, not to mention knowledge I've gained in the past. I've been in the business long enough to know how to do it right. You have to learn something if you spend all those years pulling apart old boats and rebuilding them. You take that knowledge and apply it to new boats to avoid making the mistakes made in the past. The boats I build now are built to last."

Months later, in the summer of 1987, Gary Weisenburger moved his operation from New London to Groton, Connecticut. The past winter's project, the fiberglass boat, was in commission, but much, much work remained to be done and Weisenburger and a crew of helpers were doing it. The boat was built for oceanography education, and its owner, an organization called Project Oceanology, had allowed Weisenburger to set up his unfinished Whitehall — the sixth in a series — in a small dockside shop. Weisenburger worked on it a few hours here and a few hours there, whenever he could get away from his larger, more time-consuming (and more remunerative) fiberglass job.

"I must be in a rut," he said, taking a break from his work. "I've almost given up. As I realize I'm not making money on these Whitehalls, I'm tending more and more toward repair work and such, more bill-paying work. I'm thinking about doing that and building the Whitehalls part-time on speculation. At least that way I won't have customers who have given me a commission and already paid for a good part of the boat breathing down my neck.

"I'm beginning to realize that you can't build small wooden boats one at a time in a one-man shop, the way I have been doing it, and make money. I think it can be done if you work it more like a factory operation, with specialized workers doing specialized parts of the construction, but I'm not set up to do it that way. In this shop I do all of the sanding, all of the painting, all of the cutting. Much of that work could be done by anyone with reasonable woodworking skills. My time could be better used in supervising and training and helping people to do various jobs.

"But then again, I don't think a factory type operation

would produce a boat that is of the quality of one by a single boatbuilder who loves what he is doing. What's more, such a production-oriented shop would go against the very reasons I started out on my own in the first place.

"Yet to keep on running a one-man shop is a starvation project. My wife will attest to that. We have gone hand-to-mouth too damn often, and I can't let the dream stand in the way of my family's survival.

"I've had so many people drop in to see what I am doing — this is a very public place — and the first question out of their mouths is, 'How much do you get for this boat?' Since last winter, when I finally admitted to myself that I was asking too little for my work, I've taken up the notion that this boat costs $15,000. I haven't heard any more squawks when I say that than when I said $10,000.

"At the same time," he added ruefully, "I haven't had anyone step forward and volunteer to pay it, either."

Unfortunately for today's builders of small wooden boats, no matter how much craftsmanship goes into a boat, no matter how beautiful it may be, the people who buy small boats have a resistance to what they see as excessive prices. The builders may be able to prove that the prices are justified, and most can, but the buyers have difficulty swallowing them, especially when they can get a comparably sized fiberglass boat for thousands of dollars less. Not of the same quality, you understand, but that's a tradeoff that most are willing to make.

Not all, of course. There will always be a market for the type of boats built by the Weisenburgers of the world; it's just that the market won't be very large.

"Who buys my boats?" said Weisenburger. "People who like things made by hand, who want to be on the water in a boat that's appealing. People who appreciate old-fashioned craftsmanship and artistry."

The wooden boat builder as craftsman. The wooden boat builder as artist. The wooden boat builder as artisan-intellectual-historian-philosopher, keeper of the flame.

In the March/April 1985 issue of *WoodenBoat*, the magazine that has spent more than a decade trying to come to terms with the economics of wooden boat building, there was an article by Bruce Northrup entitled "I'm an Artist, Dammit!" The author, a boatbuilder who, like Weisenburger, was scratching away at a very meager living, explained why he nevertheless kept on going.

"Let those without talent or imagination reinvent the wheel daily in some stuffy office choked by neckties and tight shoes. I'll build boats, though I've nothing but a hatchet and baulks scrounged from the woodpile. It's our interior vision that makes us what we are . . . I know why we don't make any money and why we can't keep our books straight and why we take our dates for a row around the harbor instead of to a fancy dinner place. It makes my face red to admit it, but by golly, I'm just going to blurt it out. *I'M AN ARTIST!* There."

"You can call it art if you want to," said Gary Weisenburger. "What it comes down to is an honest living. If people want quality work and a boat that does more than sit in the water — a boat that is truly beautiful to look at — then they will have to realize that it is going to cost a lot of money. And if the demand for wooden boats should totally die, there's nothing I will be able to do about it. I can sit here and expound on the durability and beauty of a wooden boat, but if some guy gets it into his head that it is more economical to go the other route, there's nothing I'm going to be able to say to convince him otherwise."

A $15,000 rowboat — a Boston Whitehall — tells us much about our times. And it also poses an interesting question: Can the builders of small, high-quality wooden boats — the idealists who work in one-man shops — expect to make an honest living?

Only if the buyers demand the best and only if they are willing to pay for it.

Melbourne Smith and the Art of the Possible

As a reader of the late, great magazine *The Skipper* back in the 1960s, I remember being taken by a series of gouache paintings that appeared at various times on the cover and subsequently were offered for sale through the mail as fine-art prints. They were profiles of sailing craft — the pilot schooner *George Steers*, the schooner yacht *America*, the Friendship sloop *Amanda Morse*, the Essex pinky *Tiger*, the pungy *Amanda F. Lewis*, and others — and were characterized by an authenticity of detail seldom seen in nautical paintings of the type.

The artist's name, Melbourne, always appeared on the keel of the vessel being illustrated. The advertising that pushed the prints in *The Skipper* referred to this fellow Melbourne as Captain Melbourne Smith, though what he was captain of was never made particularly clear. He was said to have been from Canada and to have had scads of experience under sail and to have been one of the last of that breed known as *real seamen*, an Alan Villiers kind of guy. He was said to have retired from the sea to pursue a career as an artist, and sure enough, there were his paintings reproduced in living color and there was his name on the masthead of *The Skipper*: Melbourne Smith, Art Director.

It therefore stood to reason that if I bought a print of a painting by Melbourne, I was not only buying a genuine work of nautical art but also getting a summary of one man's life on the boundless ocean. This was a grizzled sea dog who could paint; an art director who could hand, reef, and steer.

In my mind's eye this Captain Melbourne Smith took on a legendary persona, especially after I heard along the waterfront that he had been at various times a smuggler and a lieutenant commander in the Guatemalan Navy, and had been shipwrecked at least once. Keep a lookout for this fellow, I said to myself. Here's an old man, probably in his sixties or seventies, no doubt with a long gray beard flowing to his knees, who can show us young fellows a thing or two.

I first came across Captain Melbourne Smith in person in 1969 upon moving to Annapolis, Maryland, where I worked as a book editor at the U.S. Naval Institute. Melbourne was still at *The Skipper* but also worked part-time at the institute as a book designer. He was a curious fellow, a whirling dervish of activity — an artist, a sailor, a designer, a boatwright, a raconteur, a marine surveyor — but he didn't look or sound the part I had imagined. He wasn't an old sea dog who walked with a rolling gait and wore a marlinspike in his belt. Neither was he a coffee-house artist, the type that wore sandals and a beard and complained loudly about the abominable state of American middle-class society. He was in his late thirties, pink-cheeked and hale of body and mind, and he looked like any other ambitious young man of the time. He could have been a junior executive of a large corporation, or an instructor of fluid dynamics at the Naval Academy, or a member of the legal staff at the Maryland State House.

Melbourne was full of nervous energy — always on the

move — but he hardly seemed as if he might have served as a deckhand on merchant ships or skippered a charter boat in the Caribbean or built boats in the jungles of Belize. He talked about those things, even told a number of outrageous-sounding anecdotes about them, but he always came across as too matter-of-fact, too offhanded. Dare I say it? He sounded like a pure promoter, someone who talked a good game, but when push might come to shove . . .

Obviously, I didn't know Melbourne Smith very well at the time.

Melbourne Smith, the consumate free-lancer, tells a story about himself that goes a long way toward explaining both his capabilities and his approach toward his work, whatever it may be.

"When I was first married," he says, "I was looking for a job as an artist. We went to New York City in an old MG with twenty-five dollars and a dog. I couldn't get a job in a commercial art studio, so I took a job as a building superintendant. Every day I tried to get a job in an art studio. I'd go for a job interview. They asked if I could do photo retouching. I said yup. Can you do typography specs? Yup. Can you do type layout? Yup. Can you do book design? Yup. Can you do this? Yup. Can you do that? Yup. I could do all these things, yet I could never get a job!

"Finally someone tipped me off. Find out exactly what they are looking for and say that's the only thing you can do. Do you do comp layup? Yup. Can you help with pastup? Nope. Can you do specs? Nope. I got the job! That's New York. You have to specialize. You can't say you can do all these things!"

In 1975 Melbourne Smith, the marine surveyor, received a call from an official in Baltimore, Maryland. It seemed that someone in California had donated a replica of a Baltimore clipper to the city, and a survey would be necessary before the gift could be accepted. Would Smith check it out? Of course he would. He was a marine surveyor, wasn't he?

Smith didn't find much of a Baltimore clipper. It turned out to be a backyard-built plywood vessel in poor condition. It was loosely based on a design from one of Howard Chapelle's books, but in no way could it be characterized as a *replica* of anything. So Melbourne returned to Baltimore and told the responsible city officials to forget it.

But Melbourne Smith, the promoter, noticed that the city officials were more than slightly disappointed. They were in the process of putting together the pieces that would lead to the restoration/yuppification of the Inner Harbor, and they thought that a catchy centerpiece would be nice, something that would symbolize the essence of a reborn city, something that said *Baltimore* and *fast* and *dynamic* and *historic* and *creative* and *heroic* all at once.

"Would you like a real Baltimore clipper?" Melbourne Smith asked.

"Oh yes," the city officials said. "We've always wanted one."

So Melbourne Smith, the artist, went to work. He made sketches and drawings and half models, putting together a package that made the project so real, so necessary, so desirable that nobody who believed in the future of the *new* Baltimore could say no. It was a brilliant presentation. Not only would the city get an eighty-four-foot Baltimore clipper, they would also get a living exhibit while the vessel was under construction — the building site would be on the edge of the Inner Harbor itself, right in front of the tourists and the media.

The city wouldn't be building the vessel, not at all. That would be the job for the experts, the builders of wooden ships. So they solicited bids. One bid, for $750,000, came from a yard in Canada. Another came from Melbourne Smith, the shipbuilder. "I told them I could have it built in ten months for $450,000," he says.

There were those, especially in the maritime museum community, who thought the job couldn't be done so quickly and for such a low cost. Where would Smith get the materials, the skilled shipwrights, the organization? "They were saying the vessel was phony, that it would never work, that the price was all wrong," says Melbourne. They didn't realize that Melbourne Smith, the expediter, would be on the case. He had built boats in Belize, after all, and he knew where to get the lumber, the fastenings, the fittings, and above all, the men. He also knew Thomas Gillmer, the naval architect, and enlisted him as the vessel's designer.

"Ten months after beginning construction I was on my way to Bermuda as the skipper of the *Pride Of Baltimore*," says Melbourne Smith, the sailor. He had built the ship and then convinced the city that it would be criminal to leave her tied to a pier for the rest of her life, which had been the original intention. The vessel should be sailed, he maintained, both to keep her alive and to spread the good word about the renaissance of Baltimore. She should be an ambassador of sail, so to speak.

The *Pride Of Baltimore* became so successful that other cities became interested in the concept. And if another city were to build a replica ship, who would they turn to? Someone without a track record who would charge an excessive amount of money, or someone with a track record who would charge a modest amount? Melbourne Smith, the replica builder, was in business.

Melbourne Smith is an impatient man. Not because he can't wait for something to get done, but because he can't wait to get something done. It's a subtle distinction. Nothing exasperates him more than knowing that a job that can be done quickly, efficiently, and inexpensively is being done slowly, inefficiently, and expensively.

"We were building a ship once," he says, "and a guy — one of the new 'craftsmen boatbuilders' out of some apprenticeship school or another — came in and said he was a mast maker. I said good, I have a mast to be made. He said he would like to quote on it. I said good, we have the tree right here in the yard. He said, the tree? I said sure. He said he had never worked from a tree before. I said, well you do it the same way. You square it and eight-side it, and sixteen-side it, and so forth. He said, oh sure.

"So I showed him the drawing and asked him how much it would cost. He said he had no idea. I said, well how much do you want to make? He said I'm not expensive, I ask only six dollars an hour. I said fine, how many hours? He said I really have no idea, but I'm working on another job right now, a mast for something or other. He said I still have three more weeks on that job.

"I called over one of my men. How long will it take you to make this mast? He looked over the plans and figured a week if he could have a boy to sand it."

Melbourne Smith was born far from the open sea in Hamilton, Ontario, in 1930. Part adventurer and part artist, he early on discovered that it was against his nature to stay in one place too long doing one thing. He quit school when he was fourteen and took a job as a sign painter in Niagara, New York, then spent four years with the Royal Canadian Sea Cadets, an organization that lies somewhere between the Sea Scouts and Naval Reserve Officer Training Corps. He put in two years in the merchant service as a deckhand on ships going transatlantic to get sea time for a master's license. He passed the exam for his papers, but never served as a master. In typical Melbourne style, he understates the case to emphasize the accomplishment. "Actually, I got limited master's papers. Panama Canal to the Arctic Circle, East and West coasts of North America."

The merchant service wasn't right for Melbourne, however. He became more interested in smaller craft. "I bought my first boat when I was twenty-three," he says. "I got it over in Georgetown, Maryland, and sailed it up north. I then sailed it to Bermuda and brought it back here to the Chesapeake over a four-year period. My ultimate dream was to go to the West Indies."

But art was becoming as important to Smith as sailing; in fact, it was through his artistic talents that he was making a living. "I always worked in the art field, wherever I was," he says. "I worked as an art director in several different advertising agencies and studios in Montreal and New York." In his spare time he was perfecting his painting style, the gouache profiles of ships and boats that he gives a three-dimensional effect by careful shading and highlighting.

Melbourne Smith's route to the West Indies, like everything he does, was indirect. He went to England with his wife and bought a seventy-two-foot Brixham trawler that needed considerable work. His intention was to live aboard the vessel while he fixed her up, supporting the endeavor by selling his paintings. It was not to be. On a passage to France, the vessel foundered in the English Channel off Cherbourg. Melbourne and his wife and crew survived; everything they owned, including hundreds of Smith's paintings, did not.

That didn't deter Melbourne. He merely added the shipwreck to his ever-expanding stock of tales of personal adventure, and carried on. A year later he bought a 105-foot, three-masted engineless schooner in Gibralter, financing her operation by smuggling whiskey into Spain, then sailing her with a Spanish crew to the Caribbean, where he entered the charter trade for a brief period.

Even though Melbourne's dream had been realized — he had made it to the West Indies — the times were tough.

Melbourne's wife had died while they were in Gibralter, and his children had gone to live with his sister in Canada. Chartering was not proving to be a piece of cake, either.

"Chartering wasn't working out as I had hoped," says Melbourne, "so I took a commission as a teniento comodoro [lieutenant commander] in the Guatemalan Navy to teach their cadets how to sail. It was the worst year of my life."

A revolution in Guatemala put him out of his misery. "I escaped over the mountains to British Honduras [now Belize]," he says. "I had to leave my boat behind, it happened so quickly, but I came back a year later and stole it back."

It was in British Honduras, hiding from the Guatemalan revolutionaries, that Smith learned the art of wooden boat and ship construction. He went to work with Simeon Young building large commercial vessels and the occasional yacht. But even though labor costs were low and building materials were abundant, the boatyard had a difficult time surviving. "I figured we would have to build three boats at a time to make money," he says, "but we could only get orders for one at a time. It was a valuable experience, though. When the time came to build the *Pride Of Baltimore*, I said to myself, hey, I know where to get the wood, I know where to find the men."

When Melbourne Smith was in his early thirties, he delivered a yacht from his boatyard in British Honduras to Annapolis, Maryland. "I had one painting with me," he says, "a portrait of a Baltimore clipper. I walked into *The Skipper* magazine and showed it to them and they bought it. They gave me a hundred dollars for it. I said to myself, I like this place." Later he would go across town and sell a series of paintings to the U.S. Naval Institute. Annapolis looked like fertile territory to Smith, and he decided to make the town his home.

Melbourne Smith is one of those people who believes he can do anything and wants to do everything. In the winter of 1987, for example, his projects included, among others, the redesign of the Revolutionary War vessel *Niagara*, the supervision of the construction of a fifteen-foot square-rigged sailing model, the design of a book or two, and several commissions for paintings. In addition, he was in the preliminary stages of various proposals for future projects, among them the design and construction of a replica of the clipper *Sea Witch* and the building of a boat in America to be delivered to Ireland.

"Why do I do all these things at once?" he says. "I want to do them all. I want to do this. I want to do that. I want to do all these things. Somebody will call me about a book design, and I'll want to do it. They'll call me about a painting, and I'll want to do that. They'll want me to build a replica ship, and I'll want to do that. It doesn't take long to do these things. It's a matter of organizing the work and getting it done.

"I think the one thing I can do well is get things done. I tell them I will finish the project, whatever it is, on time, and I finish on time. I tell them I'll finish on budget, and I finish on budget. It's like anything else. If you can get the job done on time, you will be automatically ahead of almost everyone else."

In the ten years since the *Pride Of Baltimore* was launched, the building of replica ships in America has taken on all of the elements of an industry. The success of the *Pride*, even though she was knocked down and sank in a storm a couple of years ago, pointed out the numerous advantages of building new vessels with all their attendant glamour. There is publicity and therefore potential economic gain for the sponsors of the vessels: museums, municipalities, and private groups. There are jobs for the shipwrights and caulkers and riggers who prefer traditional construction for traditional reasons. There are crew positions for the sailors who favor sail training and adventuring. (Unfortunately, there is also ample opportunity for hyperbole, a characteristic that seems to be inherent in the building and operation of replica ships.)

One of the captains of today's replica ship industry — indeed, the captain of the industry — is Melbourne Smith. Besides the *Pride*, he has to his credit two Chesapeake skipjacks, the revenue cutter *Californian*, the storeship *Globe*, the fishing schooner *Spirit Of Massachusetts* (which he designed but which was built by others), and the fifteen-foot square-rigger *Federalist*. His plans for the immediate future include building the clipper ship *Sea Witch*.

Melbourne Smith's ships, however, are not replicas in the accepted sense of the word. They are not exact copies of the originals. In fact, they are so different from the originals in many ways that they are best described as interpretations.

The storeship *Globe*, for example, is Smith's interpretation of a ship that was built in Maine in 1833 and which was laid up in California on the Sacramento waterfront during the Gold Rush. Her masts had been sent down, a roof had been built over her deck, and she had served as a floating warehouse. But the original *Globe* has been gone for years. The city fathers of Sacramento, who were in the process of restoring the waterfront, hit on the idea of building a replica of the vessel as she had been rigged as a storeship to add authenticity to their project.

In the absence of plans for the original vessel, Melbourne's building crew had to work from new plans based on contemporary photographs and drawings. It would be impossible to build an exact copy from such inexact sources. And because the replica of the *Globe* will never even be rigged for sail, never mind actually be sailed, the hull was built with a flat bottom to save on building costs. As she sits in the water, the *Globe* looks authentic, but by museum standards she is not. She maintains an interpretation of authenticity, the best she can do under the circumstances (and all she has been asked to do by her sponsors).

The diminutive *Federalist* is another example. Built in 1787, the vessel was a toy ship, fifteen feet long and square-rigged, and was to be given to George Washington in appreciation of his services to the nation. She was sailed from Baltimore down the Chesapeake and up the Potomac to Mount Vernon, but she sank in a storm. A replica of the *Federalist* was designed by Melbourne Smith for a foundation in Maryland in honor of the two-hundredth anniversary of the U.S. constitution, and it was built in a Maryland boatshop in the winter of 1987. Even though the vessel conforms in appearance to that of contemporary accounts, she is still an interpretation only, since no original plans exist. What's more, she has been strip-planked, a type of construction that did not exist in George Washington's time.

The *Californian* is another interpretive replica. Based on the design of the revenue cutter *Joe Lane*, she is shorter than the original (83 feet vs 100 feet) and wider (25 feet vs 23 feet), and her hull lines have been greatly modified. The changes were made necesary both for economic reasons and to satisfy modern Coast Guard safety require-ments. Even her hull construction is different. The *Joe Lane* had sawn frames; the *Californian*'s frames are laminated.

The key to Melbourne Smith's success in everything he does is his knowledge of sources and his open-mindedness in seeking alternatives for impossible-to-find items. In his book-design work, his trademark is the use of devices borrowed from elsewhere — rules, borders, special typography, etc. His greatest book design, that of the *Junks and Sampans of the Yangtze River* by G. R. G. Worcester, published by the Naval Institute, is full of such devices, including Chinese characters that both provide decoration and have meaning in and of themselves.

In his wooden ship construction work, he is always using offbeat sources to get better materials at a lower cost. He buys his lumber directly from Belize and Guatemala without going through a middle man. He goes down to Central America periodically and hand selects the lumber.

He will try anything within reason to keep his costs down. "If I had had the keel of the *Californian* cast out in southern California, where she was built," he says, "it would have cost $20,000. I found an excellent foundry in Pennsylvania that would do the job and ship the keel out to California for less than $12,000. You have to know your sources and shop around."

So where and how does he come up with the sources? "Drinking in the 'wrong' bars, talking to the 'wrong' people. I almost think I learn more in bars than anywhere else. I'll be sitting there talking to someone, talking about my latest problem, and many times he might suggest a solution or point out someone who might have the solution. I listen to every suggestion, no matter how harebrained it might sound at the time."

Melbourne Smith is a pragmatist more than anything else. Never one to remain wedded to the old ways if the new ways prove to be better, he is famous — and at times controversial — for his iconoclastic approach to a normally hidebound field. To save topside weight on his vessels, for example, he has had cannons cast in aluminum with steel liners in the bore. "Painted black," he says, "nobody notices the difference."

Perhaps his most notable departure from traditional wooden ship building practice is the use of laminated frames. "Laminated frames?" he says when reminded of past criticisms. "Why not? Do you want to build in rot? If so, you should build a double-framed vessel. If not, take my word for it; laminated frames are the way to go."

One advantage, of course, is that frame scantlings can be lighter because laminated frames are stronger than sawn frames. Another is that there are no unbonded joints in a laminated frame as there are in a double frame, and therefore water cannot collect in the gaps and cause rot. The greatest advantage, however, is that laminated frames can be produced and prebeveled in a factory, shipped to the building site, and quickly erected on the keel.

"I developed a source for factory produced laminated frames myself," says Melbourne. "I looked up a place in Alabama that makes wooden arches for churches and buildings like that. They had never made ship frames before, but they were willing to try."

Smith provided the factory with lofted lines on Mylar and the proper bevels for each frame. They laminated the frames with resorcinol glue to approximate shape and used the Mylar loftings as patterns to cut out the exact shape of each frame and to cut the bevels. Because the laminating was done in a factory, precise control over temperature, humidity, and clamping pressure could be maintained, and all wood could be pressure-treated with preservatives.

"Factory laminated frames are expensive," says Melbourne, "but since they do not have to be built on site and are easy to erect, labor costs are less." The result is a wash — high-quality, strong, rot-resistant frames for the price of sawn frames.

Not everyone is impressed, however. While Smith was able to use laminated frames on the *Californian*, the sponsors of the *Spirit Of Massachusetts*, designed by Smith, rejected them in favor of traditional construction. He shrugs his shoulders. "I offered to build her with laminated frames for $750,000, and they would have had a stronger, more rot-resistant vessel. They went for sawn frames and heavy construction and wound up spending $1,400,000. It was their choice."

Melbourne Smith is a promoter. Never content to let things develop on their own, he is always one to push, persuade, cajole. He decides what he wants to do and then sets out on a carefully prepared course of action to see that it will come to pass. And to ensure that it will come to pass, he is prepared to modify his concept at a moment's notice or to bring in new talent or to stay up all night revising his presentation. He is, to put it bluntly, one smart cookie. Anyone who could go from being a shipwrecked sailor to a smuggler to a charter skipper to a boatbuilder to an art director to the king of the replica builders — on his own, without any capital, working out of his house, against all odds — has to be.

Everything Melbourne has done to date, however, is small potatoes compared to what he is planning for the future: the construction of a replica of the 178-foot clipper ship *Sea Witch*, the original of which was designed by J. W. Griffiths and built in 1846.

In essence, the plan is this. Raise money to build the vessel by seeking corporate and other private sponsorship. Build the vessel using the latest in modern wood technology, including, of course, laminated frames. Choose a building site that can become an attraction in itself — a working nineteenth-century style shipyard. Launch the vessel and send her on a barnstorming voyage around the world, making money by carrying commemorative cargoes (wine from California to China, tea and china from China to London, Scotch whiskey from London to New York) and performing oceanographic and archaeological studies along the way. When the voyage is over, either lay up the ship for display much in the same way the *Cutty Sark* is in Greenwich, England, or give her to the U.S. Navy for service as the ultimate sail-training vessel.

The price? Ten million to build her; $8.5 million to pay for a three-year circumnavigation. The return? Ten years ago the estimate was over $17 million; today it would be more.

On the drawing board for years, the *Sea Witch* project is one of those unrestrained dreams that sound ludicrous at first but, upon further reflection, seem no crazier than, say, rebuilding the steam schooner *Wapama* at the National Maritime Museum in San Francisco for roughly the same amount of money with no chance of earning income later.

This may be pie-in-the-sky lunacy from someone who has been sitting too long in the noonday sun, but consider this. Melbourne Smith, the promoter, has established the American Clipper Trust, whose board of directors includes a number of high-powered people and which already has a high-powered fund-raiser who is twisting the right arms. Melbourne Smith, the artist, has painted his paintings and carved his models. Melbourne Smith, the designer, has reworked Griffiths's offsets to produce a vessel that can be built in the modern era. Melbourne Smith, the expediter and the shipbuilder, is waiting to spring into action.

Melbourne Smith, the sailor? If the *Sea Witch* should ever be launched, you can bet your seaboots that he will be at the wheel.

Welcome to Hard Times

A light rain was falling when I pulled into the driveway of the Hathaway Mill Farm in Rochester, Massachusetts. Dean Stephens, who knew more than enough to stay in out of the rain, was working inside the shop rather than outside on Bill Gilkerson's twenty-six-foot Swedish gaff cutter *Elly*, which lay covered by a tarp alongside the barn. Stephens is a boatbuilder whose deserved reputation for skillfulness surrounds him like a net, enough so that his round-trip plane fare from Wisconsin had been paid for by Gilkerson, who loves his boat with maniacal fervor and will accept — and pay for — only the best in her behalf.

Indeed he should, because *Elly* is a truly impressive, ancient craft, built at least one hundred years ago — one-inch oak lapstrake planking over sawn oak frames, trunnel fastened. Stephens showed me one of the trunnels he had withdrawn from the sheerstrake, which he was replacing along with the covering board. He was speculating on how he would cut new trunnels to match the old, because those wooden fastenings had a tapered shoulder at the head that matched exactly a bored and reamed hole in the planking.

"I'll have to turn them on a lathe," he said. "It just goes to show what I've said all along, that every boat is different and every boatbuilder today has to be able to do anything and everything, rather than be a specialist like the builders of the past. You can't be just a caulker or a plank-hanger anymore. You have to do it all."

Stephens had much to do on the *Elly* and only a couple of weeks to do it in, so I left him alone for the time being while he chiseled a frame to a pattern he had taken from the cutter's inside planking. Later, when the early spring darkness fell, Stephens knocked off for the day ("Dean likes a glass of wine and a gam around five o'clock," Bill said), and we retired, wine and whiskey in hand, to the studio over the workshop in the barn.

Gilkerson, who owned the farm (he has since sold it and moved to Nova Scotia), is a marine artist, and his studio was just the place for a conversation about boats and boatbuilding. It abounded with paintings and carvings and books and paintings, all relating to the sea in one way or another. Since it was over the workshop, the smell of freshly sawn wood mingled with painter's oils and fixatives, complementary odors that suggest what we intuitively know — that the artisinal and the artistic are many times one in the same.

Bill sat down at his drawing table ("Don't mind me; I'll just listen in while I work"), and I took an easy chair with my back to the hot stove. Stephens chose a hard-backed chair that half faced me. He seemed uncomfortable at first, since he hardly knew me, but the wine and the pleasant surroundings soon warmed him up, and he was off and running on subjects he knew best: the travails of boatbuilding and the agonies of teaching. But first I asked him to tell me a little about his early years, especially the reasons why he chose to do what he did with his life.

"I was born in 1923," he said, "in Blackfoot, Idaho, a little town on the Snake River. The town still had that old-west flavor, the people still had the frontier attitude. My family was Mormon and had lived in Utah and Idaho for a couple of generations.

"Woodworking was just another part of small-town life in those days. My first big project, though, came when I was thirteen. My father decided I was too old to sleep in the same room with my sister, so my grandfather showed me how to build a log cabin in the back of the property. I built it over the summer and then lived in it for five years until I left home. I had an axe and a saw and not much else, but that cabin is still standing and being used.

"I got out of Blackfoot as soon as I could. What made me leave? It was Idaho.

"I joined the Marine Corps right after high school, before the war started. I hated the Marines, but while I was in I got it into my mind that I wanted to be a cabinetmaker. Not just a cabinetmaker, but the best damned cabinetmaker there ever was. I was a radio operator at the time, but I carried that thought in my head wherever the Marines sent me, including Guadalcanal, where I got a little housebuilding experience. For some reason they put me in charge of building the mess hall, so we stole a bunch of lumber from the Seabees and put her up.

"When the war was over and I was discharged, I made up my mind I would apprentice myself to a cabinetmaker. I moved back to Idaho (I had a wife and a child by then) and went to work for a local fellow. I found out later that my training with him was pretty poor. He didn't have a sound background in the techniques — he was just getting by. He wasn't a good teacher but I was a good observer, so I learned by watching and doing. I worked for him almost four years, but we had a falling out after I ran his car into a train one night, so I quit."

Stephens looked matter-of-factly over at me or Bill from time to time with the baleful eyes of a basset hound. ("Dean has bags on the bags under his eyes," Gilkerson

77

said later, "and they increase and decrease in number with his mood. A five-bagger means he's really down.") But for the most part he stared expressionlessly at the floor while he told the most outrageous stories about his life. ("Luckily the train was standing still," he said, "or I would have been a goner.")

He set up his own shop in a nearby town and built a house, only to close down and move to St. Helena, California, where he opened another cabinet shop. He wasn't very successful in either place.

"I was completely outfitted with power tools. At that time a salesman would come around and sell you the whole shop on time if you wanted, but I only bought one or two tools at a time. Still, I had a lot more machinery then than I have now. I didn't even give any thought to hand tools versus power tools. It seemed clear at the time: if you have power tools, you're in business. If you don't, you're not." Under his eyes were four-baggers.

Fully equipped or not, Stephens packed it in as an independent cabinetmaker. He moved back to Idaho for a few months to help out his father in the dry cleaning business. But that didn't work out either, so in 1953 he moved his family to Alameda, California, just across the bay from San Francisco.

"I ended up in a shop where I really learned the cabinetmaking trade. It was a place where they made bars and café furniture. They built the finest bars and back bars that I ever saw. They had a complete upholstery shop, a complete spray shop. They built bar stools, booths, refrigerated back bars, and all kinds of pie cases. We did work all over the western United States, even Hawaii. We built all the fixtures in the shop and then trucked them to the place they were to be installed. We lived with the bar fixtures until they were installed. We used a lot of cherry, maple, walnut, birch — all hand scraped and finished.

"I started there in 1953, and even though I had been

woodworking professionally for a number of years, I was really insecure. I had had my own shop and did what people asked me to do, and if I didn't know how to do it, I faked it to get by. I knew there was a lot I didn't know, but I couldn't even visualize it.

"The guys in there were old men — seventy to seventy-five years old — and they didn't want to teach me their trade. They had tools that I didn't even know about. They were old-timers who had been at it their entire lives. None of them were born in the United States. We had Finns, and a couple of Icelanders, some Mexican-Americans (they were really the artists), and a Swede (one of the greatest mechanics I ever saw; that fellow could make jigs for everything), and there were Germans. I watched them work and learned by it even though they were covetous of their trade.

"I was a bench hand and didn't have to use machinery, only hand tools. The foreman was a German immigrant. Nobody could work with the guy, he was so ornery. I had a pretty rough time with that foreman at first, but I made up my mind that it was either him or me. I was going to stick it out. Sometimes I couldn't sleep for a week with that guy eating at me all the time. He just rode me."

I could see that the painfulness of the experience was still felt by Stephens after all those years. He became angry just talking about it. His face came alive and he began to shout, stamping his feet, describing how he finally told the foreman off and in the process gained his respect. After all, respect was the operative word in an old-style cabinet shop, where the craftsmen came to work in suits and changed into their work clothes in front of their lockers.

"The foreman told me to come work with him," Stephens said, "I guess because he finally wanted to teach me the methods they used to build those bars. He told me everything. He told me where to put every nail, that guy did. He and I built all the bars from then on, and we got along great. When I quit after three years — they weren't paying me enough and I got a better offer — that guy cried when I left. I couldn't believe it, because he was the hardest guy I ever knew in my life.

"Right behind the shop there was a small shipyard, a place where they hauled tuna boats and small merchant vessels. A guy was building a boat there, and I used to go down there and look at that boat and wonder how in hell he got the shapes into that boat. I decided right then and there that that was the ultimate in woodworking — it just put my work into the shade — so I decided to build a boat. Even though before then I had no knowledge of boats, no experience building them, nothing."

Dean Stephens had finally begun to feel confidence as a cabinetmaker, so in 1955 he undertook to become a boatbuilder. He bought a copy of Sam Rabl's *Boatbuilding in Your Own Backyard* and in nine months had built the famed hard-chine Picaroon, a tiny pocket cruiser.

"I bought Rabl's book because it was cheap and it was simple. Sam Rabl was a great guy (I got to know him by letter) who designed boats that could be built out of a lumberyard. There's a hell of an approach. With Sam's instructions a fifteen-year-old kid could put himself together a little boat. His designs didn't sail all that good, but they were fun. Sam had a heart for young kids — they were the ones he really designed those boats for. My Picaroon was a nice little boat. You can see a picture of her in the second edition of Sam's book. She was too small, though, so I sold her.

"In the meantime, I started working professionally on boats — repairs, remodeling, that sort of thing. I built in my spare time the thirty-four-foot Jonquil designed by William Atkin, a pretty heavy boat rigged as a ketch. Then my entire family moved onto the boat. I raised four kids on that boat. We lived aboard for ten years. Whenever someone wanted a boat built, up or down the coast, I'd sail

80

there and set up on a vacant lot and build a boat."

There it was: "I'd set up on a vacant lot and build a boat." That short statement is the essence of the legend that has built up on the West Coast about Dean Stephens, the boatbuilder. This little man — short, wiry body, bearded face, devastatingly sad eyes — roamed the Pacific coast building custom boats, finishing off boats, repairing and restoring boats, so many he has lost count of them. He became possessed by the notion of building boats. I shook my head in disbelief, not that I didn't believe that he had done it, but that I couldn't believe that it was as simple as he made it sound. I asked him how he could possibly have picked up all the information he would need — the knowledge of design, the traditions of the sea, the secrets of weatherfast joints, all of it. Gilkerson stopped painting for a moment and peered over his glasses, first at Stephens, then at me. Stephens had the blank look of a man who has just been asked an immensely stupid question.

"Hell," he said, "I just talked to a lot of people. I talked to caulkers and shipbuilders and everyone else. I'd go around and try to pick other boatbuilders' brains. Many of them were just miserable, didn't want to talk to you, were mad all the time. But others, especially those in the Alameda area, were the finest kind — people like Johnny Linderman, Al Silva, Em Doble, Johnny Guenther, and Jack Erehorn really contributed to my boatbuilding. They were so good they make my work look like crap.

"One time I worked for a guy who had built tuna boats for fifty years. I learned how to use an adze from him. He had been a dubber for fifty years. He had a big hump on his back and his arms were skinny, but he could adze from any position. Hell, you could hang him from his feet and he could dub a boat. I thought I knew how to use an adze before then, but I didn't. He showed me how.

"I had to pour a lead keel once — ten thousand pounds — and didn't know how, and none of the boatbuilders I knew had done one that big so they couldn't help me. But I found a book on the subject and followed the instructions and sketches and that's all I needed."

I nodded in agreement, still not doubting him, but suggested that we can all talk to boatbuilders and read textbooks, but there is no guarantee we will become accomplished boatbuilders as a result. Stephens thought about that for a moment. He obviously had something direct to say, but he didn't want to be careless in saying it lest he hurt my feelings or create a wrong impression.

"Have you ever wondered why you know how to do some things, and you've never done them before, and you just don't know how you learned them? Well, there are a lot of things that come up in a man's life. Like I'd never slaughtered a hog before and I did one last fall — a four-hundred-pound hog — but I knew how. I don't even remember reading any books on it. I don't even remember seeing anyone do it." (Gilkerson, whose face was buried in his work, said, "Some philosophers believe you have a past memory in the culture into which you are born — that all men know everything.")

"Yes, I believe there are some past memories that allow you to do things with your hands, that you are inherently born with them. I believe that much of what I can do was within myself from the beginning and something set it free. I'm called on to do things, year after year, that I've never done before and I find methods to do them."

So Dean Stephens made the transition from cabinet-maker to boatbuilder, or so it would seem. In fact, he didn't see it that way at all. As he talked his mood alternated between sadness and anger.

"You've got it all wrong. I didn't just build boats. I never made a living building boats. Nobody makes a living building boats." This said in anger, in a tone that suggested that what he said was a terribly unjust truth. "The boatbuilders in Alameda were only just barely making it, and they were dropping out as the years went by and went into house carpentry and such. Boatbuilding in my area was going downhill even before the advent of fiberglass.

"You just do everything you can to make a living. I kept building bars and all kinds of stuff. I even worked in wineries making wine presses and barrels, anything out of wood, so I always considered myself a woodworker. If I happened to be building boats from time to time, I guess you could call me a boatbuilder during those times.

"It wasn't possible to make a living building boats, because for one thing I only had a boat to build every three years. And this despite the fact that I was pretty well known. Even when I had a yard down in Santa Barbara it was difficult to come up with a steady stream of boats to build. I didn't build small boats. I've built mostly boats that averaged thirty-six feet or so, and they are expensive toys and consequently there isn't a great demand for them. Even when I had a boat to build, or a hull to finish for someone, the hourly rate was very low. For a long time I impoverished my family because I wanted to build boats. Nobody I knew could build new boats alone and make a living. They had to rely on repair work and other jobs to keep going."

This shouldn't be taken to mean that Dean Stephens didn't build a lot of boats, because he did. And those that he built established for him the reputation for being among the best wooden boat builders on the West Coast. What they didn't establish for him was the reputation for being a financially successful boatbuilder, in the West or anywhere else. Gilkerson, who had given up all hope of just listening while he painted, thought he knew why. "With all due respect for you," he said to Stephens, "and I mean this as a compliment, you care more about the boat, even though it isn't yours, than you care about the money."

Stephens didn't disagree. Instead, in a very quiet, tired voice, he confirmed that observation. "Well, naturally. I'm a lousy businessman. The last several boats I built turned sour just on account of money. I usually charged for my work by the hour rather than on a flat rate. But I would give the owner an estimate because I know how long something will take, and I try to stay within that estimate. The owner would pay for the materials. Yet I really think that if I had asked more by the hour for my work, the owners wouldn't have been able to afford the boats."

He cited as an example a recent boat he was building at his regular hourly rate for a man who seemed to be wealthy enough to handle the cost. When the boat was nearing completion, the owner came to him and said he had too much money in the project and couldn't afford any more. He said he would take the boat unfinished and have it completed by a builder who charged less. Stephens said no, feeling the owner would be dissatisfied with the quality of the work and blame him. "I told him I would work six weeks for nothing to finish the boat, and I did. Yet after doing that for him, at the end he beat me out of five hundred dollars." (Under his breath, Gilkerson muttered, "I rest my case.")

"Look," said Stephens, "I don't want to sound pessimistic, but I don't think the economy of this country is going in the direction of supporting significant new boatbuilding in wood. Maybe I'm foolish. Maybe I don't know what is really selling on the market."

So Stephens spent years getting in and out of boatbuilding, filling in with boat repair and woodworking to pay the bills. In the late 1960s, he had a boatshop and yard in Santa Barbara that included a small foundry to cast essential fittings that were becoming difficult to buy off the shelf, but wooden boat building in southern California at that time had become marginal at best, and besides, his marriage had foundered. ("I got up one Sunday morning, piled a few things in my truck, left the yard to this guy who worked with me, left everything else to my wife, and headed on out.") He drifted from job to job.

The early 1970s found Dean Stephens living on a northern California mountainside in a tepee with his second wife.

"I saw this nice little ranch with a lot of outbuildings near Mendocino. I was able to rent it from the owner, and it seemed to me to be perfect as the base for a woodworking apprenticeship school.

"Why did I decide to take on apprentices? I did it because I had so many young people come to me when I was building boats who wanted me to teach them. I couldn't do it, because the owners of the boats didn't want them around. I had hundreds of them — most with college educations — and they wanted to learn how to really do something. I decided to help them by setting up this program on the farm rather than try to get the owners to go along with having apprentices on the boats."

Stephens gave me that low, baggy eyed look of his, the one I have seen from any number of craftsmen who grew up in the Depression and found it difficult to believe someone with an education and a virtually guaranteed job would find himself lost in a world of endless opportunity compared to that of the 1930s. He had come squarely up against the New Age — where manual work was seen as artistic expression, not as gritty, hands-to-the-tool survival — and didn't really understand it. To his credit and to the good fortune of his apprentices, he didn't ignore it either. With words laced with incredulity he described the task he willingly assigned himself.

"My college-educated apprentices didn't even know how to get along. They didn't even know how to chop wood. I had to teach them everything on that farm, everything I could think of. They learned not only woodworking but also subsistence farming, because to get them woodworking clients, we had to ask for a low wage for their work. Making them more or less self-sufficient in the food department freed them up to work for less and still do their very best. We raised goats, cows, chickens, and gardens. We raised rabbits, even. I taught them how to kill and skin rabbits. They didn't know people did things like that. Why, they didn't even know where the water came from.

"We grew our own food because we had to. They were really turned on to that. They wanted to learn how to live. They got down to the realities of work. My function was to teach them what work really is, not what they might think work is. And it seemed to have worked, because I had a total of twenty-one woodworking apprentices and all but one continued with woodworking."

Stephens was a driver. He figured that if work is what these fellows want, then work they will do. ("Well, I wasn't all that easy on them," he said with the slightest hint of a smile.) One of the first things he did when he set up the school was to put a sign over the gate to the ranch: *Welcome to Hard Times*.

"The hell of it is, the harder I drove them, the harder they worked. And the harder they worked, the closer together they got. Those guys got really close. I couldn't believe it. If I should get down on one of them, they would all be mad at me. We built quarters for them and a kitchen/dining area called The Café, which became their hangout.

"I had six apprentices at a time and we made just about everything — we built stage sets, two or three houses, even coffins at one time. We had two shops on the place. Whenever someone approached me for a job, I told them I would require so much money plus they would have to take six apprentices. We worked for our money, and they worked for their training.

"I still had boatbuilding in my mind, though, so in 1976 when the last group in the woodworking apprenticeship program left, I decided to try to solicit some boatbuilding work and take on six boatbuilding apprentices. I tried to get clients to order boats from my school but couldn't. I'll tell you the type of clients I was being approached by. Three or four said they would put up the money to buy materials if I would use my apprentices to build them a boat. I said no — I'm not going to give you a boat. It takes not only their energy but also mine. If we're going to do this for you, we're going to get paid, a small wage anyway. I had these people try to chisel me and my apprentices, and it just pissed me off. They wanted to chisel me because they thought I had some free labor.

"I said to hell with it and borrowed some money from a friend and put it with some money of my own, and we started two boats on speculation — a twenty-five-foot motor-powered salmon boat and a twenty-seven-foot Atkin cutter. This time the apprentices weren't being paid because no money was coming in. They were paying me. Each was paying one dollar an hour for instruction, which means I was getting six dollars an hour among the six of them. They had to furnish their own support — clothes, food, spending money."

I could tell by the way Stephens was talking that the boatbuilding school meant a lot to him. I could also sense from the layer of darkness that spread across his face that it didn't work out. In fact, I could figure it out for myself: six dollars an hour doesn't go far when you have a ranch to support and two large wooden boats being built side by side on speculation. But first I wanted Stephens to tell me — given his previously stated feelings about the viability of building new, large wooden boats — what he told prospective apprentices who applied to his boatbuilding school.

"The first thing I would say is why do you want to be a boatbuilder? Don't you know boatbuilding is a dead trade? Saying that really encouraged them. They wanted to do it even more.

"Besides, if someone wants to do something, I'll never

be the one to discourage him. I think more good things are gone to hell because you tell somebody your idea and they get down on it. I didn't ever discourage them in any way. If I could help them build something or do something, I never really would discourage them. I told them at the beginning this really isn't a way to make a living, but most of them had an attitude like mine — if you can build a boat, then you can build anything. So they weren't limited to boatbuilding, which I am sure is the way that most of them saw it.

"I think I had the best boatbuilding school going. We put out some fine vessels, and they weren't little vessels either. I didn't teach peapod building. And those boys did good work. They were careful, they were enthusiastic, they weren't goofing off. The only problem with them is they wanted to work all the time. I tried to teach them every trick I could think of, all the stuff the old-timers wouldn't show me, even though I was teaching apprentices who could conceivably go out afterward and compete with me for what little work there was available.

"I always felt as if I should share in what I had learned and knew. I felt I could make their apprenticeship a lot shorter by turning them on to things I had learned by watching and digging."

What more could you ask for? A committed teacher teaching dedicated students in what amounts to an idyllic setting. But it didn't work out. Even at one dollar an hour, the apprentices couldn't afford to keep paying Stephens, and one by one they were forced to drop out of the program.

Stephens believed in teaching boatbuilding from start to finish, so he refused to take on new apprentices in the middle of a project ("That wouldn't be right for them.") He and a couple of remaining apprentices finished the salmon boat, which was sold some time later at a loss. Then he turned his attention to the Atkin cutter alone.

"I had to give up the apprentice school in 1978 because I hadn't sold this one boat and I was beating my brains out to get her finished. I got to worrying a lot. She was a gorgeous boat, all beaded inside, bronze fittings we cast ourselves, trunnel-fastened ironbark backbone. I worked on her alone after the apprentices left for nine months, fourteen hours a day, seven days a week. And when I finally sold her — after a year and a half of waiting—I got a dollar and seventy-eight cents an hour for my labor.

"When it was over, I didn't go back to the original woodworking apprenticeship program, which worked, because I was pretty tired out by then. I was strung out.

"I had a guy tell me that my trouble was that I needed a business agent. He said I couldn't sell my own work. That's true. I was trying to do it all and you can't — teach, keep books, order materials, sell boats. If a guy buries himself in his work, he shouldn't have to sell it."

The wind had come up and was driving the rain against the windowpanes of the studio, adding emphasis to one of the saddest stories I had heard in a long time. Gilkerson got up from his drawing board and threw another log into the stove. "Everything Dean has told you is absolutely true," he said, "because I was there at the time. He hasn't exaggerated or understated anything."

As if you couldn't tell by now, Dean Stephens was not one to give up. He made a permanent-lease offer, which was turned down by the owner, on the Abalobadiah Ranch. But farming — like boatbuilding — was in his blood.

"I couldn't afford land on the West Coast, but I had a friend who had some land in Wisconsin who wanted to sell half of it because he couldn't keep the payments up. I had never been to Wisconsin but figured I might as well try it, so we moved out there in 1978. It turned out to be better than what I had hoped, and as a result I've been there three years. I've been putting up buildings, clearing land and

89

farming it. I've been supporting myself with odds and ends of work — remodeling a farmhouse, furniture work, built a couple of Whitehalls on order from clients in southern California. I even set up a sawmill for milling lumber from my trees."

Gilkerson said, "You cut the logs?"

"Yes."

"You mill them yourself in your own sawmill unassisted?"

"Yes."

"How many trees do you think you've cut?"

"I don't know. About seventy."

"By the way, what do you weigh?"

"One-hundred-thirty-pounds."

The gales of laughter inside the studio beat back the sounds of the storm outside.

"That's why I'm so tired."

Afterword: Dean Stephens eventually gave up the farm life in Wisconsin and moved back to northern California. He lives in Fort Bragg, on the coast, and is building and repairing boats.

A Cloud of Sawdust and . . .
Simon Watts Strikes Again

I received a letter a few years ago from a fellow named
Simon Watts. He said he would be teaching wooden boat
building to amateurs at the Rockport Apprenticeshop and,
knowing that I lived just down the road from that school,
thought I might be interested in dropping by during the
course of the course to see how it was going.

It may sound uppity to say so, but I get letters like that
all the time. People think that because I have written a
number of articles about boatbuilders I must know a lot
about boatbuilding, and because I once spent a considerable amount of time in the presence of educators I must
know something about education. I don't. But I do know
that you can't teach a class of greenhorns enough about
boatbuilding for them to construct a ten-foot lapstrake
pram in a week. Mr. Watts, in his letter, claimed he could.

It sounded like a stunt, like teaching a bullfrog to walk
upright on stilts while playing the French horn in a marching
band. It also seemed totally out of character for the Rockport Apprenticeshop, an institution notorious for the leisurely
pace of its boatbuilding projects. In short, it sounded like
an iconoclastic send-up. My curiosity was piqued.

Other responsibilities intervened, however, and I missed the course, though I managed to visit the Apprenticeshop briefly on the next-to-last day. I expected to find a pack of disorganized students rushing around, getting in each other's way and tripping over power-tool cords while the instructor, Mr. Watts, looked on in dismay. Instead I found a planked, framed, kneed, thwarted, inwaled, gunwaled, and transomed ten-foot pram — a dainty little thing — about to be primed and painted. The next day it would be launched into the harbor just outside the shop door and begin its career as a yacht tender. The students, who claimed never to have built a boat before, were relaxed and exceedingly proud of themselves. Mr. Watts was perched on a shop bench drinking a cup of coffee.

Zounds! This wasn't a stunt. This wasn't guerilla theater. This was a brand-new lick in the never-ending struggle to keep the knowledge of wooden boat building techniques alive.

Classes in boatbuilding are a modern-day phenomenon. With the exception of a very few vocational school curriculums, they didn't exist fifteen to twenty years ago. Before then, under the best of circumstances, if you wanted to become an amateur boatbuilder, you learned from your Uncle Fred, who as a boy may have worked part-time in a boatshop sweeping up sawdust and straightening out bent nails. Under the worst of circumstances, you bought a copy of Sam Rabl's *Boatbuilding in Your Own Backyard* or Howard Chapelle's *Boatbuilding* and taught yourself. Now there are a number of schools where you can undertake a course of instruction that may not necessarily lead to a Bachelor of Arts in Boatbuilding, but at least will make you competent enough to get that long-contemplated boatbuilding project off the ground and into the water. Among other places, you can study at the Rockport Apprenticeshop, the Apprenticeshop of the Maine Maritime Museum, the Center for Wooden Boats, the Center for Wood Arts, the Mystic Seaport Museum, the Wooden Boat School, the Landing Boatshop, the North Carolina Maritime Museum, and the Northeast School of Boatbuilding.

Most of these schools conduct courses on the principle of longevity — the longer you hang around, the more you learn. (To be sure, many teach short courses on various subjects, but few would presume to build a ten-foot lapstrake boat in a week.) Their cachet is The Revelation of the Mysterious Truths of Wooden Boat Building. Their strengths are experienced staffs and a track record of accomplishment. Their weaknesses are centralization — the students must come to them — and institutionalization.

Simon Watts is wary of institutions. An Englishman, he studied civil engineering at Cambridge University and architecture at the Massachusetts Institute of Technology. He became neither an engineer nor an architect; rather, he opened a custom woodworking shop in Putney, Vermont. He worked alone, or with an apprentice or two, for close to twenty years. That was about as institutionalized as he wanted to get — in fact, it was too much. A few years ago he closed his shop, worked in Joel White's boatshop in Maine for a few months, and then moved to California, where he began to write about boatbuilding and woodworking techniques, primarily for *Fine Woodworking* magazine, and to teach boatbuilding.

He didn't become simply a teacher of boatbuilding, however. He became an itinerant teacher of boatbuilding. The students don't come to Watts; Watts comes to the students. He has no affiliations, no staff position, no certification, no permanent workshop address. He's a free-lancer — a hit-and-run artist like Johnny Appleseed — and he will set up a boatbuilding course anywhere you like, even in a shed behind a pool hall in Boise, Idaho, if it comes down to that. The sponsor of the course could even be the owner of the pool hall, if it should come down to that.

Watts's theory behind all this is that the more people who are exposed to the techniques of wooden boat building, the more likely the art is to survive. The institutions that teach boatbuilding only draw students from the immediate area or those with enough time and money to travel to the immediate area. If wooden boat building is to be universally practiced, it must be brought to the hinterlands. The only way it can be brought to the hinterlands is by itinerant teachers. Watts has taught rank amateurs how to build boats in San Diego, San Francisco, Berkeley, Seattle, Nova Scotia, Maine, North Carolina, and places in between.

Simon Watts's basic shtick is a one-week course on how to build a pram, a Chamberlain dory, a recreational rowing shell, or a sailing skiff. The featured construction method is lapstrake, and the emphasis is on the use of hand tools, though some power tools are used. Sponsors — museums, craft centers, tool stores — set up the workshop space, recruit the students, collect the tuition fees, and pay the instructor his fee and put him up for the duration of the course. The only prerequisites for the students are that they be reasonably facile at woodworking, have their own hand tools, and be prepared to work like demons for a week. The only promises Simon Watts makes are that he will strip away the mysteries and mumbo-jumbos of lapstrake boatbuilding and instill confidence in his students. He doesn't claim to turn hackers into boatbuilders in a week; his goal is simply to convince his students that they have within themselves the ability to become competent amateur boatbuilders.

There are many people who don't understand that goal, as I found out in the summer of 1986 while sitting in on another of Simon Watts's courses at the Rockport Apprenticeshop, this one a twelve-day event on the building of a 12 1/2-foot lapstrake sailing skiff. (The extra days beyond a week were necessary because this boat required a centerboard case, centerboard, spars, tiller, rudder, etc. Even so, the job was finished on the eleventh day and most of the students went home early.) People who claimed knowledge of boatbuilding and boatbuilding education were in and out continually. Some of them applauded Mr. Watts's efforts and congratulated his students. Plenty of them grumbled to each other about the sinfulness of it all. Look at all those guys prancing around with folding rules in their back pockets, thinking they're boatbuilders and they don't even know the difference between a bearding line and a horn timber! Look at that instructor, standing back and letting them make mistakes and not pointing out the mistakes until they've been made! Whoever heard of building a lapstrake sailing skiff in twelve days?

Indeed, who has? At 7:55 A.M. on the morning of the first day of the course, the students looked a little doubtful themselves. Here they were, grown men — an illustrator, a dentist, an airline pilot, a school principal, a carpenter, among others — and they were as nervous and as unsure of themselves as any class of incoming high school freshmen. Most of them had read a bit about boatbuilding from a reading list that Mr. Watts had provided before-hand, but what they had learned from that only served to underscore how difficult the task before them would be.

The day before, Simon Watts had built the molds for the boat, a Nova Scotian model for which no conventional plans exist, and had set up a spruce backbone held together with drywall screws. This mock backbone was in place only for demonstration purposes; the real thing would be built in oak by the students.

At 8 A.M. sharp Mr. Watts appeared, introduced himself all around, walked over to the mockup, and said, "Take a good look at the connections so you can see how the backbone goes together." So everyone took a good look at the connections. They weren't too certain what they were looking at or why, but they got on with it.

Nowhere in my notes for that day do I have written down exactly what Simon Watts said by way of introduction to the project. I do remember that he talked slowly and deliberately, not at all as one would expect under the circumstances. He didn't seem to be in much of a rush; neither did he seem concerned about whether or not the students understood the terminology he was using. He spoke about rabbets and forefoots and transom knees and keel battens and lining off and things like that. Everyone stood around nodding their heads in perfect agreement, but you knew full well nobody had any idea what he was talking about.

Mr. Watts knew it too. About five minutes into his little talk he merely said, "OK, let's go. A couple of you start dismantling the mocked-up backbone, some of you get the timber together to build one out of oak, and the rest of you start figuring the plank lines." It was then that the parts began to cry out to be defined.

"What's this?" asked one.

"That's the keelson," said another.

"No," said Watts, "That's a keel batten. There's a difference, small but real."

"Hey, how many planks to a side?"

"What do you think?" asked Watts.

"Five, six?"

"Why do you say that?"

"Seems reasonable."

"Here," said Watts. "Let's quickly go over the relationship of girth to the number of planks. This is your boat, our boat, and we can plank it any way we want. We are not going by a textbook, so we are free to do what we want."

He then sent a crew off to make battens for lining off the planks. The instructions were no more thorough than,

"Find some lumber that we can use for making battens and let's make them."

At one point he held back one of the more skilled students — a professional woodworker — from a particularly difficult task. In an aside, he said, "The temptation is to rely on the best workers to get the job going. But I force myself to give difficult jobs to people who aren't quite ready for them. These people are here to learn how to do something they couldn't do before, not the other way around."

Exactly an hour after Watts walked in the door, the class was going full tilt. Watts was standing off to one side, watching students struggle with lining off the planks. None of them had ever done it and most of them had never heard of the concept before that day. Some thought the lines were fair, some thought they weren't.

"Let them argue," said Watts. "Then they'll have to develop a consensus."

"What do you think?" a student asked.

"What do you think?" Watts shot back.

The student looked surprised, perturbed, but then asserted himself. "I think it looks pretty good."

"Well then," said Watts, "so do I." (He turned to me and said, "Let them make the decisions. They're the ones who have to live with them. I'm here to keep them from getting out of control and to provide advice.")

"Do we have to use a daggerboard?"

"No. Would you rather build a centerboard?"

"Yes."

"Then we'll do it."

And so it went. By 2 P.M. the planks had been lined off, a mock-up of the centerboard trunk had been built, the stem had been cut and fitted to the keel, the centerboard slot had been cut, the stern post, including tenon, had been made, and the transom was well underway. Watts stood overseeing it all — commenting, exhorting, prodding, the picture of confidence that all would work out.

A student went over to the keel to test a piece of wood to see if it was the right size for the centerboard trunk posts. He tried it. He looked over to Watts for approval. He didn't get it. He asked. Watts looked at him awhile. Then he merely said, "Does it fit?"

"Yes."

"Then it's good." (To me, he said with a smile, "It's like bringing up children.")

On the second day the class was supposed to have started at 8:30 A.M. I arrived at 8:26. Five students were already at work, and they looked as if they had been there for a long time. Watts nodded over to them and said, "They were lost yesterday. They want to take charge today. In a few days, you'll know they will be ready to graduate when they start to resent advice from the instructor."

By the morning of the fifth day, the backbone had been completed, the rabbet cut, the transom in place and beveled, seven planks had been hung, another was ready to go, and several more had been roughed out. The crew — for that was what this once-random bunch had become — was cheerful, joking, whistling, confident, self-reliant. The boat was a little rough around the gills, but as Watts said, "I let them make mistakes so they can learn from them. We leave the mistakes where they are as reminders of what has to be done differently the next time around."

The seventh day found the boat rightside up and primed on the inside. This was framing day. Watts gave a short speech on the principles of steaming and bending frames, then finished with a statement to the effect that the entire job would be completed inside an hour. Again, nobody believed him. Again, he was right.

By the tenth day the inside and outside had been painted, a Canadian flag was flying from a staff at the stern, and the crew was working on the final details — thwarts, breasthook, knees, mast, sprit, etc. By the eleventh day, just about everything was done. On day twelve it was over. Simon Watts and his pickup crew had proved the tire kickers wrong again.

Does he get tired of doing this over and over again, starting with greenhorns from scratch?

"No. I learn something new on every outing."

Does he get tired of sleeping in borrowed quarters and living out of a satchel?

"Sometimes, yes. But it is the only way I can reach students who have never been exposed to this type of thing before."

Does he yearn for a change of pace?

"Definitely. I want to get away from the coasts, where the boatbuilding tradition already exists to a certain extent. I want to get some classes going in St. Louis, perhaps. Anywhere in the Midwest, where there is a need for this type of thing and no other way to fulfill it. All I need are the sponsors."

Three Friends

I first encountered the Vermont boatbuilding scene in, of all places, Rhode Island. Tom Hill, of Charlotte, just south of Burlington in northern Vermont, was unloading canoes for display at the Newport Wooden Boat Show. Most other exhibitors had to enlist an army of warm bodies to help them move their heavy, traditionally constructed boats. Hill — who is quite short and built like one of those high school wingbacks who specialize in the flea-flicker and end-around but wouldn't stand a chance off-tackle into the line — merely tucked his canoes under his arm or hooked them over his shoulder, laying them in display stands that looked barely capable of supporting a plastic bag of dry leaves.

Not a few onlookers took notice, and soon several students of the light boat were clustered around, hefting the tiny craft and muttering things like, "Eleven and a half feet and twenty-five pounds?" (Hill: "Give or take a few ounces") and "How do you get these things to hold together?" (Hill: "Tight seams and epoxy glue"), and — from the true aficionados—"Do you know Carl Bausch?" (Hill: "He is my mentor").

Bausch . . . Bausch . . . I remembered seeing a Bausch canoe once. It was lying in a field next to the Stillwater River in Orono, Maine. The wind was gusting that day, and the tiny canoe was fluttering and trembling on the ground as if it were made of papier-mâché and weighed only ten or so pounds. As I got closer, I realized it was built of lapstrake plywood, and when I hefted it, I discovered that ten pounds was no exaggeration. If the wind had gotten any stronger, that 9 1/2-foot canoe would have become a UFO.

The quality of the craftsmanship in that Bausch canoe was nothing to write home about — in fact, it was incredibly crude — but the eggshell lightness with strength was an achievement matched only by J. Henry Rushton, a nineteenth century canoe and boat builder noted for the excellence of his work. The Bruynzeel plywood planking was four millimeters thick (for all you metrignoramuses, that's a little more than an eighth inch), the laps were glued, the framing was nonexistent, and there was not a metal fastening in the boat. Despite this almost reckless disregard for conventional scantling rules, the canoe looked as if it could easily top Rushton's comparable *Sairy Gamp* and *Nessmuk No. 2* in the abuse-in-use department. (Later I was to hear that Carl Bausch in a rage pulled one of his canoes off the car roof-rack and threw it as far as he could. It bounced once and vibrated like a tuning fork.)

Tom Hill's canoes look like Bausch's (as we shall see, they are Bausch canoes), but they are a little heavier and much more finely finished. They, too, are four-millimeter plywood, but the keel, stems, breasthooks, rails, and thwarts have more heft to them and hence produce stronger craft. The final touches — the matching of grain, the careful chamfering, the deep varnish, the smooth paint — add to the fascination.

To get to Vermont from Maine you have to cross New Hampshire, the home of low taxes and cheap liquor. The best road west is Route 2, though it is not much more than a two-lane snake that would be classified anywhere else — even in Delaware — as a couple of notches below secondary, and the towns along the way, with few exceptions, could easily serve as sets for the remake of *High Plains Drifter* in a Great Depression setting.

So it comes as something of a relief to rattle across the bridge spanning the Connecticut River and revel in Vermont, a progressive state, an enlightened state. Perhaps it's only my imagination, but I can feel the difference, even though Route 2 continues to meander and the towns along the way are not what you would call prosperous. Vermont, you see, has a record of liberal conservatism or conservative liberalism unmatched by any other state except perhaps Oregon, and it shows. Vermont was one of the first states to ban billboards, one of the first with a bottle-redemption law, one of the only states to enact development-control laws before the developers were through "improving" things. You can actually see the Green Mountains.

Of course there are all those jokes about Vermont, that it is the only state with more cows than people, that its native citizens, famous for their lack of toleration for outsiders, insist "you can't get there from here." But for the most part they are benign jokes related by people who love Vermont's bucolic countryside and gorgeous mountains and civilized cities and breathtaking Lake Champlain. Every person there, if backed against the wall, would speechify about Vermont's tradition of educational excellence and its small-town democracy-in-action and everything else in the American Dream that the state holds dear. They would talk about the maple sugar bush, ski resorts, the stalwart farmer hauling loads of hay down idyllic winding roads. They probably wouldn't add boatbuilders to the list because serious watercraft are ever-so-slightly incongruous for such a rural state, but they should, for they are blessed with some of the best.

The leaves were down but Indian summer was in full reign when I visited Tom Hill, Boatbuilder, who plied his trade at the foot of Mt. Philo, a foothill of the Green Mountains in Charlotte (accent on the second syllable, please), not far from Lake Champlain but far enough to be farmland country rather than summertime lakefront, if you know what I mean. A huge turkey hobbled around Hill's yard with the haunted look of a bird who knows what is coming up in just a month or so. He was certainly more picturesque than Hill's shop, which is merely a garage with a workbench, a couple of machine tools and a few hand tools, and canoe molds in the rafters. Despite the down-home appearances, however, Hill is an enlightened progressive, just like the state he lives in, though he would probably be the last to claim such a description.

"Let's go over to Carl's," Tom said, and we did, driving up into the hills, where there were vistas of Lake Champlain to the west, the Green Mountains to the east. It was proof enough that Vermont is the very soul of New England. Streams tumbled down from the hills to the lake, but at this time of year they were low and impassable by canoe. In the spring they run high, swelling over the banks and into the fields and woods. I was beginning to appreciate the need for light, strong, small, maneuverable canoes. While we drove and I contemplated the pumpkins and the cornstalks, Tom talked about his background.

"I was brought up here in Vermont. I guess I'm what you might call a dropout since I never went to college or took up a conventional career. My high school years were 1968, '69, '70, '71; the Vietnam War, protest, Kent State. Vermont was like everywhere else then, perhaps even more so. My generation was looking for something else. I wanted to learn, but not necessarily what we were expected to learn.

"I started out as a carpenter, working on houses. Carpentry is a typical Vermont getting-by occupation, and I did it to keep from starving to death. But I wanted to do something else, and when I heard Carl Bausch needed help I asked him for a job. He took me on as an apprentice at twenty-five dollars per week, forty hours. I lived up in the mountains about twenty-five miles from here and rode a motorcycle to work. It was 1972 and I was seventeen years old.

"Carl was building strip-planked canoes at the time. It was the heyday of the stripper, and somehow he got hooked up with Orvis, the high-class fishing-tackle suppliers. They were selling Carl's boats as the Orvis Canoe. There were almost always eight to ten boats on order, so Carl and I and another fellow, who eventually became a fine furniture maker, went crazy. We built a hell of a lot of boats.

"It was hard, grueling work, and it eventually became boring. Strip planking is messy and repetitive. We were always up to our elbows in glue, which came to worry me after awhile — the health aspects — especially after Carl developed a detached retina in his eye. I've always wondered whether that was caused by the constant contact with epoxy glue.

"Anyway, Carl's health became a problem, so he had to stop building strippers. He began experimenting with plywood lapstrake construction because he has this thing about light boats and he thought that technique might produce something worthwhile. You have to understand Carl. He only builds light boats — no heavy boat has ever come out of his shop — and he is a compulsive experimenter. He's also an antitraditionalist. He had a motto in his shop: 'Tradition is for breaking.'

"When the strippers stopped, so did my apprenticeship, so I went to work in a boatyard down on the lake. I did typical maintenance and repair work.

"I soon got sick of painting boats. I'd just plain had it. My experience with Carl taught me that I preferred building boats, not fixing them, so I decided to go into the boatbuilding business, even though I didn't have much of a plan for how I would do it. I had $1,500 saved up to get started, and my landlord let me convert the garage to a shop. I started out by building traditional boats, nothing like what I am doing now."

Carl Bausch's place, which was only a few miles from Hill's, had a hardscrabble look to it — not rundown, just temporary. There was a main house, a studio (Carl's wife is an artist), and a boatshop. Not to mention a barking dog, a fixture of the rural environment. Up there in the woods, you would never expect to see boats of any kind, but under a shed roof jutting from the shop were a few, plus at least one failed experiment rotting off in the bushes. If an old-timer had appeared, picking a banjo and drinking sour-mash from a stone crock, I wouldn't have been surprised.

Instead, standing in the shop doorway was the next best thing, the legendary Carl Bausch. Tall, gaunt, wearing work clothes that were stiff in places from solidified epoxy, he was one of those men whose age is next to impossible to determine. He could have been fifty, he could have been seventy, but he had the shaking hands that made getting his cigarette to his mouth an act of sheer willpower, and a body build reminiscent of the guy who gets sand kicked in his face at the beach. (I later learned that he was in his sixties.) To look at this man, you would never imagine that his avocation was building radio-controlled model airplanes (strength and lightness) and that his vocation was building small boats (uncounted hundreds since he began professionally in 1971). He was just too fragile.

His shop was much like Hill's, only a little bigger and not as neat. There were few tools around — an old Sears band saw and some dull hand tools — but plenty of patterns and jigs and pieces of plywood and gobs of hardened glue. In the middle of the shop was a boat in progress, a plywood pocket cruiser based on a design by Steve Redmond of Burlington, Vermont. "That's Redmond's Elver," said Bausch, "but I'm sure he would never acknowledge it. He calls for rounded topsides and a dead-flat bottom, and a centerboard right down the middle. I think it's too heavy, and that centerboard gets in the way; and I've had it with strip planking. So I've lightened it up with chined plywood construction, rockered bottom, and leeboards. Is it too light? Perhaps, but I've incorporated water ballast."

The boat was less than half the weight Redmond intended, yet when I mentioned that to Redmond a day or two later, he merely shrugged his shoulders and said what everybody says. "Carl's an experimenter. He starts with someone's design and radicalizes it." That's progress, I suppose.

The Bausch-Hill relationship goes beyond mentor-apprentice. It's more of a true friendship, even though they are generations apart. Actually, they are closer than one would think, because both are dropouts — it's just that Bausch did his dropping out later in life than did Hill.

"I started out as an architect, houses and commercial buildings," said Bausch. "I came to Vermont right after World War II from Rochester, New York. I've been a canoeist since I was a kid. While I was working as an architect, I started experimenting with strip-building canoes, built a couple in my house. So about ten, twelve years ago when I decided to drop the architecture thing, it seemed only natural to become a canoe builder.

"I had been building professionally for about six months when the Orvis deal came through. By then I had worked out various improvements to make construction simpler and the boats better, like a plank garboard to even things out so the topsides could be planked with parallel strips to the sheer. But I didn't build just straight canoes. I stripped everything — double-paddle canoes, Adirondack guideboats, you name it.

"My deal with Orvis was no great shakes. I built all the canoes and they made all the money. Plus I was bored with strippers. Plus I was dissatisfied with the types of fits you could get unless you took excessive amounts of time to do the job. Plus I was developing health problems. Caused by glue? I don't know. But there sure was a hell of a lot of glue running around this shop when we were building those strippers. I decided to quit and fool around in another direction, absolute lightness.

"Why light? Nobody else was building light. Besides, I needed a light boat — I'm not the strongest fellow in the world."

Carl Bausch's idea of fooling around in another direction was to start with some of J. Henry Rushton's light canoe designs and modify them to his own tastes, in the areas of both performance and construction. All the while, Tom Hill was watching over his shoulder, dropping by the shop in his spare time and learning, learning, learning. "I liked to watch Carl work out a problem," said Tom. "He kept 'light' in his mind and went straight for it."

"Well, not quite straight," said Bausch with understated good humor. "My bad eye makes me see crooked lines as fair, and there's nothing I can do about it. But I'm not much on finishes, anyway. I figure a boat is a working tool, not a visual feast.

"I can't remember why, but I figured lapstrake plywood, radically thin, was the key. I read *Dinghy Building* by Richard Creagh-Osborne and thought his chapter on lapstrake ply was a ponderous method. Too much left to chance. So I devised a building jig with rigid, spaced battens and a tool for trimming planks and beveling laps — on the boat, after the planks have been glued on. No real spiling is necessary, yet the planks come out exactly as you want them."

Carl Bausch's canoes — frameless and with minimum scantlings all the way around — turned out to be so light they were creepy, and Bausch turned into something of an underground legend for his accomplishments. Just the right subject for a big-city Sunday-supplement magazine writer looking for a character/craftsman plying his trade up in them thar quaint hills of Vermont. The article came out in the design section of the *New York Times Magazine*, November 12, 1978 ("The dream of the canoeing enthusiast is a lightweight craft . . .").

You guessed it. "I got about two hundred responses in two weeks," said Bausch, "and I was back in the same position I was in building strippers. I tried to keep up with it as best I could, but eventually it tired me right out."

It was about this time that Tom Hill set up shop as an independent boatbuilder. He was struggling to get enough business to pay his overhead, never mind feed his family, when Carl Bausch showed up at his door. "Take them, take them all," said Bausch, " — my forms, my orders, my future orders." Tom Hill became the legatee of the ultralight canoe.

Tom Hill is unlike most boatbuilders I have met. The way he shows off his accomplishments is to show off his teachers. His emphasis is on influences (the people he admires), not results (the boats he builds). So just in case I got the idea that he learned everything he knows — which is considerable — from Carl Bausch, he took me over to see Ed Sturges, another Charlotte boatbuilder of a quite different stripe.

We drove further into the hills, the early afternoon sun shining on the green grass and the rust-colored leaves, past apple orchards and small farms and old cellar holes yawning through the brush, deeper into territory that made *Vermont Life* cover photographs look like snapshots of the Dakota badlands.

"Ed is just the opposite of Carl," said Hill. "He's a very traditional boatbuilder. His canoes are all wood-canvas, and his idea of a good small craft is a Maine peapod, plank-on-frame, the more heavily built the better. He and Carl are friends, even though each thinks the other's boats are too extreme.

"I'm constantly getting input from both men. I've worked in Ed's shop, too, but not for money. My boats come somewhere between the lightness of Carl's and the strength of Ed's. I've struck a compromise between these two guys I've watched over the years. On the one hand, I like the way Carl thinks. For example, his house is built to last just as long as he is going to last. But then again, I like the way Ed thinks. If he were to build a house, he would try to build it to last forever, a house that would have its own tradition, separate from Ed himself. Does one resent the influence of the other on my boats? No, I don't think so. They're both strong willed and good hearted at the same time."

Ed Sturges. If there ever was a vision of what we all wish we could be in our late seventies, here he was, coming around the corner of the barn as we turned off the road: short, vigorous, unruly gray-white hair, woolen shirt, Scott Nearing/Robert Frost down on the farm. He had a physique that could only be described as rawboned robust, and his handshake was a cross between a gentle touch and a hydraulic press.

His younger friends talk about his strength and endurance with awe. Tom Hill describes a 250-mile canoe trip with Sturges about ten years ago down Ontario's Missinaibi River. They were portaging across a long stretch, the canoe having soaked up enough water to weigh about one hundred pounds. Hill carried the canoe a short distance and collapsed. Sturges picked it up as if it were a Bausch featherweight and ran on ahead. "By the time I got to the campsite," says Hill, "Ed had his tent pitched and was building a fire."

Ed Sturges, who lived alone, welcomed the opportunity to show off his boats, various ruggedly constructed north woods wood-canvas canoes and a couple of stout peapods, one a John Gardner rowing model and the other a Walt Simmons-Howard Chapelle rowing/sailing model. They were beautifully built and plainly finished, their handsomeness enhanced by the patina of use. ("This canoe was the one I used on my expedition to Labrador last year." Labrador! Doesn't this guy know that people who are pushing eighty are supposed to be down in St. Petersburg playing Chinese checkers in the park?)

Sturges builds his boats and keeps them ("People get mad at me for that"), or gives them away (they must love him for that); never sells them because he doesn't have to. There's money in his past, though you would never know it to look around — the barn and outbuildings are dicey, his house is a tiny one-room-with-rootcellar, his bed is a sleeping bag in the corner, and the closest he comes to a modern convenience is when he rides his bicycle down to the store, which isn't very often because he grows most of what he eats. Henry David Thoreau would be impressed.

"I'm originally from Connecticut," said Sturges. "I've had two lives, one in salt water, this one in fresh. In my first life I sailed across the Atlantic a couple of times, and up and down the coast. I've been all around. About fifteen years ago I met Harold Blanchard, a canoe builder in Greenville, Maine, and bought a canoe from him. I loved the boat and liked Harold's shop so much that I asked him if I could stick around while he taught me how to build canoes. He agreed, though he wouldn't take money for his time. I wound up giving him a fancy trout rod, but it wasn't nearly enough to pay for all I learned. I built only canoes until about three years ago, when I started building peapods because I wanted one so badly."

For years Sturges has been repaying Harold Blanchard's favor in the best way possible: by teaching other people how to build canoes. Tom Hill, of course, is his most avid student — certainly his most successful — but there have been many others. They hear about Sturges through the grapevine and stop by; if he is in the mood and they seem serious and are willing to pay for their materials, he'll build a canoe with them.

"I met a fellow in the mountains once, hiking up on Camel's Hump," said Ed, shaking his head in amazement. "Somehow he found out I was a canoe builder and asked me if I would help him build a canoe. I agreed. He lived on a farm in a trailer until we were done. Then he said, 'How do I get to Alaska from here?' I said, 'What do you mean?' He said, 'I built this canoe, and now I want to paddle it to Alaska.' And by God he did it."

Have you ever tried a light canoe? I mean a really light canoe — one that you alone can lift onto the roof of your car without slipping a disc or having it leverage you onto your back on the ground with your left elbow wrapped around your right ear. One that allows you to stop by the side of the road next to a body of water — any body of water more than three inches deep — and in a matter of minutes be exploring it. One that can be packed through miles of woods to that mythical mountain lake where the trout are so big and tame that they think the fly at the end of the line is real and the canoe it is coming from is just a big brother. One that is so easy to carry that you can run with it across private property to the shore and be in the water and away before the trespassee can identify you as a trespasser.

Tom Hill builds ultralight canoes like that. They may have evolved from the nineteenth-century designs of J. Henry Rushton, and they may look like Carl Bausch's, and they may contain within them the strength of Ed Sturges's, but they are uniquely Hill's own. They are a synthesis of ideas and materials, a coming together of thin plywood for lightness and dimensional stability, epoxy glue for watertight integrity and strength, spruce for lightness and flexibility, Xynole cloth for bottom abrasion resistance. They can be driven on top of your car down the New Jersey Turnpike at fifty-five miles an hour in the hot summer sun without drying out so much that they sink when you launch them, and they can be so easily maintained that you'll never, ever consider going second-class again because first-class seemed to require so much work.

We stood out in the yard, Tom Hill and I, as the Thanksgiving turkey ran free, and talked about Carl Bausch and Ed Sturges and their contributions to the education of a young boatbuilder. Tom nodded his head and said, "Yes, Carl and Ed tolerated me in their shops, and I gained everything as a result. They felt a certain responsibility to pass on what they know, and I guess I do, too. This summer I'm teaching a course in canoe building at the Appalachian School for the Crafts in Tennessee, and the day will come when I take on an apprentice just like Carl did me." An enlightened progressive talking if I ever heard one.

Afterword: Tom Hill is still building ultralight canoes and boats in the Green Mountains, though he has moved his operation from Charlotte to the town of Huntington. Ed Sturges still lives on the farm and still builds wood-and-canvas canoes. Carl Bausch, I'm sad to say, died in the summer of 1988.

113

Quick and . . . er . . . Dirty Boatbuilding

Sikaflex.

There, I said it. But in the interest of artistic integrity, that is the last time, at least for a while, because we're treading the fine line between advertising and editorial. To show my lack of bias, I'll call it Kumquat.

"Kumquat?" asked Dynamite Payson as he climbed down from his garden tractor. He had been fixing the headlight switch when we hove into view. ("You'll never know when you want to plow your garden at night," he said with a straight face.)

"Looks more like gunk to me," said Amy Payson, who has always been one to call a spade a spade.

"Actually, it's a miracle marine sealer/adhesive," said John Hanson. And so the Quick & Dirty Boatbuilding Contest, a.k.a. the Sika Challenge Cup, was under way.

It all began when the Sika Corporation's interest in promoting Kumquat coincided with John Hanson's desire to hold a quick and dirty boatbuilding contest. Hanson, then head of *WoodenBoat*'s advertising department, had this strange notion that boatbuilding could be fast and fun — a notion that is in direct conflict with a good many of the tenets at the core of the Wooden Boat Revival. It goes along with his feeling that the music of Adam and the Ants has social significance.

With not much more than a few vague promises that a contest featuring lashed-together boats would make Kumquat a household word around the land, the folks at Sika agreed to put up a Challenge Cup and pay for the necessary materials. Hanson agreed to organize the event. Payson got into the act because a technical advisor was needed, and nobody knows more about instant boatbuilding than that gentleman. In fact, he wrote the book.

Dynamite Payson is a skeptic, however, and he wasn't going to get involved in a boatbuilding contest that relied on Kumquat to hold the craft together unless he was satisfied the stuff really worked. So we overlapped the ends of two pieces of plywood with a copious amount of Kumquat in between. During the twenty minutes or so that it took the gunk to set up, Dynamite laconically described all the miracle adhesives he had tried that never came close to living up to expectations. Then we destroyed the plywood while trying to break the Kumquat joint. Then Dynamite became our technical advisor.

The rules of the contest, as determined during a marathon session around Dynamite's shop stove, were to be as simple as reasonable: two boatbuilders to a team, two teams to compete head to head at a time, each team to be provided with two sheets of plywood, a pound of trap nails, four eight-foot 2 x 4s, and all the Kumquat they could use. The contest, to be held at the Newport (Rhode Island) Wooden Boat Show in August, would be in two parts: first part to be the boatbuilding itself, the second to be a race using the boats built in the first. Combined points earned in the two parts would determine the Sika Challenge Cup's winner, who would earn the right to the title King of the Quick & Dirty Boat.

We realized this was all pretty weird stuff — that there

may be few people out there who would really understand the concept of quick and dirtiness; that nobody in his right mind would want to participate in, never mind watch, such gone-to-hell madness; that we could very well wreck our reputations, such as they were. John Hanson decided to soften the blow by calling it a "quick and simple" contest. After all, dirt is dirt, but simple . . . now there's a good, solid L. F. Herreshoff word.

Nevertheless, we were on the brink of the cold sweats from the moment in June when the contest was announced until the beginning of August when all the entries had to be submitted. After all, the Sika Corporation was putting their money and influence behind this organized craziness, and we had assured them it was going to be OK.

As the entry deadline approached and we had heard little or nothing from potential participants, John Hanson had a brief but intense flirtation with despair. He started sleeping under his truck in the barn. The seams around the corners of his eyes got deeper and darker. "I guess I'm going to have to call in some favors this time. Twist a few arms. Good God! Will I have to pay people to enter?"

He needn't have worried. The last few days of July and the first of August produced an avalanche of entries. First class, special delivery, we even got a couple Federal Express.

The rules of the contest required the submission in advance of original, nonprofessional designs. The Esteemed Panel of Judges — John Hanson, Dynamite Payson, Fingers Spectre — would select six finalists on the basis of "originality, ingenuity, and a touch of whimsy." When we actually sat down to the task, we added two other criteria: "Will the design as built actually work?" and "Does this design have a reasonable chance to win?" We expected the winner in the boatbuilding half of the contest to do the job in about two hours. As it turned out,

117

we overestimated by a factor of two.

Boy, did we ever get some deliciously weird designs. Pirogues, dories, bateaux, the expected run on the sixteen-foot double-ender, a trimaran, a guideboat, a few skiffs, a triangular wedge reminiscent of *Star Wars*, a few that defy description. And letters, such as this toss of the gauntlet from Jeff Blum of Nashville, Tennessee, who wanted to build a double-pontoon paddlewheeler: ". . . If y'all are interested in what us Southern river runners can do against all those Yankee folks that talk so strange, give us a holler and we'll pack up the pickup and meet you in Newport."

Newport. For a while there we had another attack of self-doubt. Have you ever been to Newport, Rhode Island, in the late summer? The boys in the lime-green pants were strutting the polished streets, and the women had that look of silken ease indicating both an ignorance of and an abhorrence for goop, gunk, and above all, Kumquat. Moët Champagne was sponsoring a match race between Gary Jobson and Tom Blackaller in the gold-plated wooden yachts *Cotton Blossom* and *Royono* and the so-called Victory Syndicate from England was in town with their twelve-meter, a brace of Jaguars, and matching T-shirts and shorts to practice for the next *America*'s Cup challenge.

Imagine, then, John Hanson, whose six-month-old razor had expired two days before, on the dock of the Newport Yachting Center, unloading plywood, 2 x 4s, sawhorses, and the like from his rusted yellow-paint-flaked pickup. The one with the dog drool on the dashboard and crushed beer cans under the seat.

"What are you doing?" a passerby asked.

"Getting ready for a quick and . . . er . . . simple boatbuilding race," said John.

"Oh. How nice. Say, could you direct me to the Ida Lewis Yacht Club?"

"Gentlemen, man your saws," announced the fellow from the Sika Corporation, and the four-day competition was underway. Two teams went head-to-head each day, and the "Sea Trials" were held the fourth. I don't know where they came from, or what kept them there, but the people crowded around the boatbuilders were about five layers deep most of the time. Our fears of ridicule — or worse, of indifference — turned out to be unfounded. Nobody seemed to mind that bizarre little boats were being built with enthusiasm right alongside some of the highest-quality yachts in this land.

We got what we asked for: competitors ripping 2 x 4s freehand, cutting plywood to shape with not much more than a prayer to the God of Approximation (templates and patterns were not allowed), pumping Kumquat into joints that were sometimes tight, sometimes as wide as the Ausable Chasm, maintaining good humor as the goop stuck to their hands and landed in their hair, as wisecracks looped from the crowd and the minutes ticked away. Ingenuity was the order of the day; it had to be when you consider that the fastest construction time was fifty-five minutes, eleven seconds (a fifteen-foot paddleboard), and that the slowest, at four hours, twenty-five minutes, twenty-two seconds (a twenty-two-foot W-sectioned pirogue) was unbelievably fast by anyone's standards.

For example, the rules were that all tools not provided by the race committee had to be carried aboard the completed boat in the "Sea Trials." This was intended to keep contestants from showing up with band saws and table saws. So Jim Taylor and John Judge, whose twenty-two-foot pirogue required long, thin stringers cut from 2 x 4s, built their own table saw out of plywood scraps and a hand-held power circular saw. The spectators laughed when Taylor and Judge started; they applauded when the last stringer was ripped.

For another example, Dan Greene and Dennis Pilla,

119

otherwise known as the Glues Brothers, needed a very extreme bend in the keel of their proa's outrigger. Without a steam box or the time to use one, the spruce from the allotted 2 x 4s wouldn't take the bend. So they cross-hatched the keel piece with their circular saw, bent the keel in place, then filled the gaps with Kumquat.

For yet another example, Chris Fabiszak and Lou Sauzedde, who built the winning double-ender, had to scarf their plywood to get the proper length for the boat's sides. They planed the bevels and smeared them with Kumquat, then laid the joint on a strip of steel. Nails driven through the joint hit the steel and clenched themselves, saving considerable time.

Think about it. Two sheets of plywood, four 2 x 4s, a bag of nails, all the Kumquat you can use (as it turned out, an average of six cartridges per boat). A skiff in one hour, two minutes, two seconds. A dory in two hours, forty minutes, eighteen seconds. A proa in one hour, four minutes, twenty-seven seconds. And you thought that dinghy would take you two winters of weekends.

Sunday, August 22, 1:30 P.M. It's a hot, sunny afternoon with a strengthening offshore breeze. Jobson and Black-aller are somewhere out in Narragansett Bay in *Cotton Blossom* and *Royono*, fighting it out for the Moët Masters Cup. It's just as well, because if they were to see what is about to unfold in their town, at their dock, in front of what is supposed to be their audience, they might be so appalled as to quit yachting for the rest of their lives.

Danny Greene and Dennis Pilla, the Glues Brothers, are suited up in their loincloths and Hawaiian war paint, standing by their yellow proa unofficially known as the *Golden Banana*. Dan Shaw and Mo Mancini, two professional boatbuilders who are beginning to wonder why they got involved in this madness, are trying to figure out how they will be able to stay aboard their paddleboard on this windy, choppy day. Jim Taylor and John Judge are nervously contemplating their twenty-two-foot pirogue with the nonexistent freeboard, arguing about how much or how little clothing to wear in the race, for they know they are going to get wet. Neil Husher and Allan Pickman flex the oarlock outriggers of their fast-looking shell and pray for the best. Tom and Joe Egeberg, also professional boatbuilders, test their double paddles one last time and reassure each other that brotherhood will help them match their strokes.

Chris Fabiszak and Lou Sauzedde are all confidence as they carry their light dory down to the dock and ready it for launching. They know something we all know and too often choose to forget — that in the crunch, the flashy, bizarre, imaginative designs can't hold a candle to simplicity and seaworthiness. Such is their confidence that only one of them will be rowing in the race — the other will go as passenger—and they carry a miniature cannon for their expected victory celebration.

John Hanson stands on the race committee platform, deliriously happy as he surveys the boats in front of him and listens to the shouts of encouragement from the crowd in back. Half the attendees at the Newport Wooden Boat Show are here to watch this historic race, and the other half stop what they are doing to listen to Hanson's inspired commentary over the public address system as the race unfolds. Reporters are on hand from the *New York Times*, the *New Yorker*, the *Providence Journal*, the *Newport Daily News*; there's even a television camera crew to record the event on videotape.

It's a LeMans-style start, boats on the dock, crews standing by. The course includes a short leg across the wind to a buoy, a long leg downwind toward the Yacht Club, and another long leg upwind to the finish line. This is going to be a test of both boat ability and crew strength.

Hanson gets them ready, on the mark, and lets them go.

The crowd erupts into cheers. The *Spirit Of Pythagoras*, the twenty-two-foot pirogue, hits the water and promptly sinks. So much for long, skinny, unstable boats in anything but a flat calm.

Boats bump, paddles and oars jumble together, the crews look bewildered. Then, in a flash, the light dory leaps from the pack and is gone, around the first mark before the other crews can catch their breath. The Glues Brothers dig in and pursue, not willing to give in so quickly. The *Lizdexia*, a spindly double-oared shell, picks up the beat and the competition gets hot, then hotter, as the paddleboard shows its form downwind.

But it's upwind travel that separates the men from the boys, the boats that go fast from the fast-built boats, the winners from the losers. The paddleboard falters, almost expires, but gamely continues on. The others struggle mightily, even cheer defiantly, but they know all is lost. Fabiszak's and Sauzedde's light dory drives on in leaping sweeps as the crowd goes wild. They cross the finish line in a final burst of speed, and fire their cannon in salute to their victory and in respect for their fellow competitors.

"What a day! What a race! We pulled it off!" yells John Hanson as he drinks champagne from the victor's cup, then presents it to the Kings of the Quick & Dirty Boat. The fellows from the Sika Corporation, who have never seen the likes of this before, shake hands, pat backs, and swear they'll sponsor the same event next year. Kumquat, indeed.

Sikaflex. There, I said it again.

On the Waterfront with Iain and Fabian

November 2, 1982 — Brooklin, Maine

We were sitting around the office with our feet up, looking across the dead grass of the lawn out across Eggemoggin Reach and the islands. Maynard Bray, who had just come back from England with a lot of story ideas, suggested that I go to Maldon and write about mud. Mud? "Yes," he said. It seems there is so much mud in the Blackwater River when the tide goes out that dealing with it is a way of life. Sticky, viscous stuff, deep and soft; deep-keeled boats sink right into it at low tide, float in it.

"You're not pulling my leg, are you?"

"No, I'm not."

OK, I told myself, Maynard Bray is not pulling my leg. I'll put Maldon mud on my things-to-check-out list. Just to humor him, you understand. Crackpot idea.

February 21, 1983 — Maldon, Essex

The first thing I did when I pulled into town was buy a new tire to replace the one I destroyed on the way. When I told the garage mechanic why I came, he laughed. The second thing I did was go down to the Blackwater River

123

and beat my feet on the mud. Are you kidding? I almost sank up to my knees. So I hauled myself out and started talking to people, getting mud stories. I heard that in Victorian times the mud was prized for facial packs; that some people have the ability to row across it at low tide; that it can seal a flat-bottomed barge to the bottom — as the tide rises, the barge can't break free of the mud and float, so it appears to get sucked down; that you can walk around on it with wide boards, like snowshoes, strapped to your feet.

Here we go again, I thought. Gullible American gets bamboozled by the natives. But I was a hard-nosed journalist. I demanded confirmation. Somebody said I should talk to Fabian Bush. He lives in the mud. He'll confirm everything and then some.

I found Mr. Bush at Maldon Marine, a place that sounded quaint but wasn't. They built metal boats. Grinding tools, welding torches, purple smoke with sparks arcing through it. Mr. Bush ("Call me Fabian"), the only woodworker in the place, was laminating a wooden railing for a steel staircase. Compared to the prototypical Englishman of our mind's eye, he was an apparition — long torso, short legs, wild eyes behind beat-up gold-rim glasses, full beard that to be groomed properly would have to be combed with a garden rake, clothes that looked as if they got in the way of an abstract expressionist on a rampage, then attacked by a crazed Doberman guard-dog. I'd say he was in his late twenties, early thirties.

"Mud?" he asked in mock shock, dropping his tools and dragging me out into the yard. "Forget mud. Let's talk wooden boats. Get in the car, I've got things to show you."

And so began what can only be called Fabian Bush Delirium, a movable monologue through the streets and pubs of Maldon, rushing about on one of those highs that Jack Kerouac ascribed to Neal Cassady when the pluper-fect joy of being who you are and what you are cannot be

124

contained. "I can't believe you came all the way here from America. Tell me about the Wooden Boat Revival there. No, let me tell you about the sorry state of things here. Let's go over to Heybridge Basin and see Arthur Holt. No, wait a minute, let's stop here and look at this boat. As soon as the tide is low let's go out to Osea Island and I'll show you my shop. Mud? Forget that; let's talk about important things, let's talk about boats . . . ."

By early evening I was tired by the intensity. By midevening I was exhausted. But Fabian wouldn't let up. We had to see his boatshop, which meant we had to wait for the tide to go out, which meant we had to sit in the Great Eastern pub and drink bitter ale by the pint. Osea Island, it seemed, could be reached by car over a causeway at dead low water. A motor torpedo-boat base during World War I, then an alcoholic's asylum afterward (run by a renegade member of the Charrington family — brewers, whose product created the alcoholics in the first place), Osea had become partly a farm but mostly derelict. Fabian lived on a boat wedged up in the mud in the Osea saltings and rented cheap space in an old barn to build wooden boats.

He was a British wooden boat revivalist, one of a very few at the time. He felt as if he worked in a vacuum. To me, after years of exposure to struggling, idealistic, enthusiastic young boatbuilders in America, Fabian Bush was business as usual; to the English, he was a freak. When fiberglass struck Great Britain, it made an almost-clean sweep. Most of the old-timers went out of business. The so-called hippie boatbuilders, a central part of the American scene in the 1970s, hardly existed in England. The traditionalists either hid in their closets or concentrated on the restoration and preservation of antique craft, especially the old gaffers. New wooden construction, both traditional and modern, for the most part lingered on only in backyards and nearly forgotten boatyards at the end of lost-in-the-murk back roads.

"Sure I'm a revivalist," said Fabian, "but saying I am won't pay the rent. I'm lucky to get the odd repair job, never mind a commission for a new boat." A free-lance job building a wooden stair railing in a metal boat shop was found money for him. He wasn't bitter, defeated; rather, he thought the New Jerusalem could be just around the corner if the right people would listen.

Fabian's life story, to a point, was typical professional-class English. He was born in 1953; his mother was a practicing doctor, his father a research scientist. He went to a boarding school from the age of ten, then attended Cambridge University, taking up residence in the same college as his father and his grandfather before him. His intention was to be a physicist.

"It was the understood thing," he said. "It never occurred to me to do anything other than that until my second year at university, when I rethought my goals and switched over to the social sciences." He had become something of an iconoclast, rejecting the idea of settling down to the comfortable life of an academic or a middle-class professional. The result: he graduated from Cambridge as the typical liberal arts major who was not trained for any particular occupation.

He started drifting around. He worked in a factory, then in an antiquarian bookshop, at one point as a laborer on a highway construction project. He seemed to have no goals, no aspirations. Well, not exactly none. If the truth be known, he was a card-carrying boat nut.

"I had led a sort of double life from the age of three," Fabian said, "being mad keen on boats, especially model boats." He learned to sail when he was in school and built a Mirror dinghy from a kit during one of his vacations. "I was continually drawing boats, trying to design them," he said. As a teenager he always had his own boat and even worked part-time in a boatyard when on school vacation.

126

When he was in his early twenties and people were starting to look askance at this unruly university graduate who was behaving like a shiftless day laborer — when he was starting to look askance at himself — Fabian decided to put interests in handcraftsmanship and boats together and become a boatbuilder. He built a boat on his own. "It was my design," he said. "It was a weird-looking boat, something like a sampan with a lug rig and bilge boards. I sailed it most of the way around the Thames estuary and the East Coast."

Though his decision to become a wooden boat builder coincided with the disastrous decline in commercial wooden boat building in Britain, Fabian was still able to gain an apprenticeship with Arthur Holt in Heybridge Basin, Essex. Holt was the perfect mentor. A university man who had also dropped out, he had enough work on hand of enough variety — traditional and modern — to give Fabian a good grounding in the basics of his craft.

But after three and a half years, Holt was having difficulty landing new construction commissions. Fabian, who by then had his journeyman's ticket, quit his job, rented space on Osea Island, and set up a one-man boatshop.

"I always felt you can make a living by building the right boats for the right people," Fabian said. "I knew all along that it was a trade that would only employ a tiny minority of people, but that was no problem. I just assumed that I would be one of those people."

It seemed an extremely optimistic view from a man who seemed to be so close to the edge of starvation, who had only been out on his own for about nine months and was having difficulty finding bona fide clients with the desire, and the wherewithal, to order new wooden boats. I had been in England long enough to know that this fellow was far from representative of most of the English people of the early 1980s, whose collective view was clouded by a declining industrial base, loss of overseas markets, serious unemployment, and low wages.

About 10 P.M. we drove out to Osea. It was a strange night. Damp, cold, blowing. The moon and stars were out, and ragged clouds were racing across the light. I took Fabian's word for it when he said, "Now we've left the land . . . Now we're on the causeway . . . At high tide we'd be under ten feet of water . . . ."

Startled seabirds flashed across the headlights. We crashed into potholes filled with salt water. The road, if you could call it that, twisted and turned across a sea of dark, mysterious mud. "Here's the island . . . Now we're on the beach . . . Good, we've found the farm track . . . You can relax now, Peter." If I had been a Catholic, I would have crossed myself.

We stopped at a large building and went inside. The main room was dominated by a fireplace along the far wall. Seated on a bench in front of the fire, which provided the only light, was a thin, bearded fellow drinking from a goblet. I couldn't see much of the rest of the room; if it didn't have paintings of yachts, fowling pieces, mounted stag heads on the walls, stuffed grouse and ship models on the tabletops, it should have.

"Meet Ian Outred," said Fabian. "He designs boats."

Ever the working journalist, skin full of ale or not, I got out my notebook and wrote down Ian's name. He looked at me rather wearily and said that he didn't spell his name the way I thought he did. "I use the archaic spelling," he said. "*I-a-i-n O-u-g-h-t-r-e-d.*"

"Why?" I asked.

"I like the look of it," he said. Another Englishman who had spent too much time with mad dogs under the noonday sun, I thought to myself. Then I had to revise that notion when Fabian pointed out that Iain was born in Australia.

I learned that Fabian and Iain had an informal partnership, much like Dynamite Payson and Phil Bolger in America. Iain designed small craft and Fabian built them on order. Sometimes Iain built the prototypes; sometimes Fabian. Already I could sense that it was a Simon-&-Garfunkle deal. Fabian was the realist, the pragmatist; Iain was the idealist. How could I tell? Fabian wanted to show me his boats. Iain wanted to talk about the design process — not the hows of his boats but the whys. Fabian talked about the endless search for ways to keep down the costs of boatbuilding and the prices of boats as a means of luring customers to the door. Iain talked about craftsmanship and quality and excellence, under the assumption that these elements carpet the path to a resurgence of wooden boats in Great Britain. I could smell fundamental agreement to disagree in the air.

Iain grew up in a middle-class environment, first in Melbourne, then in Sydney. An introspective loner, he found little to interest him in school and dropped out in his last year of high school. His passions were model airplanes and model boats until his teens, when he discovered the high-wire rush of performance dinghies. Sydney Harbor and environs were the perfect playground for those. But in those days Australian middle-class dropouts — at least this one, anyway — weren't allowed to while away their time playing with boats. Iain had to get a job. He went to work in a modelmaking shop that specialized in architectural models and special displays. Boats were reserved for his free time.

"I wasn't happy as a modelmaker," Iain said. "Boats, especially the high-performance type, represented freedom." He spent hours pouring over a stack of 1940s and 1950s *Rudder* magazines lent to him by a friend and became greatly influenced by the writings of L. Francis Herreshoff, who was published regularly in *Rudder* at that time.

As we all know, if modelmaking equals slavery and

boats equal freedom, the inevitable must take place. Iain quit his job to build boats, especially the National Gwen 12, a red-hot Australian dinghy racing class. He was good at it and produced several competitive boats. He was also good at racing Gwen 12s, eventually winning the national championships.

Did he have any long-term goals?

"Oh yes," he said with a deadpan expression. "I wanted to work out systems for setting spinnakers faster." (Iain was so wound into the go-fast scene that to this day he can describe his races in excrutiating detail — tactics, sail changes, wind conditions, the order of finish, everything.)

By 1964 Australia was wearing extremely thin and Iain emigrated to England. What followed next was virtually a blueprint for bohemianism, including starvation in garrets, odd jobs for small change, art school, Europe in a Volkswagen bus (yes!, yes!), across America on a motor-cycle, transcendental meditation, Findhorn, English folk music — years and years on the high and low roads of Hip. Iain went back to Australia a couple of times, worked for a naval architect or two as a draftsman, but always, always returned to England and always, always was out of step with all but a few.

Just about the same time Fabian Bush was taking a serious look at boatbuilding, Iain Oughtred, in his late thirties, was ready to take a serious look at boat design. Gone was his intensity about high-performance craft; in its place was equal intensity about traditional boats. He met Fabian through mutual friends, and the decision to collaborate soon followed. The off-center Englishman and the equally off-center English-Australian thought they might — just might — have a tilt at the Wooden Boat Revival that existed in their minds if not in fact.

We walked out into the night, Fabian, Iain, and I, trudging along a rutted path to the boatshop in the middle of the island, next to a wide field. The moon came and went behind the clouds, and the cold, damp wind cut through our heavy clothing. The shop seemed even colder. Plastic sheeting broke the single room into thirds — a space where Fabian was building a boat, another where Iain planned to build one of his own, and the other for timber storage.

The winter's project was a pair of boats designed by Iain, the Acorn Dinghy in twelve- and fifteen-foot versions, lapstrake plywood planking, glued laps, steam-bent frames. Fabian had one well underway. Iain showed me the plans for the one he would build. I was struck by the detail of the drawings. I was also struck by the American influence of the design. Whitehallian. Nothing like the heavy, apple-cheeked traditional boats of the British Isles, though the construction was reminiscent of some of the British racing dinghy classes.

Iain showed me study plans of some of his other designs. I could see Pete Culler, John Gardner, Phil Bolger, Howard Chapelle. I thought it strange that the English should emulate the Americans, then recalled that the Americans were not above emulating the English. Atkin, Gillmer, and Hess with their Falmouth quay punts. L. F. Herreshoff with his canoe yawls. Even J. Henry Rushton with his decked canoes.

But I couldn't linger over this forever. The tide was rising. I had to get out now or wait until noon the following day. Fabian invited me to sleep on his boat, but the thought of slogging through the mud to get aboard had no appeal. Besides, I had other things to do on the mainland. Iain drove me ashore and said, "I don't blame you. Osea is no place for me either."

February 22, 1983 — Maldon, Essex

I was the only overnight guest at the Great Eastern. At breakfast the owner came over to my table and drank a cup of coffee with me. He was curious about an out-of-season

American in a working-class hotel. "Osea Island?" he said. "Building wooden boats on a farm? There's no future in that."

November 2, 1984 — Brooklin, Maine
I heard from Fabian Bush and Iain Oughtred off and on as time passed. Long letters with news, photographs of their latest boats, laments about the continued decline of even the most latent interest in wooden boats in Great Britain.

Each had a different response to the problem. Iain, the idealist, saw perfection as the goal, even if few people would buy his boats. ("In many ways I have compromised too much, and this makes compromises harder to accept.") He starved while seeking perfection. Fabian, the realist, figured that building and selling boats was the goal, that perfection would be fine after survival was assured. ("You have to balance perfection against earning a living.")

I could visualize the two of them on the *Titanic*. Iain would figure that if the ship were to go down, it should go down in style, with the orchestra playing and the captain still romancing the debutantes. Fabian would forget about style and tell everyone to bail like hell. Neither would be able to go so far as to declare that it was everyone for himself.

An excerpt from today's letter from Fabian Bush: " . . . It sounds as though it's boom time for wooden boats in the USA, which must make you all feel quite bright. In the UK, I feel it is quite the opposite (and this may last), and this casts quite a pall over the way people are thinking. I feel the market for new boats is small and not growing. That doesn't mean that there is no work — but it does mean that it is very thin and one can't quite see where it is coming from, or whether one should try and expand. A number of established builders seem to be doing OK —

ticking over — and a number of newcomers like myself are sort of doing OK, but many are not. Really, activity around the Blackwater seems pretty dead . . . ."

March 5, 1985 — Heybridge Basin, Essex

While I waited for the tide to go out, Arthur Holt, boatbuilder, gave me a short course on the difficulties of being a wooden boat builder in Britain during the modern era. Once one of the more prolific builders on the Blackwater, he felt lucky now to get repair work, no matter what material the boat was built of. Fabian Bush apprenticed here. Arthur spoke of him with proprietary affection.

Arthur said to be careful on the causeway to Osea. So far this winter two drivers weren't. They barely escaped after their cars stalled out on an incoming tide. They ran for their lives while the rising waters claimed the vehicles. Several new layers of paranoia wrapped themselves around my usual hardened core.

The land around the Blackwater was low and flat, of the sinking-into-the-sea variety. Shoal-draft boats were understandably king, followed closely by those with bilge keels or at least legs that allowed them to stand upright on *the hard*, as the locals called anything that resembled ground at low tide. I hesitated to drive out on the causeway but bit the bullet and went. I muttered under my breath about the madness of boatbuilders who set themselves up in inaccessible locations and wondered why nobody came to see them. In mitigation, Fabian could at least bet his boots that anyone who would chance losing his car to the tide must be a serious client. Someone should have erected a sign out there in the mud — *Osea Island Causeway: The Tire Kicker's Waterloo*.

Fabian was the same man he had been two years previously, though he looked a mite chunkier, buried as he was in an indeterminate number of layers of coarse British wool to keep out the damp cold. Iain, who came up from

133

London, where he lived, had a more cosmopolitan air. His clothes looked less warm but more refined; ditto for his companion, Welmoed Bouhuys, a pleasant woman from Holland, who as part of her own escape got involved in building two of Iain's boats.

We walked together out to the shop. Fabian had been busy, on his own, without even the design partnership of Iain. In the shop was an almost-finished rowing dory for an upcoming two-person Atlantic crossing by a pair of London masochists. Designed and built by Fabian, it was plainly but strongly built — "A Grade H job," he said. "These particular clients aren't so much interested in looks as in survivability." You could tell by Iain's expression that if he were in charge, they would get both.

Out in the yard was the prototype of a boat Fabian called the Blackwater Sailing Canoe. "Another boat I didn't design," Iain said with good humor. It was a twenty-foot daysailer, multichined plywood with stringers backing up the laps. This was the craft that one boating writer called the best hope for British wooden boat building. Fabian scoffed at the idea, but he was still proud of his accomplishment. "It's my idea of the proper use of plywood," he said. "Light weight in the hull, heavy weight in the centerboard to help right her in the event of a capsize. I had banks of interest in her at the Southampton Boat Show, but nobody actually bought her."

In the evening we crossed over to the mainland and retired to a pub on the waterfront in Maldon, down by a fleet of spritsail barges laid up for the winter. The vessels — formerly freight barges, now dude cruisers — made quite a sight silhouetted against the rising tide of the Blackwater. A handful of local boatbuilders met us for a pint of ale (or two or three) before supper. I was struck by the contrast between the optimism of Fabian and Iain and the pessimism of the rest, though all were having equal difficulty keeping their boatbuilding acts together. The pessimists were little different from the optimists when you got right down to it. They only complained a bit more.

March 7, 1985 — Hurley, Berkshire

There was no complaining at Peter Freebody's boat-shop. I opened the door to a din of saws and sanders, hammers and chisels. This Thameside establishment, one of the largest wooden boat operations in Britain, was packed to the rafters with work in progress. New construction, maintenance, repair, restoration, you name it.

Fabian, who had promised to meet me there, was standing in the middle of the shop with a knot of Freebody's craftsmen. They were drinking tea from mugs and talking so fast and with such intensity that it was difficult for this New Englander to tell whether they were speaking the Queen's English or Swahili. The truth was that they were speaking boatbuilder's English, which was such music to Fabian's ears that his whole being seemed to vibrate like a tuning fork. He had been shut up alone in his own shop for a long time, so this opportunity to talk at length with men of similar mind was like opening a sluicegate that had been holding back flood waters.

Iain arrived close to quitting time, after which a small mob of boatbuilders headed up the road to the Rising Sun, a village pub. It was like a gathering of the clan, a scene in a yet-to-be-shot documentary on the yet-to-be-accomplished Wooden Boat Revival in Great Britain. There were at least five conversations going on at once, and all of them had something to do with the techniques and theories of wooden boat construction. The sum of it all? Everyone agreed that interest in wooden boats will be revitalized in Britain if the builders will be more aggressive in presenting their wares to the potential buyers, and if the potential buyers will become aware of the alternative to the mass-produced, aggressively advertised boats currently available.

March 9, 1985 — Kew Bridge, London

It happens in small ways, but it happens nevertheless. Iain took me to the Thames Steam Launch Company, a small shop that builds, restores, and installs steam engines and boilers in small craft. A new boat, designed by Iain and built by Fabian, sat in the yard waiting for its power plant, a two-cylinder compound steam engine. It was created on commission from Lord Strathcona, a steam enthusiast who wanted to sponsor a design for an easily built, easily driven launch. The prototype looked vaguely familiar, and it was — a twenty-one-foot Swampscott dory modified in shape to take the weight of a steam engine and boiler plus passengers. The stern, a radical departure from a Swampscott's tombstone, was rounded off launch-fashion after a William Garden design much admired by Iain.

Lord Strathcona hoped that the boat would stimulate more interest in steam power. Iain Oughtred hoped it would stimulate more interest in wooden boats. Bob Bossine, one of the owners of Thames Steam Launch, hoped it would stimulate more business. Nobody expected to get rich, but then again, nobody said that was the goal.

February 26, 1986 — Camden, Maine

I showed this manuscript to my wife, who read it with interest but said, with just a tad of disappointment in her voice, "I thought you went to Maldon to write about mud."

"Mud?" I said. "That was just to humor Maynard Bray. Crackpot idea."

A Matter of Family Tradition

"When I became forty years of age," says Peter Freebody, "I decided to stop working after midnight. Before then, we would be out there in the workshop sometimes until two or three in the morning. Why did I do this? I always wanted to carry on with the family tradition."

By this, Freebody doesn't mean that his family's tradition was to stay up all night, working until they collapsed at the bench, to be carried out of the shop like fallen soldiers in the boatbuilding wars. Rather, he means that his family's traditional business was boatbuilding, and if carrying on with that business during any period of economic hardship meant literally working day and night, then of course he would do it. It almost goes without saying.

Freebody is a big, burly man with an air of inevitability about him. He runs a boatbuilding and restoration shop — perhaps the largest wooden boat shop in Great Britain — in the tiny village of Hurley, between Henley and Marlow, near Maidenhead, on the Thames River west of London. He is possessed by his work in a gentle-giant sort of way; for him to take the time to talk with a visitor requires an act of willpower, but when he does, he is quiet, reflective, understanding, a gentleman.

This matter of family tradition dominates Freebody's conversations; he doesn't stop talking about his father, his grandmother, his grandfather, his great-grandfather, his ancestors who have lived on this stretch of the Thames River for hundreds of years. "My wife, Elizabeth, and I take great interest in tracing the family history, and we've discovered that we were first recorded as having been in business as ferrymen in nearby Caversham in 1257. We've been ferrymen, bargemen, and professional fishermen; we've been actual boatbuilders certainly as far back as 1809. My earliest memories of my grandmother and my grandfather and my father are of their continual reminders to me that I would be a boatbuilder." It was his legacy, his destiny, even though such a concept was quite outdated in post-World War II England, where the new realities of modern economic life left little room for employment predetermination through birthright.

The Freebody boatyard is on the Thames hard by a set of locks that detour a small weir (dam). Next door is Freebody's home, where he lives in modest comfort with his family. Hurley is an ancient spot. Nearby are the ruins of a Benedictine monastery, and up the road is one of the many inns that claim to be England's oldest. Built in 1135 A.D., it very well could be. The scenery is right out of *The Wind in the Willows*; country cottages, meandering river, winding lanes, wood smoke on a misty winter day. One almost expects to see Toad Hall set back in a hedge-enclosed field, with a motorcar parked by the door.

Bucolic backdrop notwithstanding, Freebody's shop is the genuine article, not an artful sham decorating the riverside but a true full-service boatyard where you can get a wooden boat built or an engine repaired, rent a punt, or haul a launch. It is one of the few yards in England which

138

can make that claim.

Commercial wooden boat building in England today, like nearly all industries in that country which were at one time significant producers, is hardly prosperous. Before I came to Freebody's in the late winter of 1983, I had visited several harbors and maritime centers around the country. It was not an encouraging tour for someone who had grown up believing that every seaside town in England had at least one boatbuilder of notable reputation who employed scores of people and whose shop was packed with boats of my dreams under construction and repair. I found nothing like that. I found plenty of boatshops, to be sure, but they were lightly staffed and lacking in work; some were closed permanently, others temporarily; too many had switched over to fiberglass. I saw a few one- and two-man shops with boats underway, but for the most part I was seeing what once was or what might have been, not the happy land of serious wooden boat building I wished it were.

So it came as something of a shock to pick my way through a graveyard of broken-down Thames launches, punts, skiffs, even a retired Gypsy caravan — thinking all the while, "Here we go again, Pete; another damp, drafty shop with a couple of years' worth of cobwebs immobilizing the thickness planer" — and step into Peter Freebody's boatshop for the first time. From the outside it might be considered a neighborhood eyesore, if it weren't buried at the end of a lane, hidden from view by trees and walls. On the inside it went against the grain of almost everything I had ever seen before, including ninety-nine percent of the shops I have visited in America. The building was filled with workers (actually *craftsmen*, as Peter Freebody deferentially calls them), with humming machinery, boats being built, boats being restored, patternmakers at their benches, mechanics tinkering with steam and gas engines, inboards and outboards. (Freebody was to say later that his customers were either millionaires or bus drivers; the steam-engine department served the former, the outboard department the latter.) The workmanship was excellent, the materials were of the finest grade, the tenor of the place was of confidence and productivity. It was enough to make anyone who considered himself a front-rank boatbuilder reassess his priorities.

How all this came to be is bound up in Peter Freebody's past and his view of it, as well as his philosophies of boatbuilding and business management, which keep the place going.

"My grandfather," says Freebody, "whose boatyard was over in Caversham, had three sons, and they didn't get on with each other very well. So he thought the best thing was to find another place for one of his sons. This bit of land here in Hurley, which is now the boatyard, was bought by my grandfather in 1933 at an auction to set up his son, my father, in business.

"My grandfather's very successful boatbuilding business was the eventual result of the advent of the Great Western Railway, which ran from London, west. It brought people from the city to the small river towns for their holiday and brought about an upsurge of small boat building on the river. After the Great Western came through, our family business in Caversham had over two hundred small craft available for hire, and many riverside boating families had equal numbers of craft.

"The Freebodys tended to specialize in skiffs, punts, and dinghies, and a few electric launches. No cruising craft of the more recent development. The skiffs and dinghies were clinker construction; the electric launches would usually have had the inner skin laid in a diagonal fashion and the outer planking laid fore and aft.

"Though Freebody boats were quite similar to other boats that were being built anywhere on the river, my grandfather, in the late 1920s and early 1930s, specialized in a boat that became quite popular. It was a compromise between a skiff and a dinghy. The Thames skiff may be ideal for the chap who's rowing it, because it is very easy to pull through the water, but it's not a boat that you can comfortably move about in. So to gain stability, my grandfather developed a model with a wider transom. The boat was not flat-bottomed, but certainly flattened out in section, so it was more stable and comfortable.

"I was born here in Hurley in 1934. My father was running this place as a boatyard and used this house as a hotel before the Second World War. During the war he had a contract with the Admiralty to build clinker rowing dinghies. His was a reserved occupation, it was so important; he couldn't have fought if he had wanted to.

"My education was typical of a boy in my position. I went to a good school, and I left having a quite satisfactory command of English, an elementary knowledge of mathematics, and a certain amount of mechanical engineering. I left school at age fifteen in 1950 to become a boatbuilder's apprentice.

"Though I had helped out in my father's shop as a young boy, it wasn't thought to be a proper thing for me to apprentice with him. My godfather — my uncle — arranged for me to apprentice at Wooten Brothers, a yard in Cookham Dean on the Thames. At that time, they were building a lot of small sailing craft; in fact, we built the Laurent Giles-designed *Sopranino*, which Patrick Ellam and Colin Mudie sailed across the Atlantic. In all, we built about nine of the Sopranino class.

"My apprenticeship, which lasted for five years, consisted of going to my place of work and working alongside boatbuilders, taking what initiative and what opportunities presented themselves."

In short, Peter Freebody followed exactly the path that his background suggested he should follow. He quite rightly expected to join the family business as a journey-man. But events, both within his family and without, conspired against him. Come the end of his apprentice-ship, he was to spend many years in the wilderness, at many times with only his fatalism to keep him going ("I feel we are free to make day-to-day decisions, but the real direction — I think that's set somewhere else").

Peter Freebody's grandfather had died in the late 1940s, leaving his grandmother the owner of both the Caversham boatyard and the property on which his father's boatyard sat. His grandmother tended toward eccentricity. She feuded with her sons, she was vague about her business intentions, she was demanding and at times unreasonable. She wanted Peter to work at her Caversham yard, not with his father at Hurley, but when he gave in she made his life so unpleasant that he quit after five weeks and took a full-time job back at Wooten's.

Wooden boat building in England, as in America, had begun its long, steady decline. The great Thames River boatbuilding concerns, including Freebody's and Wooten's, fell on hard times. Fewer and fewer new boats were being built, and the yards were having trouble keeping going on just repair work and seasonal storage. Wooten's was no exception to this situation, and in 1958 Freebody quit and went back to Hurley, not entirely sure what he should do.

What could he do? His father had a weakness for whiskey, which meant that his business didn't develop very much after World War II. "We got on well," says Peter, "but he wasn't interested in getting the business really going. He was building a few boats, and did mooring and hauling. I set up on my own here at Hurley in a very, very small way, helping my father and doing a few small jobs on my own." One of his small jobs turned into a large one and even took him away from boatbuilding for a couple of years. He worked free-lance for a harpsichord maker, building the actions (an extremely demanding operation) and installing them in the bodies of the instruments.

All the while, his grandmother, who still owned the property, was demanding rent, which he found difficult to pay. "I had no right to be here," says Freebody, "except I felt I had a birthright. After all, my father was here. My grandmother kept writing, 'What about the rent?' and I was saying to her, 'What for? I'll pay you rent, but you must give me status.' " By status, he meant the right to buy her out, for Freebody had come to the conclusion that he must own his yard to be free to do what he wanted to do, what he was destined to do, the decline of wooden boat building notwithstanding. "I was interested in a feeling of security, and I wanted to be invincible."

When Peter Freebody finally convinced his grand-mother to sell the Hurley yard to him in 1962, he felt neither invincible nor secure; he had too few resources and too little work to be either. Perhaps relieved would be a better way to describe his feelings. On the day the papers were finally signed, a keen listener probably could have heard a long sigh drift across the Thames, followed by the sounds of boatyard activity spurred on by confidence in the future.

"I didn't deliberately set out with an ambitious plan to have a big yard and employ sixteen people, as I do now," says Freebody. "Simply put, once I got going I found that people were admiring what I did and asking me to do more and more. What you must understand is that I have never advertised for anyone to come and work with me. Just as customers have come and asked me to do work on their boats, so boatbuilders have come and asked if they could work with me on those very same boats."

Then how would it come to pass that a young man with no track record and little capital in a declining industry in an industrially troubled country could succeed where so many have failed?

"I'll tell you how it started here," says Freebody, with a light in his eye. "I was working in an old pumphouse, building those harpsichords, when there was a knock on the door. A chap had discovered me. He was an ex-Royal Navy captain who wanted an old lifeboat fitted out and who had been referred to me by Wooten's, which was no longer doing that type of work. It was the very first big job that I had. I did the whole job without any power tools, out in the open under a very scanty canvas cover supported by battens.

"I saw myself as running a general service boatyard. I didn't say that I would only build new boats, with that limitation. I will do anything that is asked of me. I was asked to fit out a lifeboat. I did. Later, I got a phone call from a nautical school that had been donated a marine engine. They wanted a boat built around the engine, a small rescue boat that could also serve as a rowing training boat. So I designed them a boat that would hold fourteen people for rowing, but when those fourteen people were not in it, it would sink low enough in the water at the stern to keep the propeller properly submerged and perform as a rescue boat, which the school also needed."

One well-done job led to another, so that in a few years' time Peter Freebody's boatyard in Hurley became one of those unpublicized places where you could get a good job done — the best job done — no matter what it was. During this time, however, the fiberglass revolution was sweeping England the same way it was America. The changeover in Britain seemed to be even more all encompassing, despite our perception of the Old World as being a place steeped in unwavering tradition and resistance to change. But while wooden boat building was sinking all around him in response to the fiberglass challenge, Peter Freebody's business was strangely unaffected; in fact, it increased at an accelerating pace.

"Of course," says Freebody, "I've been aware of the

decline of wooden boat building in this country and elsewhere, but is hasn't affected me. I have always had too much to do. Since a boy I have understood boat building with wood. So you might want to say, 'Well, all those other wooden boat builders, the ones who have failed or whose businesses have declined, they all have the same philosophy, they all loved their craft.' Somewhere there is a difference between them and me, but I don't really know what that difference is."

Well, perhaps Freebody really doesn't know, but I have a fair idea myself of the difference. Simply put, it is his ability to maintain a balance among his own aspirations, the abilities of his workforce, the requirements of his customers, and the fashions of the times. In the latter area, the fashions and trends, he came on the scene at the right time. Among his early jobs were a number of boat restoration commissions. They came just at the beginning of a revival of interest in old river and lake launches, especially the steam-powered variety. He not only was able to restore these craft to their former glory — in many cases even beyond their former glory — but he was also able to understand the needs of his customers, whether those customers had a firm grasp of their needs or not. He didn't patronize them; neither did he allow them to bully him into doing a job that would reflect badly on his yard.

"I try to understand what the customer should be asking me for," says Freebody. "Very, very rarely do people, after a couple of years, go out of the yard with exactly what they thought they were asking for two years earlier. You have to be very patient, and once you have a good customer or prospect, you must very gently educate him into what he should be asking you to do. After all, they can't pick up a magazine like *Motor Boat* and *Yachting* and actually be educated in what they should be asking the boatyard for. It's up to the boatyard proprietor to gently point out to the customer, without embarrassing him, the

145

inadequacy of his knowledge, let him look around, feed ideas to him. I give a customer my best advice, always. There's a different reason for every job in my shop right now, but whatever the initial reason, the result is that the customers are thrilled with the beautiful things that are being created.

"Though I have my own standards for work on a boat, I've never, never had an argument with a customer that ends with, 'I don't care whether I lose this job or not, I will not do it the way you suggest.' I would think that I would have failed miserably if I had gotten into that situation. I approach my customers very diplomatically.

"I find that customers enjoy being told very confidently, by someone they concede knows about these things, exactly how a job should be done. On the other hand, no matter how forceful my argument may be, some customers must have their way. We had that recently. A customer was determined to have standing headroom in a launch we were restoring. The original did not have standing headroom, and the alteration would have been out of keeping with the aesthetics of the rest of the boat. We were presented with a situation where we either produce what the customer wants or give up the job. We compromised by making other modifications that would allow the extra headroom without raising the coach roof too much. The customer got what he wanted, and we satisfied our own sense of proportion."

The restoration of antique wooden boats in close consultation and cooperation with the boats' owners became Freebody's stock in trade. But they weren't to be slavish restorations; rather, they were interpretations of existing boats with improvements and embellishments to make them better.

Says Freebody, "Most of the people we are dealing with aren't really looking for a restoration — that is, the rebuilding of a boat to its exact condition the day it was built — and we aren't in the business of giving it to them. We are giving them a new boat with an aura of the old. For example, we tend to restore to a higher standard than the original would have been built to. It is a question of value added to the article. We're living in expensive times, and if you're putting thousands of pounds of work into a boat, you're bound to feel that you must protect your customer's investment by selecting better timber, or using screws where there would have been nails before. We work to a higher standard simply to protect the money that is going into the boat. Most of our customers see this nice hull, and they ask what it was, what it could be. Then we show them an engine, or a boiler, fittings, fairleads, flagstaff sockets, and things go on from there. They get a boat with an authentic sense of the past, not a pure restoration."

Luckily for his customers, Freebody has an innate ability to see how the parts of a boat must converge into the aesthetics of the whole. He has an almost classical sense of what looks right — a sense that cannot be acquired but must be within a person from the day he was born. (When I mention this to Freebody, he smiles and quietly reiterates the occupations of his ancestors.) He is a stylist, and his customers, and everyone else who see his boats, appreciate it.

"I have a very simple yardstick when it comes to styling in our boats," says Freebody. "Everything must flow together. Obviously, like other builders, I am concerned with the way the grain should run, the makeup of the deck and bulkhead panels, and all this sort of thing. But that's just detail stuff. Overall I just try to preserve as clean a line from one end of the boat to the other as possible and avoid breaking it up. If you can get certain components of the boat to run from one end to the other, then those who don't know anything about boatbuilding will still be able to regard it as a beautiful thing. That's important. It doesn't matter if they don't know why they like it as long as they are thrilled by the work.

"My boats have a certain old-fashioned look to them. Of course, the restorations would have to be that way, but even my new boats are reminiscent of the past. This look was the result of evolution; it reached its peak about 1910 or so in this country. It is a very pretty style. There are certain aspects of it that I enjoy emulating from that period, one of them being beveled glass windows, for example. Once you take a piece of quarter-inch plate glass and put a bevel on it, the bevel has to run into slender stiles and the beading has to be a particular proportion. Whether you like it or not, you're back in the Edwardian era and you have your lovely saloon with the light mullions. I wouldn't want to evolve away from that; I am perfectly happy with it."

Though restoration work predominates in Peter Freebody's shop, he has always had at least one new boat under construction. New construction — especially to his own design — is Freebody's passion, and he looks forward to the day when he will be building more new boats than he will be restoring old ones. But distinguishing one of his new boats from an antique may be difficult for the casual observer, because Freebody is committed to classical line and detail — for very good reason.

"I'm not a fashionable designer," says Freebody. "Even though I have not had a formal design education, I have my own ideas on hull forms, especially for low-speed displacement powerboats. I can design boats that don't create too much wash, give the maximum speed for the minimum of power, and maintain a nice attitude in the water when they're going along. Right now, for example, my yard seems to be very deep into steam launches, which have developed a shape over the years that is sensible. A steam launch carries a very heavy payload and has very low power, so the whole thing has to be carried through the water both as sweetly and as efficiently as possible. I don't know that this is true, but I would imagine that if you were to feed the facts into a computer that has been programmed to do the job, it would turn out a lines drawing that is quite similar to the boats that I build."

How did Freebody learn to design boats? "I've been designing them ever since I was an apprentice, when my employer asked that I draw up a set of lines for a twenty-foot gig. He handed me a copy of Howard Chapelle's *Yacht Designing and Planning*. I had never done anything like that in my life, but I turned to the chapter on drawing lines and discovered that the author virtually holds your hand through the process. I got the job right on my second attempt."

Old boat or new, designed by Freebody or not, the production of steam launches, complete with power plants, has made this small yard in Hurley a mecca for well-heeled enthusiasts. The renaissance of interest in steam-powered craft is now quite strong in England, perhaps more so than in America. There are suggestions that it is inspired by dissatisfaction with a mundane way of life, or by the desire to own something different from the run-of-the-mill, or as a way to recall a quieter era. Whatever has caused it, Peter Freebody has responded to it in ways other builders would not, or could not. He could take care of the boat; he could take care of the engine, too.

"In the early days of steam revival," says Freebody, "we were usually approached by an out-and-out enthusiast who wanted a boat built or restored to accommodate his engine. He would come with the engine and would know all about it. He often would look after his own engine and boiler installation because he understood the mechanics. But now we are seeing wealthy people who are perhaps at the moment technically ignorant (I don't mean that unkindly) who are looking to us to provide the expertise. To stay in business and be competitive, we must be capable of that.

"Sometimes our customers will come to us with the complete engine system, or with just an engine, or just a boiler. The supply of restorable engines is beginning to dwindle in this country, however, what with the popularity of steam power, so to satisfy our customers who do not have an engine, we have looked toward building our own from scratch.

"It's a very, very expensive business, tooling up for producing your own steam engine, but we decided to do it when the proper opportunity came up. We had an order for a steam launch for a customer in Switzerland. Before I could set about designing the hull, I had to know how heavy the power unit was going to be, the boiler and the engine. So we had to find an engine. I turned up an engine that had been made in 1895, for which I had to pay £5,300 because it was a collector's item. It seemed a very silly thing to overhaul it, put it in a boat, and send it to Switzerland. We decided that, while we've got it, we'll take it apart, draw up plans for it, and make a set of patterns. That is what we are doing right now. When the day comes, we'll have the option of delivering the boat with the original engine or a new one patterned after it."

Above all else, Freebody's is a service yard, a place where the needs of the customers are served. In the early years, Freebody built his reputation on customer service as much as on excellent workmanship, even if it meant working hours that most boatbuilders would find ridiculous.

"We worked hard because we had the work to be done," says Freebody, "and there was always pressure of a sort from our customers. If a customer could afford a lot of work on his boat, he was usually rather a pushy person. So we would work until two or three in the morning to keep him satisfied — anything for a quiet life — and the result was that the pressure kept us strong. We were living in fear of our customers who were coming down for the weekend. Some were such super people that you felt you had to get their boats out for them by Friday afternoon. And others were such terrible people that you *knew* you had to get their boats out by Friday afternoon.

"But, of course, there are some proprietors who don't respond to that sort of pressure. They simply turn the key in the lock at half past five and go away. They have a house away from the yard, and they come back at eight the next morning and start where they left off. They say, 'Well, what's not done isn't done.' With that attitude, there's no wonder that they went out of business during wooden boat building's decline."

Yet is wasn't just to get the work done that Freebody's was open when other boatshops were closed. It was also to allow the customers to visit the yard when they had free time, a practice that continues to this day. "Some boatyard managers have a chip on their shoulders about their position, their status, and they are rigid about their prerogatives," says Freebody. "They open their firms at a certain time in the morning and close it at a certain time at night. They close on weekends. I am saying that a successful boatyard cannot be run by rigidly being open just from eight in the morning until five-thirty at night and shutting your doors over the weekend. You must realize that this is a recreation trade, and therefore you must be about when people have free time."

Though this may seem to be a curious concept for most boatbuilders, perhaps even revolutionary in a trade that guards its prerogatives carefully, it is not quite as remarkable as Peter Freebody's attitude toward his workers. "There is no hierarchy in this shop," he says emphatically. "I never thought layers of management were necessary. These craftsmen work with me, not for me. I see every man on my staff running his own show, running his own business. They all meet their own customers; it's very important to me and important to them."

The effect of this attitude is to create a feeling of shared goals in the workshop, to make it a place where you want to work, not where you have to work. A key element in a job of any kind. The results show up in the quality of the workmanship that goes into the boats. A visitor once asked a craftsman at Freebody's what made him apply for a job there. "He smiled at me. 'You don't apply for a job, you just hang around and hope you'll be allowed to work here — I was lucky.' "

Luck, indeed. Peter Freebody would say it was destiny.

A Week on the Thames

I stole the first book I ever saw about the River Thames. That would be thirty years or so ago. I was in a bookstore in my home town, idling my way through a stack of so-called "classic" paperbacks — you know the type: unexpurgated, annotated texts with thirty-five-page introductions by professors of comparative literature at Bowling Green State University — when I came across a title that was so obscure it had neither an erudite introduction nor a single cover line proclaiming it to be the rightful successor to *Lord Jim* or *Huckleberry Finn*. It had a blue cover with a rather abstract black-and-maroon illustration. It was called *Three Men in a Boat* and was written by Jerome K. Jerome.

The polite thing to say would be that I was young and didn't know what I was doing and should therefore be excused. The truth is that my larceny was cold-bloodedly calculated and shamelessly executed. I had found the only book in town with *boat* in the title, and as a card-carrying boat-loving manic-obsessive, I most assuredly deserved to have it. Immediately. Now. This minute. Even though I was broke.

Three Men in a Boat turned out to be unlike any boat book I had ever read. A stylized comedy centered around a boating holiday on the Thames during the Victorian era, it had characters — Harris, George, "J" (the author), and Montmorency (the dog) — who goofed and gabbed, mocked propriety and satirized convention, and rowed, towed, and paddled their camping skiff through the heart of England. I remember finding the book mildly amusing in places and hilarious in others, and being confused by innumerable asides that had nothing to do with boats and little to do with life as I knew it. The best part to my mind, however, was the boat journey. Before then I had thought a skiff was merely something you used to get from shore to your real boat. Jerome K. Jerome indicated otherwise. One of these days, I resolved, I would give that a try.

Monday, September 29, 1986

We join our skiff in Oxford, just above Osney Lock. Mark Edwards, proprietor of Constable's Boathouse downriver in Hampton, meets us to check over the boat, show us the ropes, and answer our questions. *The Tar Skiff*, she's called; about twenty-three feet long, stable, genteel without preciousness, said to have been built in the late 1860s. She's fitted with tholepinned rowlocks, a tiller-roped rudder, and a cushioned passenger thwart. She carries three pairs of elegantly spoonbladed oars, a full range of camping gear, a canvas cover supported by gunwale-to-gunwale hoops, a selection of river guides and charts, water jugs, a foam pad for the sculler's derriere, and a can of rowlock grease inscribed *Tallow, Winter Mixture*.

Eileen lays claim to the passenger seat by throwing her bag of knitting supplies onto the cushion. I lay claim to the sculler's thwart by adjusting the footstretcher to my legs.

Our destination is nowhere in particular; our direction is downriver. Twenty-eight miles to Goring. Forty-eight miles to Henley. Eighty-eight miles to Hampton. Who

154

knows how far we'll get in a week? Who cares?

Since it's midafternoon before we're ready to push off, we decide to go upriver for a couple of hours, then back down to Oxford for the night. Eileen gets out her knitting. I get out the Tallow, Winter Mixture.

It takes power to get *The Tar Skiff* going, but once you do, momentum keeps her that way. It's a good thing, too, because I'm used to medium-length, nonfeathering oars in bronze oarlocks. Here we have long, feathering oars between tholepins. Much thunking, splashing, banging awkwardness for a mile or so. Then I switch places with Eileen. "Scullers feather their oars," I say. "It's easier when you don't," she says. She rows the way she knits — deliberately, pacing herself, unselfconsciously.

Back on the oars, I take a page from her book and vow to feather only in a headwind or when experts are watching. Immediately, a natural rhythm develops — THUNK bic-Chuck . . . THUNK bic-Chuck . . . THUNK bic-Chuck . . . and we glide across glassy water, past horses and cows in a wide meadow, walkers on the towpath, swans and geese and ducks and coots and who knows what all. This is what we came for, and this is what we get.

We turn back about a mile past Godstow Lock, and as dusk falls slide through the backyards of Oxford to the town landing above Osney Lock. We moor the skiff securely to the riverbank, then walk down the street to the Holly Bush pub for bitter ale, steak-and-kidney pie, and chips. Later, we take up residence in a bed-and-breakfast on the Abingdon Road. No aches, no pains, no blisters.

" . . . There can be no prettier sight of its kind," wrote R. O. Rawlins in 1882, "than when a dozen boats of every size and form, from the Rob Roy canoe to the family barge, are framed within the stone walls of a lock, to look down upon them, and note the gay but mostly well assorted colours in the dress of the ladies, contrasting with the white boating suits, relieved by crimson socks, of the gentlemen, and then when the gates open, to see them scattering over the river."

From the 1880s to 1914, it was as fashionable to go boating on the Thames as it is fashionable today to go jogging in Central Park. But unlike jogging, river boating had an elegance — a stylishness and a formality — that put its practice at the level of high art. It was cultured leisureliness, with customs, traditions, and rules that only the fashionable could understand and the unfashionable could betray.

Men and women went to the river to see and be seen. They didn't go to exert themselves, to sweat like the mob. They poled punts up quiet backwaters, where they passed among lillies and under weeping willows that cascaded into silent pools. They glided downriver in their gigs and skiffs, double-rowing slowly, perhaps, while one or two of their party reclined amidship amongst pillows and carpets and assorted fluffiness. They would step daintily ashore to newly mown meadows with their wicker picnic hampers, from which would issue goblets and silver, wine and cold meat pies, cloth napkins and scented waters.

Thousands of people went boating on the Thames, where there were thousands of boats to accommodate them. Wherries, shallops, gigs, skiffs, Canadian canoes, steam canoes, electric canoes, launches, punts, dinghies: it was a riot of small craft on a river that was so carefully locked and dammed — civilized, in other words — that it looked like a Romantic painting brought to life.

It wasn't always that way. There were pleasure craft on the river before the 1880s, to be sure, but the Fashionable People hadn't found them yet. The discovery came with the expansion of the railroads from London out to the river towns. What once had been a long journey by coach or carriage now became a fast journey by train. The consequent explosion of river use and the demand for river craft can be seen in the numbers. In 1888, 8,000 small craft were registered by the Thames Conservancy, the organization with jurisdiction over the river. A year later 12,000 boats were registered. River tolls tell the same story. In 1879, barges paid £1,779 while pleasure boats paid £1,647. In 1889, barges paid only £1,174, while pleasure craft paid £3,805. On Ascot Sunday in 1888, 800 skiffs, punts, and canoes passed through Boulter's Lock.

Tuesday, September 30, 1986

The morning comes overcast, with a damp chill in the air. *The Tar Skiff* lies where we left her, untouched and undamaged despite having spent the night in the middle of Oxford, a small city. We clean out a cupful or so of fallen willow leaves, load our baggage fore and aft, cast off, shove off, and take off.

Eileen gets out her knitting. I concentrate on feathering the oars, since there are watchers on the shore and I don't want to be reported to the Society for the Encouragement and Preservation of Proper Sculling Technique in Great Britain. In no time we're successfully through Osney Lock, though it is dicey for a moment when a tug and barge come very close to crushing us against the side wall.

The river below the lock is boat free at this hour, but the towpath is peppered with joggers and dog-walkers and a fellow who declaims poetry to the waterfowl and the trees. We pass under Folly Bridge, filled with commuter traffic, take a long look at the passenger boats at the famous Salters boatyard, and enter a stupendous straight-away flanked by Christchurch Meadow, at the end of which is a row of university boathouses. A few scullers and kayakers are out, but they're too busy concentrating on their own technique to appreciate mine. We've reached the countryside anyway, so I drop the feathering business for a Maine coast fisherman's stroke. I pick it up again for a short time before Iffley Lock in deference to George

Harris & Son, racing shell builders, whose shop lies to starboard.

I would like to report that the river below Sandford Lock, where we stop at the King's Arms for lunch, is extraordinarily scenic, but it isn't. There's not much to look at except water-rat holes in the bank and not much to worry about except a headwind that slows us down. No towpath-walkers; no riverbank fishermen. Just when I remark that this is getting boring, the Radley College boathouse comes into view and we're surrounded by the flashing oars of teenaged scullers who sprint past us with a supercilious air. Their coach, in a motorboat, turns his bullhorn on us and shouts across the water, "London is down the river that way. If you want, you can keep on going to France." Sure thing, coach.

The sun starts to shine through the mist, and the knitting needles slip from Eileen's fingers as she dozes off. And then in the distance between the trees I can see a church steeple. We pass through a lock and enter a stretch of meadows and come to a bridge and — bang — just like that — we're in the heart of Abingdon. It's like going instantaneously from a country lane to the New Jersey Turnpike. We moor in front of the Upper Reaches Hotel, drag our baggage upstairs, and engage in a short discussion over who gets the bubble bath first.

The boat of choice on the Thames until the 1830s was the wherry, which was used mostly by professional watermen for ferrying and other work. It was a relatively heavily built boat, suitable for hard work but too large and difficult to handle for pleasure boating. It was superseded by the gig, which was influenced mostly by the wherry and partly by naval craft. The gig's heyday was from the 1830s to the 1870s, when vast numbers of people began to flock to the river and created a demand for a light, strong boat that would be easily handled no matter the rower's skill.

The Thames skiff, which in the years between the 1880s and World War I was built by the thousands, succeeded the gig for pleasure use, just as the gig had succeeded the wherry. No single boatbuilder or designer was responsible for its creation; like most traditional craft, it simply evolved. Though the Thames skiff existed as an identifiable type, each builder — and there were many of them — had his own distinguishing marks, either in the shape of the boat or in its detailing. But in general, all skiffs shared certain characteristics.

Strictly speaking, a *skiff* was a boat built for double sculling; i.e., there were two rowing stations for two oarsmen, each of whom used two oars. A boat designed for a single sculler was, therefore, not called a skiff but simply a *single*. A *treble* was a boat designed for three scullers. A *randan* was a fashionable variation: a single sculler sat amidship, and two oarsmen — one forward and the other aft — would row with a single oar apiece.

The standard double-sculled skiff was about twenty-five feet long and four feet wide, though many builders built slightly longer or shorter versions. Salters, for example, built three different models: twenty-five feet long, four feet wide; twenty-three feet long, four feet six inches wide; and twenty feet long, five feet wide. Besides the two scullers, there was room in the stern for two passengers and in the bow for one.

Wednesday, October 1, 1986

Eileen puts down her knitting, stands up, stretches, looks thoughtfully at a brace of swans floating nearby, and says, "Sitting in a boat like this makes you soooo stiff." I keep hauling on the oars and deliberately fail to rise to the bait.

The fish in the river aren't rising to the bait, either. We pass fishermen, hundreds of fishermen, and never see one of them land a fish. They sit on little stools by the riverbank, staring intently at their bobbers, looking neither up nor down, left nor right. "Hi, there, how you doing?" No reply. "Nice day. How's the fishing going?" No reply.

The people on the passing pleasure motorboats are no different. They placidly ignore us, even in the locks. What happened to the brotherhood and sisterhood of the boat? The concept that we're all in this together? The working stiffs on the river are the saving grace — the lock keepers, the Thames Water tug and barge men, the dredgers. They look up and see us in a rowboat, for goodness sakes, and realize we're doing this because we want to, not because we're too poor or too cheap to hire a motorboat.

Eileen yanks me out of this anguish with a passage from Jerome K. Jerome, written in 1889: "Round Clifton Hampden, itself a wonderfully pretty village, old-fashioned, peaceful, and dainty with flowers, the river scenery is rich and beautiful. If you stay the night on land at Clifton, you cannot do better than put up at the Barley Mow. It is, without exception, I should say, the quaintest, most old-world inn up the river. It stands on the right of the bridge, quite away from the village. Its low-pitched gables and thatched roof and latticed windows give it quite a story-book appearance, while inside it is even more once-upon-a-timeyfied."

We moor by the Clifton Hampden bridge at noon, too soon in the day to think about staying overnight but just in time for lunch. The Barley Mow and the village in 1986 match Jerome's description from 1889, right down to the thatch on the roofs (though the inn was rebuilt following a fire in 1976). Lunch is a pleasure. Ditto for the afternoon on the river that follows, even though the sky is overcast and mist hangs in the air.

We take a room in a hotel by the Shillingford Bridge in the late afternoon. Ever the boat nut, I empty *The Tar Skiff* of gear, even the floorboards, and wash her down and polish her up. Then we walk two miles down the road to the Cricketeer Arms in Warborough, a pub that is reputed to have good food. It does.

The construction of Thames skiffs was a fine art, practiced by craftsmen who virtually grew up with tools in their hands. All skiffs were lapstrake planked with sawn frames and six strakes to a side, finished off with a top strake, the saxboard. The latter was heavier than the other strakes, presumably to take the abuse of coming alongside. The saxboard is also said to be a holdover from Viking times, when the top strake was made heavier for holding axes and swords. (*Saxboard* is thought to be a corruption of *sea axe board.*)

The saxboard was a continuous plank that swelled up to create the rowlocks, where it was notched to take the tholepins. About ninety percent of the skiffs were built with these fixed rowlocks; the rest were built with swivel rowlocks. Many of the boats with fixed rowlocks were modified during the 1940s and 1950s for swivels.

The normal method of construction was first to set up the keel, stem, and sternpost and build the boat rightside up. The transom and three or more molds were put in place. Four planks were hung, then the floors fitted, followed by the remaining planks and the saxboard. The sheerstrake, the last before the saxboard, provided the final shape to the sheer. The thwarts went in before the side timbers (about forty in all), and then the final fitting out would commence.

Though the molds provided much of the shape of the boat, the below-the-waterline shape was controlled by the fitting of the garboards. The garboards were "tweaked in" as they were hung to provide concavity fore and aft, and hence fineness at the waterline. Lands were cut on each edge of mating planks, unlike typical lapstrake construction in which the land was cut on only one plank edge. Butt blocks were not used; rather, long strakes were scarfed in a lazy *S*, without a nib, in cross section. Fastenings were copper rivets.

Skiffs, even many of those intended for livery use, were finished quite fancily. They were varnished inside and out, beaded and gold leafed with black shadow lines, fitted with velvet-covered horsehair cushions, and provided with wool carpets conforming to the shape of the floorboards. The back of the passenger thwart was of woven rush, wrought iron, or finely figured wood. Camping skiffs were even more elaborate, with storage compartments for gear and accessories, and, of course, folding iron hoops and a canvas top that made them look like floating Conestoga wagons.

Thursday, October 2, 1986

Nick Rogers meets us early in the morning by the Shillingford Bridge. A professional photographer, he examines the boat and checks the light while he screws lenses into camera bodies hung on straps around his neck.

"Tell me," he says. "Is this going to be one of those postcard stories — bucolic countryside, weeping willows by the river, still water with mist rising, Olde English thatched-roof cottages — or are we going to tell the truth?"

I think about that awhile, then tell him to go ahead and shoot his photographs. "When you're done," I say, "you'll have both."

In a sense that's the essence, but there's one scene, common to every stretch of the river, that only the most heartless journalist would want to record on film, and it typifies the paradox of modern English life. A photograph of this scene would show a gorgeous manor-type house — twenty-five rooms plus gazebo, let's say — sitting on fifteen acres of putting-green lawn sweeping down to the river, formal gardens in full blossom, a Jaguar under the portico, teak lawn furniture surrounding a table set for afternoon

162

tea. In front of this tasteful scene would be the squire's very own boat, moored to the riverbank. White, with a black rubrail peeling away in places and fuel-oil stains running down the sides, it would be boxy and top-heavy and look as if it had been designed by Conan the Barbarian and built by Attilla the Hun. Such a scene is not an anomaly on the River Thames.

In the afternoon, we row from Goring to Pangbourne. There's not the slightest breeze, and the sun shines warmly through a light mist. The river, winding through a long, shallow valley, is as still as glass. I pull on the oars and pause, pull on the oars and pause, and *The Tar Skiff* slides past autumn-touched trees and rafts of wildfowl and cows standing in the shallows.

The river straightens as we approach Pangbourne, and the starboard bank picks up a car-filled road and railroad tracks carrying fast trains that blast their way down to London and up to Oxford. We pass the naval college as the boys are struggling with lifeboat exercises and man-overboard drills, and stop in the center of town, where we moor the boat by a riverside pub for the night.

"I do hate steam launches," wrote Jerome K. Jerome in 1889. "I suppose every rowing man does. I never see a steam launch but I feel I should like to lure it to a lone part of the river, and there, in the silence and solitude, strangle it."

Jerome may have thought steam launches were noisy and dirty, and that the people who operated them were crass and inconsiderate, but he didn't know how fortunate he was. At the time he wrote *Three Men in a Boat*, the only powered craft on the Thames he and his friends had to contend with were steam and electric launches, rather benign craft compared to those that would follow. Only a few years later, in 1894, the first motorboat — a gasoline-powered paddle-wheel punt — was launched into the

Thames at Oxford. There were no fireworks or marching bands to mark the occasion, but there should have been, because the introduction of the motorboat marked the beginning of the end for the recreational rowing boat.

Who would have thought it? Who would have imagined that a boat that coughed, thumped, vibrated, and stank, that disturbed the very tranquility it sought to explore, would supplant another that was quiet, elegant, and a tribute to the river itself?

Thousands of words and reams of paper have been expended in describing the revolution wrought by the internal combustion engine on transportation in general and boats in specific, and there is no need for me to add to them now. It is sufficient to say that by the end of World War I, motorcraft were in and rowing boats were out on the Thames. For that matter, by the end of the war the very idea of Thames boating as high fashion, no matter whether the boat was powered or unpowered, was passé. The gentlemen and the ladies, the sports and the watermaids, moved on to other fashions in other places. To the unfashionable they left the skiffs and punts in decline, and the motorboats in ascension.

Before 1914, there were over 3,000 skiffs, punts, and dinghies in the hire-boat fleet in Richmond, near London, and over 300 professional boatmen found employment there. Just a few miles upriver in Hampton, there were over 1,000 small craft for hire. At Constable's, in Hampton, 300 private boats were stored; at the livery next door, 300 more were available for hire. Following World War I, that fleet, and the other fleets up and down the Thames, gradually dwindled through attrition. (The end of true skiff building at Constable's, for example, came long before World War II.) By the late 1940s there was so little interest in Thames skiffs that it was difficult to give them away. By the 1970s only nostalgic eccentrics paid them any mind.

164

Friday, October 3, 1986

We're on the river at Pangbourne before the keeper of the Whitchurch Lock comes on duty, so as the sun burns off the morning mist I work the lock myself. Crank open the upriver sluice to fill the lock with water; close the sluice; crank open the upriver lock gate; pull *The Tar Skiff* into the lock with the bow painter; crank shut the upriver lock gate; open the downriver sluice to drain the lock; close the sluice and open the downriver lock gate; tow the skiff out of the lock; crank shut the downriver lock gate; climb down into the boat and begin the monotonous yet invigorating rhythym: THUNK bic-Chuck . . . THUNK bic-Chuck . . . THUNK bic-Chuck . . .

The morning light gives the river a fairyland quality, and I half expect to see Kenneth Grahame's Rattie and Mole come double-sculling out of a backwater to challenge us to a quarter mile off the line. It's just as well they don't, because I'm tired enough to lose and I need my strength for our destination, twelve miles away.

The scenery flattens out as we proceed, until we reach a straightaway below the Mapledurham Lock that seems to go on forever. It's a daunting sight, but Eileen cheers me on with a tidbit from the river guide: there's a pub at the bend.

In my mind the river becomes the Yellow Brick Road, and the pub, the Roebuck, becomes the Emerald City. But when we arrive we find it to be a working-class saloon set between the road and the tracks. A sign on the door says *No Bikers*. The crowd inside puts the lie to the prohibition, but who's going to mess with a long-distance rower accompanied by a world-class knitter? Nobody, it seems, and we eat our lunch to the sounds of rockabilly and an electronic gambling machine that mostly swallows and sometimes spits ten-pence coins.

The afternoon turns into a trial by headwind, a sharp

breeze right on the nose of the skiff. Every bend in the river seems to presage a long, windswept straightaway, and I go back to feathering the oars in self-defense. It's grunt and pull, grunt and pull. I keep my concentration up by telling Eileen yarns about great feats of rowing — Howard Blackburn, whose hands became frozen to his oar handles off Newfoundland; Ridgeway and Blythe, who rowed across the Atlantic; Nathaniel Bishop, who rowed down the Mississippi in a Barnegat sneakbox; Horatio Hornblower, who escaped from France in a rowboat; Peter Spectre, who reached the Caversham Lock in Reading despite a headwind . . . .

We pass through the twin cities of Caversham and Reading, fight some more wind, and finally, in the late afternoon, settle into a fine, contemplative calm. Tired, indeed, but charmed by the village of Sonning, the end of the line for the day.

We moor where the river meets the lawn of the French Horn Hotel, just around the corner from Sonning Bridge. The woman who shows us to our room says, "I'm sorry. We only serve breakfast in bed." Aw, shucks.

Nobody would be so bold as to claim that the revival of interest in rowing traditional craft on the River Thames was brought about by Mark Edwards of Constable's Boathouse in Hampton, but few would deny that he is a key influence. At this moment, Constable's is the only establishment on the river specializing in restoring, building, and renting wooden skiffs, punts, and dinghies from the Golden Era.

Edwards, thirty-one years old, grew up in Hampton during the years when the last traditional small craft were on their last legs. Most of the hire fleets left were shifting over to fiberglass rowing boats of inferior model or to motor cruisers, or getting out of the business entirely. The few old-style firms that hung on, including Constable's, which was founded in 1867, did so only marginally — their boats were old and in poor repair, and they had no demand to build new boats. They were caught in a double bind: they had few customers and therefore little money to spend on repairs; because their boats were in such poor repair, they had few customers.

Edwards, in the meantime, was one of those boys who was fascinated by the waterfront. When he was about fifteen years old, he was given an old Thames skiff, which he restored on his own and used on the river. He took to hanging around Constable's, where he was allowed to use the workshop. Soon he was doing the odd repair job for skiff owners who had nowhere else to go, and he was trying his hand at new construction — his first boat being a camping wherry for himself.

Agriculture, however, was Edwards's prime interest at the time, so off he went to agricultural college, and that, presumably, was that. But when he got out and came back to the river to pick up his boat, he found there was a long line of people who had boats to be repaired and restored, and no one with the abilities and incentive to do the work. It seems that while he was gone a small revival of interest in traditional craft had taken place, and he came back on the scene at the right time with the right experience.

A promising agricultural career ended then and there. Edwards picked up his tools, negotiated a lease with the owner of the boathouse (who by then had given up on the business), hired a shop crew, and revived Constable's. He searched out old, neglected boats to restore, built new ones (eight to order in the last two years), and organized a rental fleet.

Mark Edwards has no illusions about traditional small craft on the Thames in the modern era. He doesn't expect to see a day when rowing becomes as fashionable as it was in Victorian times, but he does believe there is a future in his chosen business, perhaps even for a few more boathouses to spring up in response to a moderate but strong interest in seeing the river in a "proper boat." Today, he has Thames classics for rent by the day or the week and which can be rowed down to London or up to the head of navigation in Cricklade. Plenty of people take him up on the offer, and none of them come back with complaints about the experience.

Saturday, October 4, 1986

Our last day on the Thames comes cool and a tad breezy, but the first few miles are protected from the wind. The open countryside gradually gives way to more and more riverside homes, and the closer we get to Henley, the more rowing craft we see. Nobody is using them, you understand, at least not at the moment, but we see Thames skiffs in boathouses, various types of pulling boats moored by the riverbank, and even racing shells here and there. Strange as it seems, the only rowers we have come across in six days are competition scullers working out for the next race and one fellow in a yellow plywood canoe rigged with swivel rowlocks.

As we approach Henley, the river traffic picks up and we see more and more joggers and walkers on the towpath. We are still dogged by fiberglass motor cruisers, but now we have the opportunity to admire fine wooden steam launches, slipper-sterned motorboats, and a day-sailer or two.

It's Saturday, and Henley is jumping, stomping, steaming. We moor by the bridge, pounding with traffic, and wonder whether it's wise to reenter society as we used to know it, even if it's only for a brief lunch. We do but wish we hadn't, and afterwards return to *The Tar Skiff* and the river with a great deal of relief, even though the wind is up and straight at our head.

So we row and talk and joke and smile, because this is our last afternoon and the living is easy. The pauses between strokes become longer and the rests by the riverbank become more frequent — not because we are tired but because we hate to see the journey come to an end. It's a long afternoon, a short afternoon, if you know what I mean.

But then it comes, the end. We round a bend and the entrance to Hurley Lock comes into view. As we stare ahead — incredulously — out of the lock comes a Thames skiff, oars flashing in the soft sunlight. It's like a mirror image of ourselves; a woman at the oars, a man in the passenger seat. We pass and wave, and then take our turn in the lock.

Later, after mooring *The Tar Skiff* at Peter Freebody's boatyard, where it will be retrieved by Mark Edwards, we take the bus back to Oxford. The ride up takes an hour and a half; the ride down took six days. The fastest, even if it were in a Porsche, is nowhere near the best.

Warrior's Figurehead

For three weeks or more I had been carrying around a clipping from the *Wall Street Journal* about a pair of figurehead carvers, among the last professionals in their trade in the world. The story told all about them but didn't say where they lived — only that they were temporarily working in a shop by the sea on the Isle of Wight. I'd pull the ragged piece of newsprint from my pocket and unfold it and show it to whomever would look. "Do you know these guys?" ("No, but I know of a pair in Cornwall who rebuild wagon wheels" or "Didn't I read somewhere that the oldest one died a few years back?")

Nobody seemed to be able to help, but at least I was closing in on the territory. I was in Cowes, on the Isle of Wight, talking with the founder of Structural Polymers, a resin and glue manufacturer — sort of an English version of Gougeon Brothers or Chem Tech or Industrial Formulators. It had been a high-tech day. The walls of the office were stark white and the edges of the sales literature were accented with bold colors. The air was filled with words like *ergosynergistic polyphenalesters* and *carbonaceous vinylbuterates*. I was getting restless.

"Say," I said, "Is there a boatshop around here that uses your product?" You know what I was after. A quick dose of Stockholm tar to counteract the chlorinated thermoplastics.

There was and there wasn't, if you know what I mean. Down the road there was a shop that was coating plywood with unidirectional fibers and grinding the surface smooth with disc sanders, and across town there was a builder who was vacuum-bagging foam-core IOR racers. But the nearest quasi-traditional boatbuilder was a ferryboat ride and long drive away.

"Of course, there are a couple of figurehead carvers over at Spencer's who have been using our glue . . . ."

It was a curious coincidence. A year or so previously Elwood Root had regaled me with stories about Harry Spencer's shop — that it was one of the last honest-to-gosh old-fashioned sparmaking establishments in the British Isles, that they could build anything you wanted — thick, thin, hollow, solid, round, oval, the works.

I was expecting something special and I found it: a long warehouse-type building right on the waterfront next to Clare Lallow's yacht yard. An assortment of watercraft ranged along the quay behind the shop, and the legendary sail loft of Ratsey and Lapthorn was across the street. There were stacks of long timbers in the yard, and milling machines surrounded by mounds of sawdust by the loading platform. A couple of workers were running rough lumber through machines and pulling out finished stock.

Inside was a large open shop, well lighted by high windows. Huge spars, some finished, some roughly shaped, lay on racks to the side, and on the floor was a jig for a round, hollow spar that tapered at both ends. In a corner, woodworkers were making mast hoops big enough for a lion to leap through. (I was to discover later that the spars and the hoops were for the restoration of I. K. Brunel's iron steamship *Great Britain*, originally built in 1843.)

Sawdust, wood shavings. I could forget about polymerized hydrocarbons.

Dominating the shop, making this larger-than-life sparmaking operation seem puny by comparison, was a colossal figurehead depicting a gladiator with sword in one hand, upraised shield in the other. The bearded warrior wore a plumed helmet and a mailed tunic, with a chain running like a bandolier across his chest. A fellow with a tweed cap and silk scarf around his neck was sharpening sculpting tools at a bench. Another in dark blue coveralls was perched on a stepladder using a gouge and mallet to carve away at an unfinished section of the figurehead. The tool sharpener was Jack Whitehead, sixty-nine years old and a picture, at the outside, of fifty. His partner was Norman Gaches, forty-four years old, with a face that was startlingly similar to that of the figurehead he was carving.

When people caterwaul about the death of wooden ship and boat building, they greatly exaggerate the condition, as we all well know. A more accurate word would be *decline*, which indicates that things have not been totally lost; they just aren't what they used to be. To say that the art of figurehead carving is dead, however, is to exaggerate only slightly. After all, any trade whose professional practitioners worldwide can be counted on your fingers has to be declared nearly extinct, if not totally extinct, for most practical purposes. The reason is obvious: there aren't many figureheads that need carving these days. The last era, when nearly every merchant ship and naval ship of consequence sported a figurehead — not to mention trailboards, stern decorations, and other carvings — as a matter of course, passed almost one hundred years ago. To be sure, the odd ship here and there has been fitted with a carved head from time to time, but the work has almost always been done by a craftsman temporarily recruited for a one-time job. A sculptor, perhaps, or a model maker with the vision to work at greater than scale. But you won't find many men who make their livings by carving genuine figureheads for real ships, not yachts or barroom walls. They are as rare as the whooping crane or the California condor.

You wouldn't get that impression from talking to Norman Gaches and Jack Whitehead, though. Both men work at their trade as if it were the most natural occupation in the world. Ever since they took mallet in hand, their expertise has been in almost continuous demand. Of course, they don't have much competition, and what competition they do have would be hard pressed to match, never mind surpass, the artistry of their work.

Surprisingly, neither man was trained as a shipcarver. They came to the occupation from other, related work, not by the time-honored tradition of apprenticeship to a master. (Nobody knows who the last classically trained shipcarver was, but according to M. V. Brewington, the last Canadian was John Rogerson, who died in 1925, and the last American was Holman Waldron Chaloner, who died at about the same time.)

Jack Whitehead began his working career as, of all things, an agricultural auctioneer. He took up wood carving to help regain strength in his hand after it was injured by a propeller when he was in the Royal Air Force during World War II. After the war he took up puppetry, designing and hand-carving his own puppets and performing with them on a television show. He became a shipcarver when a friend on the Isle of Wight asked him to carve a mermaid figurehead for a yacht he was building. As chance would have it, a photograph of the completed work was published in a British yachting magazine, and inquiries flooded in from people who had thought that figurehead carving was a lost art.

Norman Gaches also came out of left field into the

ship-carving business. He worked for a mail-order company in London, then moved to the Isle of Wight when his mother moved there. He, too, developed an interest in wood carving, eventually specializing in hand-carved signs. Gaches and Whitehead became acquainted through their mutual interest and eventually formed a loose partnership when Whitehead's figurehead commissions became too many for one person to handle alone.

Though their initial commissions were for yachts, they soon began to be offered ship projects as well. As fortune would have it, they had entered their trade at just the right time — there was a resurgence of interest in ship restoration and replication, and many of the vessels required figureheads and other fancy carvings. They became itinerant specialists, traveling extensively to work on projects wherever they were needed. Their many carvings include those for replicas of the *Golden Hinde* and *Nonsuch*, the school ships *Sir Winston Churchill* and *Malcolm Miller*, the *Royalist*, the *Captain Scott*, and the *Centurion*. For the most part, they would work separately on each project; that is, one might carve the stern decorations while the other did the trailboards. On occasion they would work independently of each other. Jack Whitehead carved the figurehead for the museum ship *Falls Of Clyde* in Hawaii, while Norman Gaches carved a coat of arms for the Captain Cook Hotel in Anchorage, Alaska. They have also done ship carvings for shore display, among them a replica for the Buckler's Hard Maritime Museum of the figurehead originally mounted on HMS *Gladiator*.

The figurehead in Harry Spencer's spar shop is typical of their commissions. It was being done for the Ships Preservation Trust of Hartlepool, England, for the restoration of HMS *Warrior*, one of the most ambitious maritime preservation projects underway in the world.

HMS *Warrior* was one of those few ships in world history that can be termed a breakthrough design, one that singlehandedly closed out one era and began a new one. According to Admiral G. A. Ballard, author of *The Black Battlefleet*, "Some 170 successors have flown the white ensign since that day, but of not one of all these vessels, nor of any vessel before her since the reign of Henry VII, could it be said, as it was said of the *Warrior*, that at the date of her launching she was in herself a match for all her existing line-of-battle consorts put together." *Warrior*, launched in 1860, was the largest (418 feet), fastest (14.3 knots steam, 13 knots sail, 17.5 knots steam and sail), most powerful, and best protected battleship afloat. Her building kicked off a surge in warship design that would result in the creation of the modern navies of the two world wars. Ironically, it kicked off her quick demise as well, since her innovations promoted new innovations in succeeding battleships, making her obsolete less than fifteen years after her launching.

HMS *Warrior* was taken out of active service. She became a reserve ship, then a torpedo training school, then an auxiliary workshop, finally a floating pontoon for oil tankers at Pembroke, South Wales. In 1979, recognized as a truly historic ship worthy of preservation as a symbol of the days when Britannia ruled the waves, the mastless, engineless, stripped-out hulk was towed to Hartlepool on England's northeast coast for restoration. The intention was to put her on display in a floating berth in Portsmouth near HMS *Victory*.

Like other naval ships of her time, *Warrior* was fitted with a figurehead, though it and the structure required to support it were severely detrimental to her performance. "The chief defect for the *Warrior*" according to Admiral Ballard, "was the distribution of weights at full load, which brought her down nearly a foot at the bows . . . . Quite unnecessary was the long, heavy iron knee at her bow, which answered no useful purpose and detracted alike from her seagoing and fighting efficiency . . . . It owed its existence solely to the conventions of the period as to the proper profile of a ship's bow above water."

And a proper profile required a proper figurehead — in this case, a huge three-quarter figure of a gladiator, painted white with gilded accents to contrast spectacularly with the ship's black hull. It is said to have been carved by a member of the Hellyer family, which did considerable work for the navy; nine years later, a Hellyer carved the figurehead of the clipper *Cutty Sark*. Come restoration time, however, *Warrior's* original figurehead was long gone, so Whitehead and Gaches were commissioned to carve a replica.

Carving a figurehead the size of *Warrior's* is no easy task. Think about it. The carving is fifteen feet long; from the floor to the tip of the gladiator's plume is eleven feet; the finished sculpture weighs two tons. (The original block of glued-up planks weighed three tons — Whitehead and Gaches removed with hand tools one ton of wood chips!) The project from beginning to end took almost a year.

"Before we started the job," said Whitehead, "Norman made a scale model of the figurehead, at one-twelfth scale, carved out of a solid piece of limewood. The model is highly finished so we could take off dimensions from it and enlarge them. From the model we made a full-size profile drawing of the figurehead, so we could take measurements from that as well.

"Since we did not have the original to work from, and since no working drawings of the figurehead exist, we had to work from contemporary photographs. We were lucky. We had photographs that were taken in 1879, of extremely good quality so they could stand enlargement.

"The first actual full-size work we did was to make a

template of the bow of the ship. We went up to Hartlepool, where the ship was lying, to get our dimensions. Actually, the original bow of the ship had been knocked off in a collision, so the crew up there had to build a new one. We worked from the same drawings they did.

"The figurehead is not a solid piece of timber. It's glued up from planks. We used Canadian pine because it carves very well and is durable and light in weight. We began with fifteen-foot lengths, 3 x 12 inches, quite well seasoned. We glued them around the mock-up of the bow because that dimension is important, and with a bit of luck the finished figurehead will slide onto the bow of the ship.

"The planks were planed on all four sides on a power planer to get exact gluing surfaces, and then Norman worked out from his model a method of contouring them to get the rough shape of the figurehead. As you can see, the planks do not all run in the same direction. It was planned that way. It is very difficult to carve end grain, so the planks were laid out to avoid it as much as possible in critical areas, such as the face and beard. We also wanted the grain to flow with the folds of the robe.

"There are no metal fastenings of any kind holding the laminations together — only glue and a few hardwood pegs in critical places. Actually, many of the pegs are replacements for coach screws that were used to hold some of the planks together while the glue set. We used Structural Polymer's epoxy glue for this job, though usually we use resorcinol. Even though we had no control over heat and humidity in this shop, we had no problems with the glue. Of course, we have had a few checks in the wood; you really can't expect to avoid them in a piece of glued-up timber this size. But they will all be filled, and the whole of the figurehead will be soaked in a thin resin solution before any painting is done. That should make the wood reasonably stable.

"We haven't worried that much about temperature and

humidity. We glued it up when the weather was cold, then worked on it in the heat of the summer, and now it is cold and damp. No problems. However, we took the partially completed figurehead to the London Boat Show this winter for publicity for the *Warrior* restoration. There was a complete lack of humidity in the show building and we had problems. It cracked open in one or two places. We sprayed water over it and covered it with a plastic sheet. All the cracks closed back up when we got the carving back to this shop. There shouldn't be any problems when the figurehead is finally mounted on the ship, because it is going to be moored in the water.

"We're building this figurehead just as they did the original, though in the old days they did not use glue but rather pegged the pieces together with wooden pins. I expect they probably used bigger pieces of timber than we have. We use the same tools they did for the rough work at the start. Some of our carving tools are probably as old as the figurehead was.

"Parts of the figurehead are carved separately, then mounted on the main body later. For example, the arms are on sliding, tapered joints so we can take them on and off. When we are done, they will be fixed permanently.

"I think this figurehead is probably the largest one that's been carved in this country, this century. The great difficulty of working at this scale is not being able to move the piece around at will to get at it. We've alleviated that a bit by designing and having a special trolley built, on which the carving is mounted. It has six wheels, with the two in the middle mounted slightly lower, which allows us to spin it around.

"This shop, which was kindly offered to us by Harry Spencer, is very good for us because it has good lighting and allows us to get back from the figurehead to get a good look. If you're working right on top of it, you're liable to lose your sense of proportion. The original figurehead was slightly out of proportion — his arms are too short. The artist probably carved in a workshop where he couldn't get back far enough to see the whole thing."

Jack Whitehead and Norman Gaches finished HMS *Warrior*'s figurehead in 1983, at which time it was brought across the Solent to the Portsmouth Dockyard. Painted white, accented with gold, it was put on display with a collection of original figureheads, including those of the first *Warrior* (1781), the *Tremendous* (1784), the *Bellerophon*, and of course, Nelson's *Victory*. It has since been mounted on the bow of the restored *Warrior*, which is now a floating historical exhibit in Portsmouth, England.

"Do You Have a Moment?"
He Asked

Someone told me — or I seem to remember someone telling me — that the tidal range in Liverpool's Mersey River was in the area of thirty feet. I'm equivocating somewhat, because from where I sit now, thousands of miles from the Mersey, such a number seems like a hallucination.

Think about it for a moment. The tide goes out: miles of mud. The tide comes in: the mud is thirty feet underwater.

The Liverpudlians have gone to great lengths to deal with these extremes. One of the most fascinating marvels their engineers have contrived is a huge landing stage on the riverfront facing Birkenhead. The size of a football field or two, this device floats on the river and is held away from the shore with immense hydraulic arms that automatically adjust for vertical motion.

Upriver and downriver from the landing stage are acres and acres of docks — not piers jutting out from the shore, but lagoons built into the shore, surrounded by quays, insulated from the rise and fall of the tide by heavy steel lock gates. Ships as big as they come are warped into the docks at high tide, and the gates are shut. The river falls away, and six hours later, there you have it — oceangoing ships still floating tranquilly thirty feet above the mud.

Behind the landing stage is a row of three edifices: the Cunard, Dock Company, and Royal Liver buildings. The latter is a massive structure, at the top of which, looming over the city, perches a grotesque gilded bird. It looks like one of those prehistoric monsters whose bones were dug out of a dry lakebed on the Serengeti Plain, wired together, filled out with plaster of paris, dipped into a tub of molten gold, and polished for three days with jewelers' rouge.

Everything in Liverpool is like that. Larger than life. The main city museum, for example, is so imposing it probably intimidates as many visitors from entering as it encourages. One of several Victorian structures surrounding a park, it looks like the Great Hall of Justice in which the common man will find none.

I wasn't intimidated. I got to walk in the back door with Michael Stammers, whose title at the time was Keeper of Maritime History. Stammers was somewhat embarrassed by the title, which brought to mind the keeper of the zoo, but he was proud of the maritime history he kept, and I could see why. Few cities in the world have a maritime heritage as rich as Liverpool's, and it is a distinction that should override all other claims to fame, the Fab Four and the occasional football riot notwithstanding.

Stammers showed me around his maritime collection, which filled a couple of modest-sized rooms. (The rest of the museum was given over to non-nautical relics of Liverpool's past.) There were some impressive ship models, a few tastefully designed and intelligently labeled displays, interesting artifacts, lots of photographs and paintings. To be frank, though, it didn't seem like much when you consider that Liverpool was and has been as recently as World War II one of the principal ports of

Europe. Stammers must have sensed my disappointment. As we sat down to lunch at the museum cafeteria, he quietly mentioned that the city museum owned the second largest ship model collection in the world.

I would have been the last to say I had been everywhere and seen everything, but I was confident I had seen more ship models in any number of small museums than I had seen so far in Liverpool, and, between sips of tea, so informed the keeper.

Stammers, to his credit always the English gentleman, carefully folded his napkin and placed his fork on it. "Do you have a moment?" he asked. Of course I did. So, after promising on my Scout's honor that I would never reveal the directions to our destination — the museum's storage building — or its address when we got there, we drove across town.

The stories you hear about Liverpool are sometimes true, sometimes not. Yes, unemployment is very high. No, the center city doesn't look like Wheeling, West Virginia, after a flood. The section we went to was full of tired industrial buildings and old warehouses, but it looked as if it were safer to walk through alone than most American cities, even at night — though I wouldn't recommend parading around with a placard pledging allegiance to, say, Birminghams' football club. Nevertheless, the museum carefully maintains a low profile for its storage facility, located in this neighborhood, because you never know when one of the local boys might develop a hankering for a piece or two of nautical memorabilia.

We parked next to a very large two-story brick building of nineteenth-century origin and walked around front. It seems to me that Stammers said it was once a mill where undertakers built coffins, but I can find nothing about that in my notes. No matter. There were large barn doors in the front, bolted and padlocked, with no sign or symbol or anything else to indicate what would be found inside. To

183

the right was a small door and a doorbell. Stammers pressed it. We could hear "I'm coming" in the best Liverpudlian accent on the other side, shuffling feet, and the squealing of hinges as the door opened. I peered into the gloom.

What can I say? It was like opening up the household freezer and discovering a virgin five-gallon tub of chocolate Haagen Dazs.

We entered a huge room packed to the rafters with ship models. Most of them were hidden in shipping crates, but a few — enough to get a sense of what was going on — were standing free. First and foremost of the latter was the original builder's display model of the *Titanic*. At twenty feet, it was big enough to sail down the Mersey and out into the Irish Sea. I could see rank upon rank of ship models, half-models, various full-sized small craft, anchors, steam engines, blocks, winches, buoys, barrels, shipbuilders' tools, casting patterns, cannons — all stowed more or less by category, but to me, taken by surprise, it was a chaotic grab bag of nautical memorabilia to make even the most jaded waterfront crawler weak in the knees.

Stammers, to his credit always the English gentleman, refrained from mentioning all those little museums I had visited, and squired me around, politely introducing the curatorial staff and pointing out some of the highlights.

"Before World War II," he explained, "there was a larger display of maritime materials in the county museum. Among the collection was the old shipping gallery, which contained about four hundred huge shipbuilders' models. Most of these, and most of the models now in the packing crates, were exhibition models built by the shipyard modelmakers to be set up in the owners' offices. At the outbreak of the war, the county museum building was evacuated to protect the treasures from German bombs. The models were taken to a country house in north Wales. Most of them were simply shipped out in the original glass-

and-wood cases they were displayed in. After the war, they were stored in a house in south Liverpool, eventually coming here in 1969. They are in packing cases now, because the original display cases started to deteriorate and we had to provide protection."

The keeper was quite matter-of-fact about it all — "There are about 1,200 models in the building, ranging from the *Titanic* at twenty feet to tiny ones that are literally a half inch long" — gesturing to make a point while threading his way among the crates to find a particularly noteworthy specimen. ("I just know you'll love this one.")

"After the war," he went on, "the idea of having a separate maritime museum was being evolved, but money was a problem. Very little of the county museum building survived the war; only the frontage really remained. It took about thirty years to get the main building back to the way it was before the war. In the meantime, all this has gone unseen and unappreciated, except the small amount now on display in the reconstructed county museum."

Only Stammers and a few members of his staff have seen all of the models out of their crates. "We had a campaign for a while to open all the crates and photograph and catalog the contents," he said. "We had to do it, because, after the confusion of moving them from one place to another, we weren't certain what we had and what we didn't have."

Most of the models were donated by shipping and shipbuilding companies when they went out of business, or by private shipowners and masters as a provision in their wills. Almost all are directly connected with the maritime history of Liverpool and its environs — the ships they represent either having been built or owned there, or having Liverpool their principal port of call.

"One distinct part of the collection, for example," said Stammers, "consists of half-models of every ship in one company's coastal fleet. These are decorative models, rigged realistically. When the company went out of business, they gave them all to the museum."

And so it went. A drawer full of tiny recognition models here, prisoner-of-war models from the Napoleonic Wars there, plating models, construction models, some without categorization — such as a mock-up of the interior of a dockside warehouse, used for legal testimony in a liability case; the model of a deck pen used for shipping cattle; even a salesman's display model of a portable cabin that could be set up 'tween decks in an emergency.

It eventually became more than I could stand — there comes a point when the brain can't accept any more, when the mouth runs out of *oobs* and *aabs* and variations of *"Isn't that great."* So while I lectured the keeper of maritime history about his obligation to do everything, anything, in his power to get that fantastic collection out of that dingy warehouse, he drove me down to the Mersey River and showed me the once-derelict Albert and Canning Docks, and explained in detail how the funds were being made available to develop the site into a new maritime museum, where the models would find their niche in public view. It would be called the Merseyside Maritime Museum.

That was several years ago. A couple of years later I went back, partly because there was something that I found fascinating about Liverpool and partly because I was curious about how the new museum was progressing. Stammers was the same, though he had a new title to go along with his increasing responsibilities. We toured the same two modest maritime rooms in the county museum. We ate lunch in the same cafeteria. And we made the same trip across town to the same warehouse, so I could regain that same feeling of discovery, of finding in a single building, without academic elaboration or interpretation, a highly refined concentration of evidence from an era I was so unfortunate to miss. Stammers seemed to understand.

When I was finished oohing and aahing, we went down to the Albert and Canning Docks, where a gang of workmen were readying the building in which a good part of that incredible collection of models would be open to the public. There was no question about it — the Merseyside Maritime Museum was turning into a fitting repository for the proof of Liverpool's nautical past. As for me, I'll never forget the warehouse.

A Perfect Boat More Perfect

"Is it so nice as all that?" asked the Mole shyly, though he was quite prepared to believe it as he leaned back in his seat and surveyed the hand-stitched leather upholstery, the instrumentation, the steering wheel, and all the fascinating fittings, and felt the engine's growl vibrate through the hull as the Water Rat flicked the throttle control.

"Nice? Are you kidding? Do you realize what one of these machines can do to you?" yelled the Water Rat with enthusiasm as the boat leaned violently into a high-speed turn. "Believe me, my young friend, there is nothing, — absolutely nothing — half so much worth doing as simply blasting around a big lake with the engine screaming like a cornered she-lion, the spray gathering into shimmering rooster tails, and the rushing airstream looping over the windshield to peel back your eyelids and flatten your ears to the side of your head."

— what Kenneth Grahame would have written in *The Wind in the Willows* if he had spent a day with Vic Carpenter

Vic Carpenter was pacing the dirt road that pierces his boatyard in Port McNicoll, Ontario, a place Mark Twain would have called a "one-horse town." I was two minutes late, only because I couldn't figure out how to detour around a freight train stopped across the road to take on grain from the huge granary that dominates the lonely countryside. Vic, who was dressed for a day of yachting — shorts, canvas porkpie hat, sweatshirt emblazoned with *Wood is Good* or some such slogan — was hot to get going. We were to take photographs of his new speed launch up in the Muskoka lakes, about an hour's drive away, and time is an unnecessary impediment when Vic has made up his mind to do something.

It was a glorious day, cloudless, warm, with only a hint of haze, and Vic was worried lest the weather degenerate before we got to the boat. ("We might as well use the opportunity to advantage," he said as we bumped out of the yard. "Hell, Kodak will make more money than I will.") All the way to Lake Rousseau he chafed about the godless weather and how it could ruin everything, throwing in a running commentary about boats and boatbuilding, and wood and glue, and speed launches and speedboats, and Ditchburns and Minetts. Especially the latter, about which I knew nothing, making Vic very happy because now he could really show me something, contribute to my education and all that. A happy Vic Carpenter is a delightful presence; with luck, the weather would hold and my greenness would continue.

Vic kept his launch under cover in a boathouse built out into the lake from the shore. It was an inconspicuous structure; just a low building with a walkway along the side. We stumbled down to it through the woods because Vic was in too much of a hurry to take the winding driveway that led off the dirt road where we parked the car.

"You are about to see one of the most magnificent

private collections of wooden boats assembled in one place," he said dramatically as he unlocked the door. Tim Smutz, the photographer, struggled with his equipment, ready to capture the moment. Hazel Carpenter, Vic's wife, fumbled for a light switch. I peered around in the murky darkness at a row of boats, rocking gently in their slips. They didn't look like much to me.

Then the lights went on. Vic clapped his hands and said, "There. Over there. That's my new Minett!" I couldn't make it out at first, partly because I didn't know a Minett from a salmon troller, but primarily because the dazzle of a roomful of mirrorlike varnish and polished chrome and stainless steel made comprehension a little slow. It was like being turned loose in a candy store and trying to pick out the chocolate cremes from the petit fours while the proprietor excitedly announced that the pecan-encrusted nougats were the special of the week. Smutz groaned with pleasure and set up his tripod. We were in photographer's heaven.

I counted eight classic boats in the house, each in mint condition and each an original, except for Vic's boat, which was a replica. The owner, who allowed Vic to keep his boat there to add luster to the collection, is a wealthy television station owner with a passion for antique boats. Like the sharp dresser with a closet full of suits who can't decide what to wear, he must have had a tough time picking his boat for the day. Later, when I was able to discern individual boats among this jungle of craft, each one screaming "Look at me, touch me, write about me," I learned that there was a small Minett speedboat, a Dispro (the famous disappearing propeller boat), a baby Ditch-burn launch, a full-size Ditchburn launch, a Greavette Streamliner ("I don't like it," said Hazel with a shake of the head. "Looks too much like a beached whale"), a Sea Bird speedboat, a Minett launch, and, of course, Vic's Minett.

While Hazel went looking for a dusting rag ("Don't

take any pictures, Tim, until I tidy her up a bit"), Vic pointed out the salient features of his boat. The gist of what he said — though I must confess that my concentration was off given the abundance of riches within the boathouse — was that this was *Era*, his interpretation of a thirty-five-foot Minett launch built in 1931. He had restored the original, named *Chimo*, for a client a couple of years back, and though Vic was a confirmed sailor, with little interest in powerboats, he was taken by the beauty of the boat, the excellence of its construction, the subtlety of its detailing. He felt compelled to build a replica on speculation, even though it would take thousands of hours and would cost so much ($90,000 Canadian in the early 1980s) that few people would be able to buy it.

H. C. (Bert) Minett was a boatbuilder in Bracebridge, Ontario, who built launches and speedboats from 1911 until 1948. His shop was noted for turning out unparalleled custom craft that had a stylishness, not to mention a durability, that was lacking in most production boats of the time. In direct competition with Ditchburn, another premiere Bracebridge custom builder, Minett carried his quest for perfection to the nth degree (it may not be unfair to say that Minett played Dusenburg to Ditchburn's Bentley). Aficionados on the Muskoka lakes — where there are to this day literally thousands of wooden speedboats and launches, and as many aficionados to appreciate them — can differentiate a Minett from a Ditchburn instantaneously, even though at first glance they appear quite similar.

To show me the difference, Vic pointed out the spray rail on his Minett replica, then compared it to a Ditchburn launch at the other end of the boathouse. The Ditchburn's rail was a separate piece, fastened directly to the planking. The Minett's was integral, carved out of the plank like a piece of sculpture. Both were flawlessly executed and eminently functional, but the Minett's rail blended into the whole while the Ditchburn's stood proud. Small differences separate the Guarneri from the Stradivari, and the Ditchburn from the Minett. According to Carpenter, Greavette, the third kingpin of the Muskoka lakes boatbuilders, doesn't even come close.

Era's dimensions and details were taken directly from *Chimo*, but Vic Carpenter in his straight-ahead manner (some would say in his egocentric manner) claims to have made a perfect boat more perfect. He pulled up the floorboards and pointed to the bilge. "In the water two months and not a drop of water. Dry as a bone. Just a little dust. Hey, Hazel. Bring that dust rag over here!"

I mentioned that cold-molded boats sure were nice that way. Vic looked shocked and offended. "Cold molded? Not on your life. This boat's single-planked over frames. Planking stock is five-eighths-inch Honduras mahogany over sheer-to-sheer laminated mahogany frames. The seams are glued. The deck is half-inch Honduras mahogany. Those look like butts in the planks but they're not. I just made them that way to be faithful to the original, butt blocks and all, but the planks are scarfed and glued. The hull is lighter and stronger than the original." It would have to be, actually, to handle the big engine installed, which was more powerful than the original and produced much higher speeds.

Tim Smutz started taking photographs, startling Vic into joining Hazel in the dusting and polishing. The Carpenters are paranoid about perfection, and in the glare of publicity they seemed to see imperfection in places that were apparent to no one but themselves. When Vic found a barely perceptible scratch on the side deck, he began to rant and rave. "Look at this, some clod must have stepped on this boat with his shoes on. I can't believe people do that. It's like walking on your piano." (Later, Tim Smutz, who has sailed with Vic many times, told me about the time a fellow climbed aboard Vic's sailboat with hard-soled shoes on. Vic got so mad he put on *his* shoes, strode to the parking lot, and walked across the hood of the fellow's Porsche.)

But we weren't going to stand around a boathouse all day, not by a long shot. Vic can't stand still for long — can't stand still at all — so he arched a look at me and said, "I hear you like fast boats." When I admitted as much, he motioned to the *Brigadoon*, an eighteen-foot Minett speedboat. "Let's leave Hazel and Tim to their chores and go for a spin." I took off my shoes.

So it began, a day at the races with Vic Carpenter, roaring around Rousseau and Muskoka lakes in a selection of fast boats, to look at fast boats, to talk about fast boats — yes, even to show off in fast boats, since above all else, Vic loves to show off. You can hardly fault him for that, since over the years his accomplishments have been monumental. Wherever we went, it was, "I restored that one . . . " or "I'm building a replica of this one . . . " or "I repaired that one . . . " or "I rebuilt this one . . . " or "This fellow wants me to build a wooden muscle boat so he can blow all these plastic switchblades off the water . . . ." We were in motion all the time, never getting around to lunch until about three o'clock, long after I ceased to care about the meal — 20 mph, 40 mph, 50 mph, 60 mph. It got to be a blur after a while, though hardly a forgettable experience. In fact, there were some clearly unforgettable experiences, many of them staged by Vic to gain attention, which he rarely failed to do.

For example, at one point we borrowed a speedboat named *Good Til Cancelled*. Vic had done some work on it. Besides customizing the dash with spectacular inlay work in a design reminiscent of Japan's rising sun, Vic had done some structural work to the bottom of the hull. We were blasting along in a straight line at 50 to 60 mph, though it seemed more like 280, when Vic told me about the problems the boat had.

"At top speed it could trip in a turn and roll over. Before modification, we could never make a turn at this speed and expect to survive. I wonder if the problem's been corrected . . . ?" He waited for a couple of seconds while that sank in, then, after checking to see if my knuckles showed the proper shade of white, threw the wheel over. We went into the tightest turn I've probably ever been in at that speed, the boat skidding sideways, the engine straining, me looking down at Vic from the high side and wondering whether to laugh or cry. When we were back on a straight course again, Vic said, "I guess it's OK." and threw the wheel over in the other direction.

At another point Tim Smutz and I were standing on a high bridge taking photographs of Vic and Hazel in *Era*. At first, Vic was just idling around near the bridge so Tim could get detail shots, but he soon became impatient with that and started running at full speed under the bridge, banking into a quick turn and coming through again, back and forth, just missing the bridge supports each time. After fifteen minutes or so, groups of people were standing on their docks watching the performance, and a few spectators were leaning over the bridge rails, wincing every time he came near the pilings. Finally, Vic roared up to the bridge and stopped, looking for all the world, with his barrel chest and mustache, like Dick Butkis at the wheel of a speedboat. "I guess I better stop. You keep running between those posts and you think all kinds of strange things." Hazel flashed a weak smile and someone down the lake started to clap.

But the joy of the day was riding in *Era*, surely the epitome of gracious speed. While flat-out speedboats like *Brigadoon* and *Good Til Cancelled* provided thrills and chills — and there's nothing wrong with that, I can assure you — *Era* made one feel like the Prince of Wales driving his bride to Balmoral in a Rolls. Comfortable speed, spacious speed, chilled-wine-and-Caspian-Sea-caviar speed — the type that allows you to carry on a conversation with your fellow passengers and walk around in the cockpit and even enjoy a Havana cigar if you should so desire.

Actually, launches like the Minetts and the Ditchburns weren't designed to be particularly fast. Something in the 20 mph range was about average with original power, and putting in bigger engines wasn't really practical because the hulls weren't capable of handling the extra strain. What's more, these launches tend to lean away from a turn, rather than banking in with it. Everyone who toyed with the idea of more power and speed quickly rejected it under the assumption that the boat would roll over in a turn.

Vic Carpenter is a daredevil, however. *Era*, built with Carpenter's trademark lightness coupled with superior strength, could take the strain of a big engine, so why not give it a try? He installed a huge Chrysler engine. To everybody's surprise, the boat seemed to stabilize at higher speeds and leaned into the turn in the proper manner.

Nevertheless, there are nonbelievers out there still. Carpenter loves to make believers out of them cold turkey. He takes them for a ride, pushes the throttle wide open, mentions quietly that it's time to turn, and "watches them stiffen right up." Dramatic surprise is Vic's forte, his weapon against those who see him as a coarse interloper in a gentle society. And there are plenty who feel that way about him. A day or two later, one Canadian sniffed to me, "This Carpenter wants to be another Minett, but he never will be. He may build like Minett, but he doesn't have the *style* of Minett."

That may or may not be true. I wouldn't know. I do know that *Era* displays a level of technical excellence that probably cannot be surpassed by any other wooden boat builder alive today. You would be hard-pressed to find another boat with edge-glued planks that didn't have expansion or compression problems a week after it went into the water. If you found one, it would probably have been built by Carpenter. You would be hard-pressed to find a boat with a bright finish so deep, so durable, so invitingly soft that it almost begs you to take a half-gainer right into it. If you found one, the finish would probably have been applied by Hazel Carpenter.

As the day wore on, Vic seemed to mellow a bit, but not enough to make him boring. We stopped at one last boathouse, looked at one last wealthy collector's unbelievably vast stable of thoroughbred lake boats — "This here's an early Greavette, that's one of the finest Ditchburns you'll ever see. Damn, Pete, ignore that one; it's just a Chris-Craft for getting the groceries. How do you like this pulling boat?" — and took the long way home. No racing around, just a steady 15 or 20 mph, enough to get us there at a reasonable hour yet allow an opportunity to look at the scenery — rocky shore, fine forestland broken at intervals by cottage clearings, high Victorian boathouses, simple yet elegant estates.

I sat up forward in the mother-in-law seat. ("Perfect place for her. With the engine between, she can be seen but not heard.") The view was spectacular, yet I couldn't keep my eyes off the boat. Under the watchful gaze of Vic, I examined every element: the deck seams, the cockpit coaming, the deck fittings, even the stitching of the upholstery. The construction was flawless.

Back at the boathouse, I took one last look before the lights went out. "Some boat," said Vic. You bet.

The Boats of Autumn

October 5, 1985 — Tuckerton, New Jersey

I wasn't sure what to expect at the Old Time Barnegat Bay Decoy & Gunning Show. Even though preshow publicity made it clear that the one-day annual event was funded in part by the New Jersey State Council on the Arts, an institution that presumably puts its imprimatur only on culturally uplifting events, I was nevertheless prepared for a crowd of gun-toting, beer-swilling, truck-driving, hairy faced bird shooters who would merely be marking time while they waited for the bass season to close and the duck season to open.

Not necessarily so, though some of the pickup trucks in the lot at Tip Seaman Park, where the main part of the show was held, did little to dispel that notion. They had gun racks in the rear windows and dog cages in the back and bumper stickers proclaiming such truths as *Flamin' Harry's Harley-Davidson, Hot American Steel* and *A Bad Day of Fishing Is Still Better than a Good Day of Work.*

Sponsored by the Ocean County Department of Parks and Recreation, the Old Time Barnegat Bay Decoy & Gunning Show (hereinafter referred to as the

OTBBD&GS) was the duck hunter's version of the Wooden Boat Revival, which is to say that most of the participants and observers were doing their best to stave off the plastic and the unreal and replace it with the organic and the real. They were there to talk good old dogs and good old decoys, good old sneakboxes and a proper pair of waders, twelve gauges and ten gauges and the good old sixteens — and to strike a blow for conservation, which in essence meant saving the wetlands for duck hunting and rail shooting, and condominiums be damned.

Camouflage was virtually the uniform of the day. Hats, scarves, vests, jackets, pants, boots, gloves — even suspenders in at least one case. I felt out of place and a trifle bewildered, especially when a prototypical water-fowler hitched up his trousers and declared that the puppy retrieving contest would be starting soon. Not being a duck hunter, I wasn't sure what he meant. I had a fleeting vision of cute little baby dogs being thrown into the pond, and some of the local boys laying aside their cans of beer long enough to retrieve the pups before they drowned. It seemed just a tad cruel to me and I said so, but nobody paid any attention. They were too busy rounding up the dogs.

Dogs, ducks, and boats — these were the central themes of the OTBBD&GS. The boats were my primary interest, but to get to them, down on the edge of Lake Pohatcong, I had to pick my way through the dogs and the ducks.

Dogs! "Hey, Joe, where'd you get that pup?" "The contest will be open to all breeds of hunting dogs; however, the contest will be strictly judged on the dogs' ability to retrieve waterfowl." "Lookit Duke take off after that stick!" There were Chesapeake retrievers, golden retrievers, labradors, flat-coat and curly-coat retrievers, Irish water spaniels, all so high-strung and raring to go that if you lit your pipe and threw the match away you were liable to get it right back covered with dog drool.

Ducks? I didn't count them, but I would estimate there were somewhere between two and five thousand. There were full-sized ducks, miniature ducks, notecards depicting ducks, records of duck calls, books on duck identification and replication, half models of ducks, rough-carved ducks, smooth-carved ducks, antique duck decoys, brand-new duck decoys, decorative ducks, paintings of ducks, duck-carving kits, duck lamps, duck hats, duck T-shirts — you name it.

I didn't see any live ducks, even though they tell me there are, indeed, such creatures along the Jersey Shore. They're just difficult to find, which is where the dogs, decoys, and boats come into the deal. At the OTBBD&GS, there were two categories of counterfeit duck: (a) working decoys and (b) decorative carvings. All in all, I'd say that category *b* outscored category *a* in volume, but according to Mike Mangum, the show director, the contests and awards were set up to encourage working decoys only. The decorative carvings were tolerated but were not allowed to get in the way of the working nature of the show. (So, too, for the dogs. You could bring your AKC Grand Champion black labrador, but if he couldn't retrieve a stick, forget it.)

The working decoys fell into three categories: wood, cork, and plastic. In this show, run and attended by traditionalists, wood was the more desirable, plastic the least, and cork okay if you didn't mind being accused of compromise. I don't recall having met anyone who admitted to using plastic decoys for anything other than a whipping post. Only wooden decoys could be entered into competition according to the contest rules. The various decoy competitions all had to do with fooling the eye of the beholder — that is to say, a live duck. The judges were human, however, and they were looking for decoys that were realistic without falling into that nether world of being merely decorative (nonfunctional decoration to traditional duck hunters is anathema), that fit into the so-called Barnegat Bay substyle as opposed to those favored in the Chesapeake and elsewhere, and that when set in the water would be self-righting (no mean feat) and would display the balance characteristics of a live duck.

The boats were significantly outnumbered by the dogs and the ducks, but they attracted at least as much attention, perhaps even more. There was a time when the Barnegat Bay area was rotten with duckboats and duckboat builders, but the outlawing of market gunning (the wholesale shooting of wild ducks for commercial gain), the development of the marshlands, and the changing habits of the sport gunners sent them into a decline from which they were never expected to recover. Until recently, the duckboat-as-petunia-planter was more common than the duckboat-as-duckboat along the Jersey Shore. But recent developments have produced a gradual change — not a revolution, you understand, but at least a shift in attitude about duck hunting and the equipment used to make it possible.

The impetus came from the traditionalists, the people responsible for the popularity of the OTBBD&GS itself. They appreciate duck hunting as ritual, as a sport slightly more refined than filling the sky with lead and hoping something edible will fall into their laps. They hearken back to the days when hunters did more than march across the wetlands (*meadows* to the hard-core duckers) and take up position in a blind, but took to the creeks and ditches in boats that were camouflaged to fit into the environment. The boats were a central part of the experience.

Of course, there's a class of hunter that feels any old boat will do. Fiberglass canoe, aluminum utility boat, outboard skiff, that type of thing. But the aficionado knows that a genuine duckboat is the best, and down on Barnegat Bay the duckboat of choice is the Barnegat sneakbox.

What's more, wooden sneakboxes are generally favored over fiberglass reproductions because they are quieter. After all, the operative condition is sneaking up on waterfowl; wood deadens sound while fiberglass amplifies it.

According to just about every sneakbox historian, the first Barnegat Bay sneakbox was designed and built in 1836 by Hazelton Seaman at West Creek, New Jersey, just down the road from Tuckerton, site of the OTBBD&GS. The boat sat so low in the water and was of such a strange, almost unnatural, shape that it came to be known as the devil's coffin long before it was given its current name. Favored by market gunners, the sneakbox was used almost exclusively for hunting waterfowl until the mid- to late nineteenth century, when it was discovered by small-boat sailors, who adapted it for cruising and racing. Perhaps the man most responsible for the sneakbox's "discovery" was Nathaniel Bishop, who took one on a voyage down the Ohio and Mississippi rivers from Pittsburgh to the Gulf of Mexico and wrote about it in *Four Months in a Sneakbox*, published in 1879. Other small-craft enthusiasts whose names became synonymous with sneakboxes were W. P. Stephens and J. Henry Rushton.

The yachting sneakbox and the gunner's version are two different boats, however. While the former evolved until its final form only slightly resembled the original, the latter remained relatively static. You have to have a sharp eye for detail to spot the differences between the earlier and the later gunning sneakboxes.

The Barnegat Bay sneakbox has the distinctive shape peculiar to boats developed for a highly specialized use. Intended for a lone gunner and his decoys, it has room for little else. Designed for travel in protected creeks and coves, it is not very seaworthy. Outfitted for versatile propulsion, it can be rowed, poled, paddled, pushed, pulled, sailed, and even driven by a small outboard motor. Capable of being handled by one man, it is light yet strong.

Every peculiar element of the sneakbox is there for a

reason. The spoon bow allows it to be pulled up onto a mudbank. The decking and canvas spray hood provide protection from the elements. The daggerboard and shallow rudder permit shoal-water navigation. The temporary washboards on the afterdeck provide stowage space for the decoys. The fold-down oarlocks allow the hunter room to swing his gun. The runners on the bottom facilitate dragging the boat across ice. The extremely low freeboard makes the boat easy to conceal in the marsh.

Traditional sneakbox construction hasn't changed appreciably since its inception. The hull is carvel planked over sawn frames, which also serve as the molds. The deckbeams are heavily crowned, and the point where the deck meets the bottom is at an acute angle, which produces the traditional feather edge. There have been non-feather-edged sneakboxes built, but few people acknowledge them to be the real thing.

Most sneakboxes today are rowed (with the rower facing forward) or driven by outboard motor out to the hunting grounds. The bow of the boat is pulled up onto the creek bank, the spray hood rigged for protection, the decks camouflaged with marsh grass, and the decoys deployed into the creek. The hunter lies low in the cockpit, ready for the action to begin.

About a dozen or so Barnegat Bay sneakboxes were on display at the OTBBD&GS. All of them to a greater or lesser degree contained the elements of the classical sneakbox, which meant that they were almost universally admired. Yes, one of the boats was strip-planked rather than carvel, and another carried a sailing rig straight out of a Sunfish, but Hazelton Seaman and Nathaniel Bishop and W. P. Stephens, if they were alive today, would recognize them instantly for what they are — not Delaware duckers, or Little Egg Harbor melonseeds, or even yachtified sneakboxes, but the genuine articles, as useful today as they were 150 years ago.

Trimaran Jim

Jim Brown — tall, a little on the gaunt side, dynamic, animated — lives in a tiny town in tidewater Virginia called North, tucked away out of sight and mind between the Rappahannock and York rivers. It's not the easiest place for a stranger to find. ("You say you're trying to get to North Virginia, sonny? Let's see now. This here's sort of southeastern Virginia, so the way I figure it, if you tend toward the northwest you should come to it sooner or later.") He and his wife Jo Anna call home the back third of a converted tin chicken house; the front two-thirds is a workshop/boatshed/garage/design studio. The house sits on a little point in a tidal river that empties into the Chesapeake, about five miles away. On one side of the point lies a trimaran pulled up out of the way of the minuscule tides; on the other is the hardscrabble home of a hardscrabble Baptist minister. A ramshackle pier falters out into the shallow river.

In the river, framed by the kitchen window, is a brand-new catamaran, shining in the morning light. Designed by Jim Brown using the Constant Camber process, it is one of three sisters that will be working, not cruising, for a

205

living. This one, the *Anna Kay*, is being fitted out for carrying day-passengers out of a Caribbean island hotel. Brown is as proud of this boat as he is of anything he has done. Inexpensive and relatively simple to build, cheap to maintain, home to a man and his wife, the platform of their living and their way of life, the *Anna Kay* is the embodiment of everything Jim Brown has tried to achieve. He can't keep his eyes off her as we talk.

Brown is reminiscing about Sausalito, California, as it was in the late 1950s. A magical place just across the Golden Gate from San Francisco, it had become a magnet for beatniks and poets, artists and drifters, winos and welders, iconoclasts, experimentalists, boat freaks — a cross-cultural soup in which the bizarre was the norm and the straight was the exception.

"It was, in the words from that wonderful old cabaret song," says Brown, 'The Greatest Place on Earth.' "

Brown was living in the old shipyard at Gate 5, down on the docks among derelict vessels and crumbling warehouses, surrounded by all sorts of debris left over from the frantic shipbuilding days of World War II. It was beatnik time, the ten-year or so warm-up for the soon-to-explode West Coast hippie scene, and people were coming over from San Francisco looking for cheap places to live. That is to say, they were taking up residence in anything that separated the outside atmosphere from the inside. Brown, for example, called home a shed he had built on a war-surplus landing craft.

"One of my neighbors," says Brown, "lived in a little tool shack out on the dock with his wife. He and I used to gab over coffee in the morning, and we developed a special little discipline, what you could call a 'can you top this?' game. He would tell me outlandish biographical yarns and I would reciprocate. Neither one would believe the other. One day I told him about a trimaran that a friend and I had built in 1957 out of welded-together oil drums in Colombia. And he said, 'Aw shucks, I've got a better one than that. We've got a guy in the next town who's building trimarans out of plywood boxes and masts out of TV antennas!' I said, 'Oh, bullshit!'

"One day I was downtown in Sausalito standing on the dock and here around the end of the dock came this contraption, a very strange, spidery looking sailing vessel, wafting around in the light airs. Someone hailed the skipper. 'Hey Art, is that the new one?' 'Yeah, it's the new one. I built her for two hundred bucks. If you don't like the color, too bad. I call it vomit yellow, left over from my garage.'

"I was standing there agape," says Brown, "looking at this thing and looking at this guy with beady little eyes, glasses, semibalding head. He hopped around his boat like a cat. There was nothing much in the way of wind until a little catspaw came along and grabbed the boat and the thing went ffuuuuuuffff out across the bay, leaving the impression of throwing a paper cup, and I just couldn't believe my eyes.

"What was that? Who was that?"

The what was a modern trimaran, an aberration so new to the western world that few people knew what to call it. The who was Arthur Piver, an eccentric yacht designer whose schemes were so outrageously left-field that if he were a medical doctor he would have been branded a quack, stripped of his license, and thrown out of the AMA. Piver and trimarans. Jim Brown, who never had any problems with iconoclasm, was hooked.

Brown looked up Piver a couple of days later and talked his way aboard Piver's sixteen-foot tri *Frolic* for a sail. "In a literal sense," he says, "my first ride quite simply blew me away. I was absolutely spellbound by the sensation of having greater power than expected generated by the sail plan, because wind could not be dumped out of the top of the sail. At the same time, the power was located over a vehicle that appeared to offer zero resistance to that power. The combination was very heady stuff to me.

"This multihull thing just woke me up. I started the next day to build one of my own."

To that point in his life, Jim Brown had been a dropped-out drifter — a shiftless knockabout who couldn't seem to get a handle on what to do with himself. The son of an FBI special agent, he was born in Chicago in 1933 and moved to New York in 1938, attending prep school in Connecticut and sailing summers on Long Island. He went to Dartmouth College briefly and quit, then college in Miami briefly and quit.

"For various reasons, I had become disenamored with formal education," he says. "I just got myself a job on a boat, and it's been boat, boat, boat ever since. It wasn't really a conscious decision that I made. It was simply that I was doing what I was doing because I had failed at everything else. It was almost like the watermelon seed getting squeezed on both sides and finally squirting out into an area where it was free to move."

Brown became a boat bum, a condition that may be typical today but was so atypical in the 1950s as to put him on the fringes of society. He went to work for Mike Burke, who had just established his pioneer windjammer cruise service in the Caribbean by buying up old sailing vessels and patching them together and taking paying passengers on so-called "barefoot" cruises among the islands.

"I was Burke's first American employee," says Brown. "Most of the crews were Bahamians. It was definitely a hard-knocks type of experience — Burke was a real scoundrel and was responsible for ruining some fine old yachts — but I learned a lot and came to understand the power of sail."

He probably would have continued in that vein, crewing for anyone in anything that wasn't staying in one place too long, except he met and became friends with a young man with a vision, a fellow named Wolfgang Crocker Von Schwartzenfeld, who was a survivor of an aristocratic German family that had been decimated by the Nazis. After the war Wolfgang felt that there must be something else besides the misery of postwar Germany. He decided he would go to sea, even though coming from Bavaria he had never seen the sea. He made his way to Rotterdam, where he made friends with an old man, a machine-shop operator. There the two of them built a boat that Wolfie designed, a twenty-four-foot pipe-framed, sheet-metal-planked catamaran.

Wolfgang Crocker Von Schwartzenfeld, the man who had never seen the sea, sailed his lashed-together little boat down the Rhine River and out into the English Channel and eventually made his way to Miami, where he met Jim Brown.

"Wolfie and I sailed together on Burke's boats," says Brown, "then we left together. He was good with a camera and I was thinking about writing, and both of us shared a fascination with island culture. My first exposure to an isolated island was back in my early days in the Caribbean when I visited Providence Island between Honduras and Jamaica. We only stopped there for a couple of days, but there were a few things that happened at the time that were formative to me and helped to seat the cruising experience. I realized that different languages and different cultures really represent different levels of consciousness and that there's often a great gulf between those levels. I wanted to bridge that gulf.

"Wolfie and I had a plan — we wanted to build a boat together and then sail down into the Caribbean Sea and photograph and write about what we saw. To get started, Wolfie was to sail back to Germany with the film footage he had taken on his voyage and sell it to German television. My mission was to go out to California and learn everything I could about the emerging fiberglass technology. Fiberglass was the latest thing then, and what we had seen of it we liked. Unfortunately it was a plan that never came together. Wolfie sailed to Germany in another catamaran — this one built of airplane wing tanks — and I went to California, but we lost touch with each other. Yet even though I never saw him again, Wolfie left me with something I hadn't had to that point: a goal."

Jim Brown found his way to California, where he learned that there was a new company in Sausalito, Coleman Boat and Plastics, that was one of the pioneers in developing the technology to build large boats in fiberglass. Small fiberglass craft were regularly being built, but not large ones because nobody had yet figured out how.

"This place turned out to be great for anyone who liked to experiment," says Brown. "All we had to go on were a bunch of shop manuals from England, some of which were barely legible, but we had money and we had time and we were given a free hand. Ted Coleman, the owner, had the wisdom to let anyone, even if he was a grunt worker like me, who had an idea to try it out. You could be turned loose with several thousand dollars worth of material to try an experiment and see the results directly. It turned out to be a marvelous education, which, of course, was what I had been looking for.

"One major thing I learned was that you could mold a part in two halves and then join it together along the centerline. I saw that technique work on a fiberglass forty-footer in 1958 and figured it would work with theoretical trimarans five years later. Twenty-five years later we would use the same principle for our Constant Camber wooden boat building method.

"Another thing I learned from working at Coleman's was to appreciate the framelessness of fiberglass boats. I figured this framelessness would be a good thing if it could be translated to wooden boats. It took us a long time and a lot of money to figure out how to do it and be economical at the same time, but we eventually did."

It was Jim Brown's chance encounter with Arthur Piver in 1958 that changed the direction of his life. Piver at the time was forty-eight years old, Brown twenty-four, and their differences in age, experience, and knowledge led to the prototypical mentor-protégé relationship.

Piver was a publisher in his business life and a boat hacker in his private life. He was a doodler, backyard tinkerer, with none of the inhibitions of the professional designer. Piver designed trimarans the way the old-style wildcatters drilled for oil. You had a hunch, you tested out the hunch, you chucked it if it turned out to be a dead end, you pursued it to the next stage if it didn't. If Piver came up with a new idea, he didn't hesitate to try it out. If trying it out meant building a boat in the garage over the weekend, to be thrown away and replaced the next weekend by an improved version, so be it. Jim Brown was charmed from the start by an attitude such as that and became Piver's disciple, joining a small group of enthusiasts centered on the man who would come to be known as the "Father of the Modern Trimaran."

"Art was without sons," says Brown, "and the nature of our relationship with him — mine and the few others in the group — was like father and son. We followed the old man's lead — once you shoved off, you could act any way you wanted and nobody cared. One minute we'd be sailing along lickety-split and the next minute the boat would self-destruct in five places. We were towed in week after week and would go home and build a new boat for the next weekend. We built them out of crab crates and packing plywood — anything to get out on the water and try again."

For all of the fun and dynamics of experimentation,

however, Brown had not forgotten the promise he had made to himself and his friend Wolfie — that he would build a boat and roam the Caribbean. "I had lost contact with Wolfie," says Brown, "but figured I better go ahead and build my own boat anyway, so I went to Arthur Piver and said I wanted to build something like the sixteen-foot *Frolic* but I wanted to go to sea in it. He thought about it for a while, assessing the idea, and said, 'You know what you're doing, I guess you could do it, I guess you could take it anywhere.' He was cautious, you see, because nobody at that time, including him, had ever taken a modern trimaran offshore. All our multihull sailing had taken place in San Francisco Bay. He pulled out the drawings he'd been working on for a twenty-four-footer and gave them to me. Instead of a design for two sheets of plywood, it was for three. We were moving up. I started building the boat.

"At that time I met Jo Anna, who became my wife, and it didn't take long for us to decide we were going to take this trip together. I was going back to the Caribbean! So we shoved off from Sausalito in this little collection of plywood and glue and headed down the western seaboard to Mexico. We didn't get very far. We ran out of money and Jo Anna was pregnant and we ran into the chubasko season — violent Mexican squalls — so we came back. It wasn't much of a voyage, but we were able to demonstrate that the boat was capable of contending with the open sea. It opened up a new era in trimaran development. The next year Arthur Piver sailed to England in a thirty-footer and the year after that he went to Australia in a thirty-five-footer.

"We returned from the voyage and I was an instant expert. No one had ever done anything like that. I was able to describe the surfing phenomenon, for example. And I was able to say yes, the boats really can go to windward in open-sea conditions, and yes you can really keep them from capsizing by using your common sense, and yes you can beach the boats in an emergency."

The Great Let's-Build-A-Boat-In-The-Backyard Cruising Trimaran Scramble and Soft Shoe Shuffle began. All sorts of people, mostly inexperienced in both sailing and boatbuilding, were turned on by the idea that you could whip up a cheap boat in the backyard in no time at all and sail off to Paradise.

"Those of us who were trimaran enthusiasts," says Brown, "had found something not only to believe in, but also something to identify ourselves with. These boats were so different that they offered a distinctiveness that was normally unapproachable in an organized society. It was very hard even in California, where you could find anything, to find something as different as a multihull sailboat. Up to then there had been none. So the boats served very well for identifying oneself as an individual. It was very seductive to be able to say, 'I am a multihull man.'

"Piver realized that there was money to be made in the trimaran business," says Brown. "It didn't take long before people started pounding on his door with money in their hands. I wouldn't be surprised to learn that during the five-year period between 1960 and 1965, his yacht design business was more lucrative than any other designer in history. We all discovered that if you had plans for sale for boats that could be built in your backyard for the price of an ordinary automobile, the world would be your oyster."

But there were minuses to go along with the pluses. For every successful trimaran built from Arthur Piver's plans, there was a disastrous one. "Piver's boats were really responsible for both the negative and positive aspects that the multihull image still carries," says Brown. "Both were well earned. The negative aspects were obvious: the plans were not sufficiently complete to avoid requiring a builder to improvise, and the improvisations were often discordant with the sea."

For all that, Jim Brown was a full-fledged trimaran convert, a monohull sailor who had seen the light. He soon became a trimaran designer himself, creating boats that were improvements on the Piver designs. "I started out designing boats for myself somewhere around 1961-1962," he says. "After building several Piver boats, I decided that I wanted to do things a little differently. I was frustrated by not being able to have it the way I wanted it. I had no training, never even took a course in mechanical drawing; I simply had a good feeling for physics and plenty of sea time. I read a lot and became fairly well conversant with the technical and semitechnical aspects of yacht design. Soon I was designing boats for friends and then for clients."

There were those who were looking to multihulls solely for speed, but Brown was looking for that and more. He designed a series of boats he called Searunner Trimarans, their principal market the disaffected landsmen of the 1960s who would escape the madness by "seasteading" instead of homesteading.

The key to the Searunners, the element that made them different from other trimarans designed to date, was the matter of comfortable cruising accommodations and good windward ability. "It was the windward aspect that was so hard for us to achieve," says Brown. "The early Piver trimarans had centerboards, but due to pressure from the buying public, it was decided to remove the centerboard trunk to relieve that constriction on the accommodations. We tried all sorts of devices — fixed skegs, keels, and other contraptions — to keep the boat from sliding off to windward. My own solution was to revert back to the centerboard — indeed, a giant centerboard — and locate the cockpit over the centerboard trunk dead amidships and put the cabins at each end of the boat. With two cabins separated by a cockpit, we had a situation that allowed people to get away from each other on a long cruise. That turned out to be a very popular aspect of the Searunner for family cruising. We had a family cruiser that would actually sail to windward."

The Searunner plans were more detailed than Piver's had been; later, when Brown became more established, he published a full-fledged construction manual that explained step by step the whys, the hows, and the wheres of building your tri and sailing off to Paradise. The ineluctable pitch? Ease of construction, comfortable accommodations, self-sufficiency at sea. Plywood, glue, and fiberglass.

Piver, of course, felt as if his territory had been impinged upon by an upstart protégé. As soon as Brown drew his first independent line on a sheet of drafting paper, a schism developed between the two men, never to be repaired. Yet when Arthur Piver went missing in one of his tris off the coast of California in 1968, Jim Brown was one of his principal mourners.

We take a break and row out to the *Anna Kay* with her owner, Fred Yeats. Almost as wide as she is long, the catamaran is steadier than the pier that we departed from. Clichés leap to mind: the Rock of Gilbralter, the Catholic Church, Boston Garden. A monohull sailor, I walk from the deck edge of one hull to its opposite on the other hull and marvel when nothing happens. Is this a boat or a dance platform set on granite posts?

Brown and Yeats and I clamber through the living spaces, bounce on the trampoline net stretched between the hulls, examine the fittings. Then we sit in the cockpit and watch the ducks and the geese fly overhead while we talk about multihull cruising and construction.

Prosperity struck Jim Brown, but by the end of the 1960s he was getting tired of watching other people buy his trimaran plans, build their boats, and sail off into the sea of their dreams. He wanted to take his family cruising for a year or two, explore both coasts of Central America, so he built his own Searunner, *Scrimshaw*, and arranged for others to run his stock-plans business while he was gone. Many people thought he was nuts.

"We had a great setup," he says. "Wonderful friends, two neat kids that were growing up, this nifty boat down in the harbor, and we were living in a huge house. We were telling everybody that we were getting ready to leave. 'What do you mean, you're getting ready to leave?' they asked. 'Stick around. What's wrong with this?' "

There wasn't anything wrong with it, really. But Brown still carried around the idea in his head that there was a need for people with hyperawareness to bridge the gap between diverse cultures. (He winces as he realizes how corny that sounds. I wince now as I write it, yet who would be so callous as to suggest it is not a noble endeavor?)

"I tend to agree with Buckminster Fuller, who once said that the principal reason for his being in the universe was to be an information gatherer," Brown says. "The information we need to gather on this planet at this time is that which allows the existence of pluralistic societies, and it can be gathered by travel. The best way to travel is by cruising boat, because long-distance cruising makes one very aware that the world's cultures are separated by both time and distance.

"Sailing offshore can be very disorienting, but it is that very disorientation that allows you to arrive in the next port, in a completely different culture from the one you left, with a very highly tuned antenna, a recipient of information. Picture yourself out there in the middle of the ocean. Let's say the sun is so bright that it is beating down on you. You've got yourself covered up with dark glasses and sun cream. You're out there being fried. Then the night comes and, Holy God, all of a sudden you can see into the universe. You can take your dark glasses off. You can live on deck without being broiled, and you can look into the sky and realize that some of the brightest stars are actually farther away than some of the dimmer ones. The night becomes the period of life; the day becomes the period of void. That's when you begin to realize that you have been going around all your life hiding under a roof in the dark. When you finally reach the next port, you're a different person, more aware of what is going on around you and therefore a superior gatherer of information. You are prepared to cross that gulf between cultures, much more so than you would ever have been if you had simply climbed aboard an airplane and been lifted to your destination in a couple of hours."

The Browns' voyage, originally planned to be not much more than a year, stretched out to three. Baja California, Mexico, Guatemala, Colombia, the Caribbean islands, Belize, Yucatan. . . all the places of their dreams and more, all the opportunities to test their theories of cross-cultural exchange and more.

"By this time we were lost souls," says Brown. "We went from the Yucatan to Miami and then — bango! — right into the southern Florida scene. Condominiums on both sides of the waterway, what amounts to flooded parking lots with boats in them. We had just come from this three-year immersion in an area where everything that would float was in constant service, and the boats were implements to the people, and our boat was an implement to us, and all of a sudden, here we were. . . I have to confess that I was really disgusted with it."

Jim Brown hadn't gone native, so to speak, but he had certainly come to see the strengths and weaknesses of the places he had visited, and what he had learned helped put the American Dream in perspective. You could say that he didn't want anything more to do with it, but at the same time he had certain responsibilities. His children's formal education, for example.

Through a process of elimination and an element of chance, he settled in North, Virginia. The Jim Brown with the big house in California had turned into the Jim Brown who lived in the converted chicken shed. ("The farmer who had owned the place got tired of keeping chickens one day and simply locked the door and walked off. Before we could do anything, we had to sweep out the thousands of chicken skeletons.")

Jim Brown, more than most people, seems to live a life ruled by fortuitous circumstance, helped along by aggressive curiosity. He may have been turned off by wasteful American consumerism, but he wasn't one to wring his hands and complain and give up. He wasn't sure what he was going to do, but he would start out by casting his net and seeing what it brought up.

He started talking with Dick Newick, the noted racing multihull designer, and Phil Weld, a wealthy New Englander "of family" who had a passion for multihulls. (Weld eventually became the first American to win the Singlehanded Transatlantic Race.)

"As it turned out," says Brown, "Newick and I had a lot in common. I was pleased to find out that he wasn't purely racing oriented, and he was pleased to find out that I wasn't purely cruising oriented.

"Dick and I were talking with each other one day in the presence of Phil about this Third World angle, about how we both wished we could somehow apply what we had learned through long-term exposure to these developmental boats. We wanted to apply our knowledge to boats that were good for something besides just cruising around or blinding speed in a race. We started talking about designing a theoretical boat for a theoretical guy who might live in a Third World village. He might use it to go fishing. He wouldn't have to spend maybe half of his income on paying off a loan on his motor or for buying fuel. We knocked the concept around a bit. We were talking about what the boat itself might look like, maybe what it would be built of. Phil Weld sat there the whole time taking it all in.

"The following week we each got a letter from Phil Weld. It was a design commission. 'What can you show me?' he asked. The next thing we knew we were building a boat.

"Just previous to that, I was sitting in what I called my office, a little shack down by the dock. Dave Dana, a friend of mine, came by and we were talking boats as usual. I said that I had been thinking about trying out a new concept — building a mold that could be used for several different hull designs. Just give it a stock curve in one direction and a stock curve in the other, making the mold the same constant curvature over the entire surface, which would mean we wouldn't have to spile individual planks. Each could be the same as the next. Dave Dana just sat there for a while and finally said, 'That'll work.' "

Constant Camber. Jim Brown came up to the Wooden Boat School in the summer of 1985 to teach a course on how to design and build boats using the patented Constant Camber system. Sure, I had read all about it, and sure, it had seemed like a novel idea, but I never did quite grasp the significance of the development until I watched Brown and his students build a cold-molded boat hull, without spiling each plank, in a couple of days.

Now, Jim Brown takes me into the little design studio tucked into a corner of his garage and shows me the plans he is working on for cold-molded Constant Camber houses. Build your house with preformed wooden panels, each panel of two layers separated by honeycomb insulation. Bolt your house together in a day!

During the period when Jim Brown was working on the Constant Camber/Third World project, he joined Phil

Weld on his trimaran *Rogue Wave* in the Caribbean for an ocean race. Also along was Mead Gougeon of Gougeon Brothers, developers of a cold-molded boatbuilding method, and Keith Taylor, editor of *Sail* magazine. All during the race, Weld, Gougeon, and Brown talked endlessly about the project — about building a modern boat at a reasonable cost that would be functional for workboat applications and very energy efficient.

"Keith Taylor listened to us go on and on," says Brown, "and in an article he later wrote for *Sail* on the race, he stuck in a paragraph about this thing we were building in a chicken coop in Virginia and had been talking about all during the race. Not more than a week after the article came out, somebody at the World Bank who occasionally picks up a copy of *Sail* magazine called me up and said, 'Hey, we're having some problems with our boats in Africa. Maybe you'd like to come and have a look.' The next thing I knew, I was in Africa. Pow! Just like that."

The problem in Burundi was simple — the fishermen on Lake Tanganyika needed boats appropriate to their needs and weren't getting them. Their government and the World Bank were trying to help. The fishing boats that had been introduced after World War II were planked-up dories, but they had reached the end of their useful life and the available wood to build them with was totally inappropriate. Steel boats with outboard motors had been tried, but they were too unwieldy for the type of fishing being done and operating expenses were too high.

This was cross-cultural exchange at its operational level. "I had just come from this Constant Camber experimental stuff," says Brown, "and I started telling Jose Schrudder, the leader of the project, about the concept and I'll be damned if he didn't get interested. The next thing I knew, Schrudder got in a meeting with the Burundi government and World Bank people and said, 'All right, if fiberglass is too expensive, I think we ought to build using

220

Jim's Constant Camber method.' "

The beauty of Constant Camber, of course, is that poor-quality wood works as well as high-grade material. Brown designed a fishing canoe, helped set up a boatshop, and taught the Burundi fishermen how to build boats that were cheap, energy efficient, and — most important — appropriate to the needs of the fishery. At last count there were 160 Constant Camber catamaran fishing canoes at work on Lake Tanganyika.

"The benefits?" asks Brown. "They would never have dreamed up Constant Camber in Burundi under the circumstances, and I would never have dreamed up the Burundi canoe unless I had gone there to see for myself the fishing tactics they used, and they would never have been able to build the boat I designed unless I went there to show them. I had something to offer, but I really think I benefited at least as much as they did. What this world really needs are exchanges like that so diverse societies can come to tolerate each other out of respect.

"Some of the things I have learned about multihulls beyond what I gained from sea experience have come from immersing myself in these cultures. Monohull vessels, for example, evolved from workboats, and for that reason they have a lot of common sense in their genes. Modern multihulls evolved from nothing. We really didn't study Polynesian and Micronesian naval architecture before developing the modern tris and cats, and consequently there are many aspects of the boats that make no sense. I think what is happening right now is that there's some hydrostatic adjustment happening here. We've got the workboat aspect entering into multihull design, and I think that's where the future exists for this type of vessel. The main reason is that they are so tremendously energy efficient.

"I have a great respect for the primitive naval architect; he knows a hell of a lot more than I ever will. I have a very high regard for the development of some of the vessels I have worked to replace. I did that only because the local people couldn't replace them themselves. The reason they can't is because the environment has changed, the logs are no longer available, the fish are farther away, the fishing tradition is changing, the young people don't want to follow the water. If technology doesn't have an answer for their plight, I don't know what does. Yet saying that, I know that technology alone doesn't have the answer."

That was only the beginning. Since the Burundi project, Jim Brown has traveled to such far-off places as the Philippines and Polynesia, living with the fishermen for as long as it takes to teach them the technology appropriate to their needs and to learn from them the techniques and attitudes relevant to his work.

Just before I leave, Jim Brown shows me a slide show based on his travels around the world. There are the usual all-stops-pulled-out color shots of trimarans silhouetted against swaying palms and mauve sunsets, ecstatic sailors running with the tradewinds in tropical seas, family and friends gathered around yet another boat being launched yet another time. But the bulk of the selection are of boatbuilding projects on the shores of Lake Tanganyika, the Philippines, Funifuci in the island nation of Tuvalu. The photographs in which Brown appears show a man who is supremely happy, who is doing exactly what he wants to be doing, regardless of the primitive conditions. Certainly the natives have seen their share of ugly Americans, but clearly this is not one of them.

"I've noticed," says Brown, "that a great deal of the development work that's going on is ineffective, particularly the well-funded, big-deal projects. The ones that are truly effective are the small ones done by private individuals. Little things. It doesn't take much. I think that a lot of money nowadays is going into the creation of exquisite

222

yachts or restorations of exquisite yachts, that the people who are financing those ventures would find themselves more fulfilled by becoming more involved themselves in Third World development work. There's plenty of development work to be done in boats. It's wide open, and it's real sailing, not aimless cruising for the sake of aimless cruising.

"Me, that's the sort of thing I'm hoping to do. I'm putting my boat back together so I can make another go at it. I just want to blow in someplace from out of the sea and say, 'Hey, are you guys having trouble with this? I've got a little polysulphide compound in a tube right here. Let's try this on your dugout and see if it'll work.' "

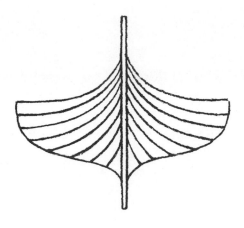

Ten Years After

Time it was,
and what a time it was,
It was . . .
A time of innocence,
A time of confidences.

"Bookends Theme," ©1967, 1968, Paul Simon, Charing Cross Music (BMI)

It was the winter of 1974, a strange time indeed. I was living in Camden, Maine, and it was there that my partner George Putz and I were meeting with a couple of pillars of the local publishing industry to discuss the putative contents of the upcoming third *Mariner's Catalog* — our eccentric annual publication that mirrored the anything-goes attitude of the late 1960s, early 1970s. One or the other of the pillars would say, "Of course, you'll be including extensive coverage of so-and-so," and the pillar who hadn't spoken would nod his head in agreeable acknowledgment, and George would give a short speech about how important that very topic seemed to be and naturally, Pete and I were on the case, and I'd write it down on my list of things to do. Naturally, we would never

225

do it. We were children of the social revolution, and we would damn well do what we damn well pleased, pillars of the publishing industry notwithstanding.

Mavericks we may have seemed, but secretly we husbanded the self-flattering concept that we were Somebodies, that we had Arrived (weren't we the toasts of the boat freaks for having made our eccentric little publication so successfully eccentric?), so when somebody at the meeting mentioned that rumor had it that some scraggle-headed long-haired teepee-dweller Down East from here was going to sell his boat and hock his tire jack so he could start a magazine about wooden boats, we joined in the self-satisfied laughter. I can't remember exactly what I said that day, but knowing me, I'm sure it was something like, "He better pray he never gets a flat, because he's not likely to see that tire jack again." I wasn't alone. Anyone with a brain in his head knew that the wooden boat industry, even here in Maine, was on the road to rapid ruin, was for all intents and purposes dead.

Putz and I gathered up our pencils and our lists of things we weren't going to do, patted each other in earnest self-congratulation for being so prescient and so very witty, and repaired to the nearest saloon.

The teepee dweller's name was Jonathan Wilson. I didn't know much about him. He had written an article on boatbuilding tools for the second *Mariner's Catalog*; the book on him said he was from Rhode Island, repaired boats at Hurricane Island Outward Bound School one winter, set up shop and built a boat Down East in Pembroke another winter, was no more or no less flaky than any other of the dropouts who had flocked back to the land as part of the latter-day homesteading movement and who could be found in the nooks and crannies of Maine — growing leeks and eating bean sprouts, building domes, yurts, lean-tos, shed-roofed, pole-framed outbuildings, what have you, and living lives that they called *alternative* and the natives called *hedonistic* when they were being polite.

A strange time, indeed. Camden, of all places, had a head shop called Le Drugstore, nearby Rockland had a natural-grains food shop that in no way resembled the Agway feed store, and Belfast looked like a Mennonite revival camp on Saturdays when the homesteaders came in from Brooks and Freedom and Unity to pick up a fresh supply of papers and Red Zinger tea. So if a guy said he was going to publish a magazine on wooden boats even though the odds of success were so long that Jimmy the Greek would have to use a Univac to calculate them, even though he wasn't a pillar of the publishing community, even though he was such a babe in the woods he didn't know a linotype machine from a blueberry rake — what the hell. He wasn't any crazier than anyone else those days, and look what was going on! A guy over in Blue Hill who didn't know much more than Wilson did had founded *Farmstead Magazine*. A bunch of back-to-the-landers had founded the Maine Organic Farmers and Gardeners Alliance. An ex-Outward Bound jock had started the Apprenticeshop at the Maine Maritime Museum. They all should have been doomed, but they weren't.

So time passed. The rumor mill cranked awhile — the magazine was off, the magazine was on, it was going to be a newsletter, no, it was to be a magazine — and then fell silent. Came the fall, however, and a friend passed through town after visiting the Newport Sailboat Show. He had in his hand a present: Volume 1, Number 1, of this thing called *The WoodenBoat*, the definite article seeming to indicate that there was more than one of them and this was the only authentic one. I enjoyed it thoroughly, even though I didn't think much of the ideology of wood (I took my boats any way I could get them) and as an editor I was appalled by the typographical errors (I was always ready to recognize others' but to forget my own). I read it cover to cover, then filed it carefully away in the bottom drawer of my desk. I ignored the full-page exhortation: "Recycle *The WoodenBoat*. If you don't want to keep it, give it to a friend. If you don't have a friend, let us know. We'll find you one." I figured only a few hundred copies at the most would see circulation, and the rest, unsold, would have to be buried in the Hampden landfill or dumped at sea some moonless night off Matinicus. What I had would be a collector's item, surely to be worth a buck and a half at a flea market two or three years hence.

The rumor mill cranked some more. It was a success, it was a failure, the bills were unpaid, not so — a second issue was in the works. Wilson was publishing the magazine out of a one-room cabin he built in the woods over in Brooksville, a town on the other side of Penobscot Bay that was so obscure not even the natives on my side had been there. The word was that conditions were so primitive he didn't even have a telephone, later revealed in *WB* No. 3 to be a half-truth. He had a phone, but not in the house. It was half a mile away nailed to a tree because he couldn't afford to have the phone lines brought in.

I think it w the telephone that captured my imagination at first, nc the magazine. Here I was, working for a pillar of the nautical book publishing community on the second floor of a three-story building, with phone lines in and phone lines out, a secretary to answer them, wall-to-wall carpeting on the floor and a coffee-maker down the hall, and actually coming home to the little lady at night and telling her what a rough time I had at the office today, dear. There Jonathan Wilson was, trudging through the knee-high snow to answer the phone, never knowing whether the fellow on the other end of the line would be a potential subscriber willing to pay up front for a magazine that could very well fold tomorrow, or a bill collector threatening to throttle him if he didn't pay up now (" . . . and don't tell me the check is in the mail; I've heard that before"). What pluck, what gumption, what grit . . . .

What foolhardiness. Everybody knew you couldn't publish a magazine that way. You needed capital, a central location, an office building, UPS service, skilled help, an IBM typewriter, knowledge. Knowledge? I heard that Wilson knew how to drive caulking into plank seams but didn't know how to punctuate a compound sentence. I reflected on how long it took me to figure out what a compound sentence was with people willing to explain it to me, and here was a guy who had fixed things so he had to teach himself, and the nearest phone was a half a mile away!

More issues were published, many at least a little late, some later than one would expect. The editor's page would contain the ritual apology, followed by a sort of breathy description of the unexpected explosion of growth, almost all by word of mouth. The original tiny circulation (two) fattened to a modest ten thousand in a year. As a reader, I could tell there was life in the magazine just by watching the masthead: an assistant editor, a Chesapeake editor, a West Coast editor, a circulation manager, U.S. advertising sales, Canadian advertising sales. By the end of the first year, the Wild Bunch no longer was in the cabin in the woods, which had become untenable as both a home to a man, wife, and babies, and as an office to a handful of counterculturalist magazine staffers. The new executive suite was South Brooksville's old Kinder House, an ex-school. There was a telephone.

My first inkling that things were — how can one say it politely? — a trifle bizarre over there in Brooksville, came when one W. Lyman (Terry) Phillips trudged up the stairs to my office. I knew Terry vaguely as an assistant editor of *Cruising World* magazine, another recently established boating journal. He was on his way to the other side of the bay to become editor of *The WoodenBoat*. He

229

said Jonathan Wilson was a bit shaken by the success and wanted to get away from it all. All? You know, the pressure from all those telephone calls, the disorientation from moving out of the peaceful woods into all the hugger-mugger of downtown South Brooksville (a post office and a general store); all the running water.

It was great. The rumor mill really started to crank and steam around the edges. Wilson was giving away the store, Wilson was going to get in touch with his feelings, Wilson was going to run away and join a commune on the coast of Scotland. He gave credence to some of this by announcing in his *WB* No. 7 editorial that his "spiritual needs have been largely ignored, and it is these that I now want to pursue," and thereby established his credentials as a card-carrying member of the New Age. He stayed on as publisher ("I discovered there were other ways to sell a magazine besides word of mouth"), then checked out the Scottish commune but decided not to stay. The rumor-mongers loved it, but it didn't last. The editor's page of *WB* No. 11 led off with, "Well, I'm back," and he was.

This business of the editor's page came to intrigue me more than the telephone nailed to the tree. The editors of other boating magazines at the time were writing about the need to revise the IOR or repeal the holding tank regulations — either that or, in fairness to all polluters, put diapers on sea gulls; the editor of the commercial-fishing newspaper down the hall were I worked was writing about the 200-mile limit or the need to find a new way to market silver hake; the editor of the local newspaper was writing about the inadequacies of the local hospital or the beauty of the sunrise over Penobscot Bay. Not the editor of *The WoodenBoat*. He was writing about his ups and downs, his successes and failures, his hopes for the future, his regrets about the past, hints and sometimes outright statements about his innermost feelings. He had a teasing ingenuousness about him that cynics found contrived and supporters found refreshing. It was almost a soap opera in a boating magazine with a *wood is good* flavor.

One morning in February 1977, Monday the seventh to be exact, I decided to get out of town. I was bored, restless, ragged from the excesses of the pillar I worked for at the time. This fellow Wilson intrigued me. I would pay him a visit.

The winter had been a hard one, and the road to Brooksville was unbelievable. Narrow and deserted, with potholes on top of frost heaves and patches of thick, black ice, it snaked its way through a countryside that was a mix of widely separated nineteenth-century marginal farms and twentieth-century hippie homesteads. General stores were few and far between; service stations were nonexistent. If my car broke down on this road, they might not find me until the spring thaw. I felt as if I were driving into the great Unknown, perhaps even the Heart of Darkness in an arctic setting. Is this any place to publish a magazine?

I found *The WoodenBoat* next to the post office in South Brooksville — Bucks Harbor, to cruising yachtsmen. It was a typical wood-framed, white-clapboarded Maine-style farmhouse, the magazine's third headquarters in as many years. I pushed upon the door. Two women were sitting on the floor surrounded by piles of envelopes and back issues of the magazine. One of them was Cynthia Curtis, who had started out as babysitter for Jonathan Wilson's children and was now subscription manager. I had heard jokes that inexperience was the only prerequisite for a job at *WoodenBoat*. Here was living proof. "Jon Wilson? He's upstairs."

I once heard a story that Spike Africa, the so-called president of the Pacific Ocean, upon being introduced to Jonathan Wilson for the first time, took a step back, looked him up and down, and exclaimed in mock disgust, "Why, he's just a boy!" I thought the same thing, although, not being a president of anything at the time, kept my observation to myself. This smooth-cheeked fellow with tousled hair and holes in the elbows of his sweater and the knees of his dungarees, shoes with lopsided heels, was editor and publisher of a magazine with a circulation of almost twenty thousand? This is the guy who had figured out he could save the world with wooden boats? My goodness. The last time I looked like that I was catching the bus to school.

He was a charming fellow nevertheless, actually a bit older than he looked, and he took full advantage of the opportunity to display generous hospitality to this visitor from so far away. We had cheese sandwiches from the general store, and I got a complete tour of the "nice little house needing lots of work."

Creative weirdness would be the best way to describe it. The rooms had stuff in them, and there were people working with the stuff, but for the most part it was difficult to tell just what it was that they were doing. Some seemed to be working on the magazine, others seemed to be doing things to the house, still others seemed to be just hanging out. It was Dan MacNaughton's first day as associate editor ("I have the required inexperience," he joked), and he looked torn by all the possibilities. There were children and dogs wandering in and out. The managing editor had gone home to stoke her woodstove or something and never came back. The advertising manager was off on some mysterious mission — nobody seemed to know what or why — and left behind a mound of empty beer cans and cigarette butts on top of his desk. The uniform of the day was modified Grandma's Attic.

So Wilson and I talked shop for a couple of hours, and I found that I liked him. He was a cross between practicality and spirituality, with a measure of idealism mixed in with his ideology. What more proof than his plans for the back room? "Here," he said with satisfaction, "is where we'll build the peapod." "The peapod?" I asked. "I thought this was a magazine." "Of course it is," he said, "but when we get tired of pushing papers around, we can always come back here and hang a plank or something." I wondered what the pillars of publishing over in Camden would think of that. I knew what I thought — this was a nice guy with a bolt loose.

But I underestimated Wilson and his staff. I think just about everybody did. They didn't build the peapod — they never even started it — instead, they survived the worst thing that can happen to a publishing company, worse even than a libel suit.

WoodenBoat (the *The* was dropped in issue No. 16) burned down in late March 1977, just before the next issue was to go to press. All of us in publishing knew full well the size of the calamity and naturally tendered expressions of sympathy and offers of assistance, but what could be done? Manuscripts gone, typeset copy incinerated, artwork destroyed, everything that could be salvaged damaged by smoke and water. A magazine lives on paper, and in a fire, paper is the first and fastest to go. By far the biggest loss was the destruction of most of the back issues, which in a way represented money in the bank. *Wooden-Boat* would have strangled financially long before if there hadn't been back issues to sell to new subscribers who wanted to own a set of the magazine from issue No. 1.

On a number scale of one to ten, I would have given the magazine a two in potential survivability beyond that point. The staff apparently didn't even think in those terms; knowing what I know now, if they were asked then they would have been dumbfounded by the question. "Survive?" John Hanson probably would have asked. "Of course we'll survive. This is the first real job I've had in two years, and I'm going to keep it."

The stories continued to filter back to Camden after

that, but this time they weren't the rumor type — you know, the "ha-ha, ho-ho, hee-hee, did you hear what those bush-league fumblefingers are up to now?" They were stories with a legendary edge; ones that would not look ridiculous if they were carved in granite and mounted in front of each of the way stations on the road to a new, permanent office building.

Yet *WoodenBoat* was on shaky financial ground. The magazine had been surviving on cash flow (though at the time Wilson was so unschooled in business that he didn't even know what cash flow was), not on money that had actually been earned. An accountant had looked at the books, shaken his head, and said, "Mr. Wilson, you haven't been running a business, you've been running a club." The magazine had to start all over again almost from scratch.

They played musical buildings. They moved into a barn, then a house down by Walker Pond, then the famous Flagpole Factory — literally a broken-down structure where flagpoles had been manufactured. At one point, John Hanson was selling advertising from a pay phone outside a barroom in Ellsworth; others were working at home, and kept bits and pieces of the magazine in their cars.

I don't mean to make this sound like an Arthurian legend, but this was loyalty and tenacity at an extraordinary level, quite beyond the then-ubiquitous stereotyped view of "those hedonistic hippies who don't want to work anymore." To put it in understandable terms, consider the "straight" company I worked for at the time. Such was my ambivalence about that place that if it burned to the ground, I would have paused only to sift through the ashes for my Brazilian rosewood felt-tipped pen and then straightaway looked for another job. If they had asked me to work in a drafty barn with an outhouse, I would have told them to go pound sand up their noses.

The invitation came in the mail in December 1978 addressed to the *Mariner's Catalog*. It said something like, "*WoodenBoat* invites you and George Putz to a Christmas Party at its new headquarters, Brooklin, Maine." The magazine had been in Brooklin since the fall of 1977, but it was not until more than a year later that the staff was ready to show off their new stuff to the outside world. It took that long to dig out from under. I called Putz. "Are you going?" "Am I going? Do hobby horses have wooden legs?"

At the time I was — how should I put it delicately? — self-employed (the pillar of the publishing industry I had worked for discovered I had more loyalty to my Brazilian rosewood felt-tipped pen than I did to him), so nobody was going to cause any trouble if I took off Down East on a weekday. Putz and I drove over to Brooklin together.

But what was this Brooklin? That *i* in the name had an ever-so-slightly pretentious ring to it, as if the residents had doctored up the spelling a bit to avoid association with another place in another state. It was reminiscent of Lucy Baines Johnson, who one day became Luci through some misguided notion that a sow's ear could be made into a silk purse by changing a *y* to an *i*.

Where was this Brooklin? Somebody in Belfast said it was past Bucksport, somebody in Bucksport said it was near Blue Hill, somebody in Blue Hill suggested that we try Sedgwick. When we finally got there, we discovered two things: (1) *WoodenBoat's* new location was more remote than its old one, and (2) the lack of a *y* wasn't the only difference between this town and a certain borough in New York.

We were charmed. The offices were in an ancient Victorian house called Mountain Ash that had been vacated by a religious community of some sort. Out back were a bunch of sagging wooden boats that bore no relationship to those pictured in the magazine; next to

235

them was an old swimming pool filled with rubble from a torn-down building. Up the street was a general store with an eclectic collection of merchandise that included, among other things, more types of bottled mustard than any store east of Boston's S.S. Pierce, and whose premises were patrolled by a creature the owner called a *guard cat* — a tom who looked like a cross between a raccoon and a panther with bleached hair. Down at the harbor was a boatyard that brought tears to the eyes, a place where they stored wooden boats, repaired wooden boats, built wooden boats, designed wooden boats, talked wooden boats. For all I knew, they prayed to wooden boats.

So we romped and stomped and talked and celebrated, and when the night was over I had a clearer understanding of why a magazine that was doomed to failure before it began did not fail and probably would not. It was a community, not a business, and was as close-knit as any place I had ever been at any time. This was my first introduction to success because of, not in spite of, the suspension of the rules. My previous view of *WoodenBoat* was changed as a result.

Not to say that it was much less eccentric than had been rumored. Not at all. As time passed and I became less of an observer and more of a participant, new levels of eccentricity seemed to reveal themselves. (I became a part-timer at the magazine in 1979; a full-timer in 1980.) Going to *WoodenBoat* became something of an adventure.

It was the people, of course, who made it that way, and foremost among them was one Terence P. Driscoll, who had become publisher of the magazine in 1977 and left for the Big Apple in 1982. I had my first conversation with Terry one winter's night in the kitchen of Mountain Ash. Revise that. I got my first lecture from Terry that night. I was eating my corned-beef hash with a poached egg on top when the door flew open and the driving snow blew in this disheveled-looking character with a black mustache and nicotine-stained fingers. He was half preppy, half deadbeat, with both sides at war with each other on a New York-Irish, educated-at-Holy-Cross battlefield. He emptied the contents of a paper bag on the table — pound of hamburger, four-pack of rolls, six-pack of beer, giant economy size sack of potato chips. He pounded the meat into four patties and fried them. "Hmm," I said to myself, "This guy's having company."

But he wasn't. He was eating alone. He ate the burgers, he ate the chips, he drank the beer, all the while waving around the sports page of the *Bangor Daily News* and defaming the star forward of the Boston Celtics. When he was done, he leaned back in his chair, belched, lit a Lucky Strike, and proceeded to tell me where I went wrong, why I went wrong, how I went wrong, when I would go wrong in the future, and all manner of other observations that were at once witty and droll.

Driscoll was maddening and abrasive, intellectual and coarse, and in his own strange way drove me to do my best work at precisely those times when I was so down and out that I would have preferred to do my worst. He had a way of needling me — everybody — not to be malicious, but to force the cream to rise to the top. Jonathan Wilson once called his style "management by walking around," and that's what it was. He'd walk around the building in a seedy bomber jacket and paint-stained chinos rolled to the knees, with a painter's cap jammed on his head catcher-style, and would act the bully or the sweet-talker as circumstances required. He'd find your weakest spot and play it like a bassoon if he thought that was what was necessary to get you to do your best. It was Terry who took the disorganized madness of the early years and created the organized madness of the middle ones, and pointed the way toward a level of professionalism that was not stifled by rules or committees.

Perhaps the most curious aspect of the people at

WoodenBoat was their marked *unboatiness*. With the exception of Jonathan Wilson, Dan MacNaughton, Maynard Bray, Terry Phillips, and John Hanson, the staff was composed of people who were no more interested in boats than they were in automobiles. They liked boats, to be sure; some even had one, of course; but their thoughts and conversations were not dominated by them. They didn't have the peculiar drift I knew so well, the I've-gotta-have-a-boat-now-or-I'll-surely-die state of mind that made the pronunciation and spelling of *Herreshoff* so easy and *Nietzsche* so hard. To me, a fellow who had worked for years with people who knew more about the origin of the Banks dory than they did about the nuclear arms nonproliferation treaty, it was a source of endless wonderment. Why were these people here, slaving like madmen and madwomen, for such a special-interest, ideologically rigid publication if they could take or leave boats? The answer, I believe, goes to the very heart of *WoodenBoat*, the community, as opposed to *WoodenBoat*, the magazine.

WoodenBoat, the community — especially during the years in Brooksville and the early years in Brooklin — was a natural extension of the social idealism of the late 1960s and early 1970s. It embodied, for example, the beliefs that the magic of place was more important than the lure of money; that the struggle for a goal thought unattainable by society at large was more exciting than the quest for predictable results; that iconoclasm for the sake of itself was no more irresponsible than conformity for the same reason; that excellence in what you did was more important than the name of what you did. If there was a uniform, commonly held view of who we were and what we were doing, it was of a band of men and women, young and old, who were strolling, not marching, happily down the road, arm in arm, toward a collectively held goal that happened to be the hoped-for success of a strange magazine about organic boats. The goal could just as easily

238

have been economic justice for Appalachian mountain folk. Dorothy and the Tin Woodsman and the Scarecrow and the Cowardly Lion meet the Wizard of Oz.

That's pretty naive, of course, and there were plenty of people, within and without, who maintained that an attitude like that wouldn't get you far in the dog-eat-dog, post-Vietnam, post-Watergate era. But it was a persistent view that was never more evident than when a new person was being considered for the staff. The question that always preceded "Are you qualified?" was "Will you fit in?" This did not mean, "Are you a conformist?" It really meant, "Do you accept the concept that a community, by definition, is diverse, and are you willing to put up with eccentric behavior if it contributes to the common good?"

The pleasures of *WoodenBoat*! You never knew what to expect from one day to the next. The staff was growing and the space was cramped. We were all jammed together in a series of rooms with paper-thin walls and a three-story uncarpeted stairwell with patched-together bannisters. Conversations ricocheted around and became tangled with others, mingling with a dual-amplifier sound system that featured MPBN (public highbrow) on one channel and WBLM (progressive rock) on the other. Given the right conditions, you could read proof with your eyes, and listen to Bach's *Brandenberg Concerto* with one ear and Jimi Hendrix's *All Along the Watchtower* with the other. Meanwhile, someone would yell down the stairwell that you had a telephone call and another would yell up the stairwell that he was going out for beer and if you wanted a bottle, place your order now.

Some of us who lived quite a distance away would sleep over at least one night a week, and during deadlines there were plenty of people who worked extra hours at night (some deadlines lasted until five in the morning), so it seemed as if the building was continuously alive, furnaces thrumming in the cellar (there were three furnaces, yet the place was deathly cold in the depth of winter). What's more, a substantial proportion of the staff lived in houses without hot water, a few without running water, so there was a constant stream of people trudging up to the third floor to take a shower.

We'd eat potluck lunches in the kitchen, skylark out in the yard, debate the qualities of this and the deficiencies of that, and work harder, happily, than those in most other organizations that were modeled after the U.S. Marine Corps. Why? I've always wondered about that, but I suspect it was because Jonathan Wilson's attitude was quite simple, though unstated: The bottom line was not how much money was made but whether the work was done; if the work was done properly, the money would be made; how the work was done was our business, just as long as it was done well and on time; if the money was made, then it would allow us to continue to work the way we wanted . . . . I had always wanted a job under those conditions, and I had found one.

Change comes to everything, *WoodenBoat* included. While the vast majority of the staff were not singleminded about boats, there were plenty who were, and in their minds there was this vision of Boat Heaven — a happy hunting ground where you could read about boats and write about boats, build boats and play with boats — almost a childlike notion rooted in the unfulfilled dreams of the past. Mountain Ash was not Boat Heaven; at best it was a dormitory just outside the Pearly Gates. Down the road, however, was a derelict estate. There was a big house, bigger than the one we were in, plus a huge barn to house the boatbuilding school Wilson had always dreamed of establishing, and there was a boathouse (great jumping Jehoshaphat!) and a farmhouse and waterfront on Eggemoggin Reach and apple orchards and fields for playing softball and a duck pond and a view of Deer Isle and Isle au Haut and the Atlantic Ocean beyond.

It was much too expensive (though cheap for any business past the marginal state, which we were not), and it was ridiculous to think we could have such a place, but then again it was ridiculous to think that a magazine about wooden boats, and wooden boats alone, could go from a circulation of two to about seventy thousand in seven years. (It is now 100,000.) I don't know what was going through Jonathan Wilson's mind at the time, but I bet it was something like this. "What the hell? I gambled the boat and the tire jack on the magazine, and somehow we pulled it off. Let's take a chance on Boat Heaven."

Lots of people, including me, were apprehensive. They thought we were developing high-falutin' ideas, that the soul of the magazine was being left behind in Mountain Ash and the Flagpole Factory and the Kinder House, even the telephone booth in the Quarterdeck Saloon in Ellsworth, or had departed with the scores of people who had worked on the magazine over the years and had gone on to other projects in other places.

All of a sudden things were different. There were fancy phone lines in and fancy phone lines out, a receptionist to answer them, a coffee-maker down in the kitchen. One day I came to work and found a crew from Bangor laying wall-to-wall carpeting in the halls. Were we becoming more establishment than the establishment? Was the Golden Era over? Were we on the threshold of bureaucratic reorganization, with reams of interoffice memos and secretaries to type them? (As inconceivable as it may seem, *WoodenBoat* has never had a secretary.) Time would tell, and it did.

As I read this over, I realize that I have been writing about *WoodenBoat* in the past tense, as if it is not the same in the present. It is and it isn't, in the same paradoxical way that things can stay the same yet change. The tight

241

community that was *WoodenBoat* has loosened a bit — it has to have, considering that the staff is larger now, older, and the counterculture is virtually extinct. But respect for each other still takes precedence over the respect for authority; the struggle for cohesiveness in the presence of eccentricity still goes on. I know it to be so when I see a half-sunk wooden skiff out in the pond — a stake rising from the thwart with a derby hat on top — presumably being used as a scarecrow to keep the loons from attacking our trout. Some people on the staff think it's symbolically inappropriate, some think it's sacrilegious, but nobody has hauled it in.

A month or two ago, I took the ferryboat from Rockland out to Vinalhaven Island, where my old pal George Putz lives. As always, we walked the beaches and explored the quarries and poked around the fish houses, all the while entertaining each other with apocryphal stories of the past and theories about the future. Come evening we stood in the dining room and watched the sun set behind the water tank across Carver's Harbor. The subject turned to *WoodenBoat*.

"You know, Pete," George said, "if *WoodenBoat* didn't exist and Jonathan Wilson walked in the door right now and said he was thinking of selling his boat and hocking his tire jack to start a magazine about wooden boats, I'd still tell him it was a dumb idea." I nodded my head in agreement.

And then we chucked each other on the shoulder and started to laugh. This time we weren't laughing at Jonathan Wilson. We were laughing at ourselves.